DOCTOR WHO

THE TOMB OF VALDEMAR
Simon Messingham

Published by BBC Worldwide Ltd
Woodlands, 80 Wood Lane
London W12 0TT

First published 2000
Copyright © Simon Messingham 2000
The moral right of the author has been asserted

Original series broadcast on the BBC
Format © BBC 1963
Doctor Who and TARDIS are trademarks of the BBC

ISBN 0 563 55591 2
Imaging by Black Sheep, copyright © BBC 2000

Printed and bound in Great Britain by Mackays of Chatham
Cover printed by Belmont Press Ltd, Northampton

This book is dedicated to
Julie, Alexander Kirk and to Mark and B's new addition,
Nina, born the day this book was completed.

Acknowledgements due to Caz – invaluable; Mike,
Stephanie and the lab; all at Tower C.

Part One

'When it had become customary to guard the entrance of houses and towns by an image of Janus, it might well be necessary to make the sentinel god look both ways, in order that nothing should escape his vigilant eye.'

The Golden Bough

Chapter One

Janua Foris. God's door. Their two-faced god, who looks both ways that nothing may escape his vigilant eye. And here you have to look both ways. The old woman would do well to remember that.

Janua Foris: also the name of an inn. This inn, this shack of light and raucousness nailed into the skirts of the Harkasal Mountains, deep in the arctic tundra. Full of trappers; so many, gathered for the annual, grudging building of their community.

The old woman does not drink. She seems barely capable of the action. Her eyes are fierce beneath the thick brown creases of her ancient skin. A white snood conceals half-glimpsed thick chestnut hair. She sits amongst them, smiling, seemingly amused by the attention.

All eyes are on her. Ponch, despite a lifetime's familiarity, can barely remember the names of the other trappers. He notes, almost unconsciously, how they lick their lips, wondering if she has anything worth stabbing for. Whether she will live long enough to be murdered. She's old, ancient. Perhaps even as much as thirty cycles.

The stars had been shedding snow when he came in sight of the Janua Foris, far below on the icy plain.

He was a mass of skins; blubbery hides cut from the backs of the snow creatures that roam this wilderness. Narbeagles to ur-mink, ice-whales to tiny furred rattlers, Ponch has the upcoming autumn to scrape and tan these hides, ready for the impossible winter. Six months of working with other trappers, any of whom might take his life for the barest of reasons. Behind him, a threadbare pony lay frozen in the snow banks, buried by Ponch, along with his improbably large sled full of more skins ready for the Gathering.

Journey's end. Ponch had urged his frozen legs down towards that tiny shack, its single plume of smoke twisting in the horizontal winds. A wind that shrieks and sends the rapidly settling icy flecks hammering at a man's face.

Once there, after making the sign of Janua, he had hauled open the door. The effluence and smoke drove Ponch almost bodily back out into the eternal snow. The stench! It had been many months since such a concentration of odours had assaulted his flared, frost-bitten nostrils. Ponch remembers reeling, tears streaming filthy tracks over his bearded cheeks. The air boiled with tobacco, ale, hot breath and worse.

It was good to be back.

'Camr'ale!' sings Ponch, after his third beaker of this thick, brackeny brew, 'Camr'ale! Let it stay in the guts 'til the Third Age!'

None present listen; all are drunk. Soon it will be the time of uneasiness, that season of togetherness when the cold air of the settlement heaves with the tearing of leather and the curses of straining men. Of murder in back corners. And the Gathering.

The new town they have grudgingly come together to build this year, as every year, is not really a community, or if it is, is of a base and suspicious kind. This is a town grown organically of necessity, when men whose instincts are for self-preservation are forced to rely upon the skills of each other. When money, that one true universal binding force, can only be conjured through the alchemy of togetherness. None like it, but all play their part. The skins, the fur, the hides, how they hate this commodity. Yet it must be done. For what else does this life have for them?

2

Not to say that daggers won't be drawn, that rough and tumble of a frightening brutality won't spill out of the camr'ale; it is expected. Still, at this moment, the novelty of other people is enough to warm them, to enjoy.

And tonight, another is amongst them. Strangers here are so rare that Ponch must search for the noun itself, his eyes blurring as they take in that too-intense thing: human features not worn smooth into the grooves of his memory.

Such abstract concepts as beauty are entirely unknown to Ponch and his cronies. However, some ancient, long-buried race memory remains sufficiently embedded for him to realise that this hag must once have been beautiful. He clutches the idol of Janua, weighted on a string around his throat.

'So it comes to this,' the old woman says in a rich, rounded voice.

It must be the camr'ale but something in that voice speaks to Ponch of faraway places, of lives distant and denser than his scratching existence. A subtone so delicate he lacks the vocabulary to interpret it.

'Watch your tongue, hag,' snaps bearded Ofrin, a giant trapper known for his extreme viciousness in a place where viciousness is always extreme. 'If you want to keep it.'

The old woman turns upon Ofrin a gaze of such withering intensity that even he pales, and sinks down to his drink. 'I have come a long way to talk to you,' she says. 'Further than you can imagine.'

'What does that mean?' asks Ponch, feeling his guts churn. How could an old woman make him feel so uneasy, so small?

'You will learn.'

Ofrin points a shaky finger. 'Perhaps you mean to steal our furs.'

There is a general slamming of tankards on benches at this. Ofrin has crossed the line. One does not speak of the furs in this way. Not out in the open.

3

'Where did you say you were from?' asks Ponch again, captivated by this woman.

'I didn't.' Once more, the gaze turns to him. 'I like you,' she says. 'You still have something. Ponch.'

Cause for general hilarity. Ponch is hot. He cools himself in the camr'ale.

'Where have you come from? The tribe beyond the mountains?'

More general hilarity. All remember the settlement beyond the mountains. How two seasons ago they marched over and burned it to the ground.

'Not exactly. You could say I come from the sky.'

'That's stupid.'

'Really? Any more stupid than believing the sky is a liquid wherein the clouds hang suspended?'

'It *is*! Woman, you are mad. Begone!' Someone hurls a tankard. Its foaming trajectory arcs towards her head. Quickly, quicker than light, the woman raises an arm and her browned fingers grip the cup as if it has found its natural resting place. The liquid within does not move.

The Janua Foris is silent. Carved icons of their god stare impassively. It is as if the woman is looking into Ponch, into all of them. He knows she can see his soul, that she knows all that he is.

'Who are you?' he whispers, feeling for the first time that he is in the presence of something, someone, greater than himself. Greater than the world.

'Gentlemen,' she whispers, still with that enigmatic smile touching her lips. 'I'm someone who's come to tell you a story. The most important story you'll ever hear. That's who I am. And you are my audience. I am going to tell you the story of Valdemar.'

Ponch freezes, he knows not why. It is as if a black breath has

4

blown over the tavern. He notes how the others are crossing themselves. He can't think why but he does it himself.

'Why does that trouble you?' she asks. 'What could you possibly know of Valdemar?'

'Don't say that name!' shrieks Ponch. 'Just... don't say it.'

'Aye, keep it shut,' growls Ofrin.

The old woman shrugs, and smiles again. 'I can't very well tell you the story unless I do mention the name. It's a major component.'

'*It's a made-your-compo-nent*,' comes a mocking voice from the back. 'We don't want to hear your stupid story anyway.'

'Aye, whoever made money out of telling stories?'

The woman pauses, taking in the crowd. Ponch knows that despite himself he'll do whatever she wants. She makes him feel sad, makes him feel he has missed out on so much. That his life up to now has meant so little.

'I'm going to tell you and you're going to listen. Partly because... well, to be honest, I'm dying and I want to do this thing before the end, but mainly because it's in your interest. It's time for the blinkers to come off. Because you will *learn*...'

'I'll tell you who Valdemar is. Or was. Are you sitting comfortably?'

There is a rush for the bar.

'Is it true then, this story?' Ponch is interested, at least for tonight. It's better than killing each other. A chorus of tankards slams on to the bench. He's not the only one.

'Pretty much. Although I have taken it upon myself to improvise when the occasion demands.'

'You've told it before then?'

'More than you can imagine. Look.' From the folds of her fur coat, the woman produces a small, soft rectangle of leaves.

Ponch sees her face wince in aged effort. 'This is a book.'

'Book?'

'Of stories.' She places the 'book' on the sodden table. 'Let's begin.'

'Hurry up, before you die, old woman.' Ofrin again. She ignores the remark. She spreads her withered hands out in the air, describing a huge circle.

'Long ago, longer than you can imagine, in another place, there was Valdemar. A god, said some; a devil, others. A vast black creature of unimaginable powers who spread his great black wings across a whole sector of this galaxy…'

'Galaxy?'

'Don't interrupt while I'm speaking, I'll lose my thread. Whole stars were swallowed up by his being; races altered and changed to become his acolytes. It was said that one glimpse of Valdemar was enough to drive a man mad, that his eyes would burn and his head would pop…'

'Like me!' roars Ofrin, bringing his giant hands together in a crushing motion. 'Starting with lying old witches! Ha ha ha!'

'I can do without the heckling. Try and keep up, there isn't much time.'

'Time for what?' asks Ponch.

'Don't confuse me with details. As I was saying, Valdemar's reign spread throughout the gala– lands. Nothing could withstand his mighty wrath. Except one man…'

'Heard it!'

'No, you haven't.'

'Who was the man?'

'Ah! A very special man, almost as powerful as Valdemar in his own way. I only knew him for a short time, very short, but it was a time I would never forget. Ever. He was a traveller, a man of great good. And occasionally of insufferable manners. A man who could travel anywhere, any time. Interfering,

6

making a nuisance of himself, helping people to see that which they needed to see. People like you lot.'

'How could he travel anywhere, any time?'

'He had a box. And he travelled inside this box. You see, the box was a magical box. A big blue box, small on the outside but inside as big as a mountain!'

'What's up with you?' Ofrin asks Ponch.

Ponch feels tears touching his cheeks, tears he hadn't noticed before. He looks through blurred eyes at his fellow trapper. 'I don't know. It must be the magic. I just love hearing about magic.'

'Bloody hell.' Ofrin shakes his head.

'Of course, he didn't travel alone. He had friends, those that others would term companions. People he trusted. A concept I understand you find difficult to credit. At this particular moment, there were two of these companions. One, a very beautiful woman...'

'Oh yeah?' As before, much hilarity and elbow jogging.

'Nothing like that. And put those thoughts of your mind. This is a clean story.'

'Uh?'

'Her name was Romanadvoratelundar...'

'Uh?'

'It's a story; names have to be as magical as anything else. You may call her Romana.'

'Romana.' Ponch repeats the word. The name is elegant, cool, charming. The very opposite of his. He starts to think that he will like this story.

'And the other companion?' asks Ofrin.

'Ah. Now the other. This one was a dog. But no ordinary dog. No. This dog was made of metal.'

'A metal dog? What? Get off.'

'Called K-9.'

'Ouch!'

The room is in uproar. 'How does that work then?' … 'Does she think we're a bunch of kids?'…'It's a man in a box…'

'I thought you said it was true?' asks Ponch.

'Apart from the lies, absolutely. Don't trouble yourself over the metal dog. It never goes down very well. It's not in the story that much.'

'Good. Hold on…'

The old woman smiles. For the first time, she realises that perhaps she has their attention. 'You have a question. Ponch?'

Ponch feels the weight of silence between him, the woman and the expectant trappers. 'You've told us the dog's name, and this Romanerverandah whatever it is…'

'Hmm…'

'What about the traveller? What do we call him?'

'Not what. Who.'

'What?'

'The Doctor. That was his name.'

'What?'

'*Doctor*…'

'Who?'

Chapter Two

Stories within stories. How do you unravel the Doctor? Perhaps even he himself could not.

Few, if any, see correctly. There are too many realities, great shifting tectonic plates of time and space, of outside and in, in the soul of a man. Only when these points converge, touch fleetingly, does chance provide an insight, a reflection of what, or who, one is.

Let's roll up our sleeves and start here.

I like to think, at the beginning at least, of the Doctor at home. What he calls home.

The TARDIS. I have called it a blue box, but it is called the TARDIS. Where the plates grind together. Where everything becomes one.

At this point in space, at this moment in time, the Doctor is moving. He is bound up in a larger story, a greater narrative he calls the search for the Key to Time – six segments of a greater whole (again) that need convergence. He has one, he needs five more. So you see, we may never know exactly where or when we are truly at the beginning.

('What is this?' bellows Ofrin. 'What are you talking about? If I wanted a sermon I'd have gone to the shaman.'

'All right, all right, calm down. Beginnings are hard. I'm doing my best. I'll switch the style. Something less pompous, how about that?'

'Whatever…')

See the Doctor, at the central console of the TARDIS, wild hair bobbing, ridiculous iridescent scarf swirling as he twists and wrestles with incomprehensible controls.

There is a noise, a disordered jumble of shrieks and whistles. Has something gone wrong? Is there a problem with the console?

No. Not this time. It's the Doctor. He is singing.

Much to the irritation of the refined Romana, who has learned much already in her time here. She is studying the first segment, perhaps wondering just what she has let herself in for. It lies on a small white table, its angular wrongness only barely positioning its mass on the teak.

Its very shape is a quandary; it is a building block, something that *slots*. It fascinates her, its bland functionality hinting at something beyond her perception. If she could just concentrate, locate the segment's meaning which dangles, hovers, just out of reach. Just concentrate…

And then the whistles and squawks ruin everything.

'Doctor?' she asks, her voice confident and haughty, refined by decades of study at the Academy on Gallifrey.

'Mmm…' (Not much of an opening line, I'll grant you, but somehow he pulls it off.)

'Must you?'

'Must I what?' he asks innocently.

'Emit that atonal racket.'

His eyes bulge (like all interesting heroes there is a touch of the cartoon, the grotesque, the over-the-top about his hyperactive manner). 'Atonal racket? *Atonal racket*? That's Ppiffer's Second Ode to the Cepholan Whale! In E minor! One of the most beautiful atonal rackets in the universe.'

'The Cepholans have three larynxes, you only one. Please stop it immediately.'

She knows he is glaring at her as she returns to her study of the segment.

The Doctor is glaring all right, wondering once again how the White Guardian has lumbered him with such an unsuitable companion. All right, she acquitted herself reasonably well on Ribos, but there was unquestionably more than the usual amount of luck involved. If it hadn't been for him…

And she is young, far too young for such a serious matter as the Key to Time. He really can't see this working.

'To have tried and failed, Romana, is nobler than to have never tried at all. You Academics – not an ounce of initiative between you.'

'A false assumption, Doctor. Trying is one thing. The fact remains that the ode is composed for a life form with three larynxes. It is not possible for you to render the piece. That proposition cannot be argued with.'

'Cannot be…? Don't tell me what I can and can't argue with.'

Romana glides to the console, unruffled, already used to this bickering. She is starting to understand them, even to like them. 'Anyway,' she continues, 'don't you think we have more important things to worry about? That we should fully focus our energies on locating the next segment?'

The Doctor, exasperated, crumples his hat. 'Romana. The first thing you should know about me is that I'm never more focused than when I appear distracted.'

'What's that then?'

An elegant finger, smooth and carefully manicured (vanity, thinks the Doctor, there's another thing) points to a flashing light.

'You don't know, do you?' she asks innocently.

'Of course I know.' Still, the way he bounds over, tripping and slamming, suggests otherwise. He glares at the light, as it were an enemy. 'I don't know,' he says. 'Now that shouldn't happen.'

'Isn't that the monitor for the dimensional stabiliser?'

The Doctor can't take his eyes off the light. It appears to obsess him. 'Which means the TARDIS is about to suffer a trans-dimensional breach…'

'Which can't happen…' Romana is up and expertly studying the controls. 'The internal dimensional units are operating within normal parameters. As normal as this machine can ever be, that's taken as read. Ergo, the light itself is malfunctioning.'

The Doctor grins. Broadly, displaying innumerable gleaming teeth, each with a life and energy of its own. The grin is genuine, confident, happy. Romana knows this means he is worried. 'Unless,' he says and she knows she is in for a lecture, 'exterior trans-dimensional forces are operating on the TARDIS.'

'Oh Doctor. That's impossible. Isn't it K-9?'

Previously hidden, ducked down in shadow in the corner as if sent there in disgrace or to hide from the singing, the little metal beast nods its head. Its radar ears waggle. Sometimes the Doctor believes the dog does that just for show. 'Mistress,' it affirms simply.

'The higher dimensions are undetectable. Even for the TARDIS. There's no instrumentation built to perceive them.'

The Doctor keeps grinning. 'Has anyone told the higher dimensions that?'

'Doctor. It's the light. It's broken.'

And then, right on time, the wave of dimensional energy smashes into the Doctor's home, sending him, Romana, K-9, and several lifetimes' worth of collected junk flying.

The source of this energy? This wave of something or other that has assailed them? In time. In time.

First, Ashkellia. Ash-kelly-ah. Roll the syllables on your tongue. Who could have named such a place? Yes, a place, different to this place. What men once called a planet. The beginning and the end of Valdemar.

You have never seen such a place. A place so inimical to life it could almost define the opposite. Though perhaps you, even you, have imagined it. Men had a word, when words still mattered to men. Hell.

However, just a place. Just a planet.

Imagine, if you can, for I know your powers are limited, a sky that really is liquid. An eternal hail and swirl of burning, yellow clouds of rubble. Acid that drifts like smoke over the boiling, unseen surface. Noisy too, with booming thunderous collisions as the muck sizzles and tumbles in the violent ether. Not a place for human beings, you might say. But human beings there are.

Specifically, one human being. A discredited novelist named Miranda Pelham.

Through the sulphur clouds, you might say *emerging* from them, a small brass bulb. Swinging like a pendulum from gigantic links, buffeted by the evil pressures surrounding it, tugged at by conflicting and deadly forces.

At this moment, at this beginning, Miranda Pelham cowers, hugs herself inside this metal bathyscape swinging down towards the surface. To the tomb. Thick glass windows visibly scar as the elements of Ashkellia scratch and scrabble, trying to find a way in, acid fingers feeling for human flesh.

Pelham, shivering despite the heat, wrapped in her flimsy cloak. Clichés ring through her head: reaping what you sow, the past that catches up with you, the one about the whirlwind that she can't quite remember.

The bathyscape bounces, jumps in one heartbeat-skipping hammer of turbulence. 'OH MY GOD!' she shrieks, her head colliding with one of the many equipment packs stuffed into this tiny bubble.

'There's nothing to worry about,' says the helmsman, a cult techie called Prahna. One of Neville's mercenaries. The yellow light transmutes his smile into something sinister, something devilish. The liquid winds howl.

'Right,' Pelham replies, wondering if the man is mad.

'They built these babies to last; same construction materials

13

as the star probes. Very expensive.' He says this with pride, as if he'd bought the bathyscape himself.

It lurches again. 'Don't worry,' says Pelham, 'I believe you. The other choice is worse.'

Worse. An interesting word. She prefers *worst*. The *worst* it could get. Meaning no more worse. Yes, she thought, let's use *worst*.

The third occupant, Erik Hass, her assistant for twelve years, lover for three, never alters his stare, his unswerving meditation on the element detector. Its blue light gives his face an entirely different sheen. Different, thinks Pelham, but equally inhuman. Like a ghost.

'Should pick up the surface density soon. You really think it's there, Miranda? After all this time?'

Valdemar. That which they seek. Her gold mine. Incredible to think that, despite this insanity, maybe their situation wasn't the worst after all. 'I never thought I'd be in a position to find out,' she replies.

'You must be really excited.'

'Ecstatic. Oh yes.'

Erik fails to catch the sarcasm and returns to his studies. He makes some adjustments to the screen.

Perhaps if I close my eyes and make a wish, Miranda thinks, I'll wake up and I'll be back in Antigua. On a beach, watching the royalties wash in like waves. No New Protectorate, no Neville, no fear. Why had she chosen Valdemar? It had all seemed so safe such a long time ago. One of those things that 'captured the spirit of the times' (the *European Review*) and made her rich.

Pelham can feel her stomach twisting, threatening to burst out of her mouth. They could have fitted this tub with anti-G, really they could have, couldn't they? But then again, she knows full well it's not the turbulence doing this to her.

'Got it!' Erik snaps. 'Hard rock. Just keep this thing steady.'

'You're joking, aren't you,' says Prahna, sweating with the effort of hauling on the levers that are supposed to stabilise the precarious vessel. 'If we corkscrew now, you can say goodbye to all this.'

'Hey Erik, that's fantastic,' Pelham says brightly. 'I can't wait to go back up there and tell Neville the news. Let's get back straight away!'

At last, Erik looks up. He is puzzled. How little he knows her. She realises that without Valdemar, they would have absolutely nothing in common. And he has absolutely no sense of humour.

'I thought you wanted to find it. It's your life's work.'

'I do! I do! It's just I feel it would be more appropriate to take things slowly. You know, correct procedures... protocol...' She feels her voice slip away. They're not going to do it, she realises, grimly. 'All right. How about if I beg?'

She looks at Prahna's stern brown face. 'I guess that wouldn't work either,' she mutters.

'You know our orders,' says Prahna. His expression has gone cold; the soldier coming through.

'Aren't you at least curious?' asks Erik.

You want the simple answer, Pelham thinks. She realises she is locked up with two madmen. All of a sudden, the bangle on her wrist itches like hell. Not yet, she thinks. Conceivably, this might not be the actual worst. Not worst enough to face... well, not yet anyway.

'OK, OK. Let's just get it over with. And in answer to your question, Erik, no I am not in the least bit curious. I'm incredibly scared. That's what I am.' Pelham feels herself starting to sob.

'We must go on,' says Erik.

'We have to go on,' says Prahna.

The bathyscape swings once more. Perhaps everything is going to be OK.

'Er…' Prahna seems sheepish. He leans back and stares at his controls.

What is she thinking? Of course everything isn't going to be OK. Pelham grabs Prahna's shoulder, digging her long, red nails into it. 'What is it? What's going on?'

Prahna spreads his hands out, indicating the dials and levers as if she's never seen them before. 'They're moving on their own,' he says. 'I'm not in control any more.'

'A chronometric pulse?' asks Romana, clearly not believing a word.

'A chronometric pulse,' the Doctor reassures her. 'A wave of dimensional energy.'

The TARDIS has stilled, for the moment. Mind you, the explosion that blew the tracer out of its nest on the console was a little worrying. Luckily, the Doctor was in just the right position to perform a dynamic double-handed catch before banging his head on the floor.

Blackened, almost chastened, the panicked travellers have hurriedly disassembled the tracer's components and are probing for damage. The Doctor squints, jeweller's glass in one eye, and hopes he can put this infernally complicated device back together again.

He waves away Romana's attempt to bandage his head.

'There's no such thing as a chronometric pulse,' she says.

'Then what you experienced was impossible. Still, not to worry. We'll just let it ride and when the universe tears itself apart you'll know that that's impossible too.'

'That's not funny.'

'I'm not joking.' The Doctor looks up, the jeweller's glass still lodged in his eye. 'What do you find so impossible? That this could have happened? Impossible is just another word for "I don't understand".'

Romana backs away, unsure of herself. She's only been with the Doctor for a short time but already she knows that events aren't always controllable, or foreseeable. She decides to check the tracer's slot on the console for damage.

'A release of trans-dimensional energy,' she mutters to herself. 'The result of a rift between the lower and higher dimensions of matter. A rift in the kinetic dance. In theory.'

'Theory my eye,' says the Doctor, the jeweller's glass dropping from his. 'It's the only possible explanation. What else could have done this to the tracer? Or the TARDIS? There, I think it's done.'

He rises, ready to plunge the tracer back into its slot. Romana looks on in horror. 'Aren't you going to test it? How do you know you've mended it correctly?'

The Doctor smiles. 'Test it? It's perfect!'

And with that he slams the tracer into place. The TARDIS lurches, tumbling once more.

'Teething troubles,' he grins, once he has untangled himself from the coat stand. Romana can only shake her head.

Almost not wanting to, they look at the console. The tracer is back in place, lights pulsing merrily.

'Seems to be functioning,' says Romana.

'Of course it is. And if I know my dimensional engineering, the location of the second segment should appear any second. Minute. Within the hour. Today.'

They wait. No readings, coordinates or information of any kind appear on the console screen.

'Doctor…' Romana warns.

'Well, it has got the entirety of space and time to search. You can't expect miracles. That's the trouble with you Academy types these days, no patience.'

Mind you, he does slam his fist down on the console and yell, 'Come on you stupid overgrown pencil!' at the innocent device, confirming Romana's view that the Doctor suffers from psychological cognitive dissonance and a fixated egocentric maturity deficiency. As Garron might have said: he's a big kid.

'Maa-ssterrr…' comes a sorry-sounding voice from the shadows.

The Doctor spins. 'K-9,' he utters, shocked. He leaps down to his forgotten companion.

'Maa-ssterr…' it says again, voice slurred, unmistakably mournful.

The Doctor hurriedly hauls the dog into the light.

'Doctor,' says Romana, frightened. 'His eyes. What's wrong with his eyes?'

The Doctor, on his knees, shuffles away. He is breathless, taken aback by the dog's plight. 'Oh, K-9. What's the matter?'

The dog's ears waggle feebly; mangled electronics grind deep inside its casing. 'Analysing tracer malfunction… Great forces… Chasms…' it says, 'breach fabling…'

'What's he saying?' asks Romana. 'Analysing the tracer?'

The Doctor strokes K-9's metal aerial, an aerial that is telescoping up and down. 'Too much initiative, too impulsive. He must have tried to run his own diagnostic program when the tracer went dead. I think he's picked up some kind of trans-dimensional feedback loop that's scrambled his circuits. Either that or he's drunk.'

There is something disturbing, something cold and remote about the black husks that seem to have grown over K-9's ocular sensors. Shining discs, like the eyes of an insect. Almost blurred, not of this reality. Romana is reminded of the segment of the Key, the way its alienness is fascinating, hypnotic.

'Don't look at him!' shrieks the Doctor suddenly and hurls himself at her. 'Look away!'

'Poor steam…' says K-9, backing away from the light. 'Meet here…'

The grinding inside ceases and its head droops.

The Doctor holds Romana tight, too tight, but he is looking at the shadows where the dog lurks. 'Doctor,' she says, smoothing back her hair. She puts on her best haughty look. Anything to cover the fear that she suspects she feels. 'I'm fine.'

'The higher dimensions,' whispers the Doctor. 'How could they… affect a machine?'

'Almost nothing is known of the higher dimensions,' says Romana. 'Except that they exist… co-exist with this universe. A part of reality…'

'A part!' The Doctor finally releases her. 'They are reality! Total reality! More reality than even pompous Time Lords can perceive. Somehow, it's made itself apparent here.'

'How?'

'The chronometric wave. A release of trans-dimensional energy. We're still on the shore. The real events are taking place out there, deep in the ocean.'

'Doctor, you're talking in riddles.'

'Am I? Sometimes that's the only way to make oneself clear.'

'Aren't you forgetting something?' Romana asks.

'Me? Forget something? Never.'

She points to the segment, miraculously still sitting placidly on the white table. 'Our task?'

The Doctor seems trapped. He stares alternately at the segment, then K-9, then back to the segment again. 'How could I…? But wait. If something is causing the higher dimensions to become apparent. Perhaps the Black Guar–'

'The what?'

'Never mind. It's just that it might be a trick. To divert us. But we can't take that chance, can we? The Key to Time must be paramount.'

A bleeping comes from the console. Romana glances over. 'Perhaps the decision has been taken for us. These coordinates. Oscillating. All over the place.'

The Doctor stares at the hesitant numbers. 'It could be that the forces are upsetting the tracer's circuitry.'

'Or you rebuilt it incorrectly.'

'Impossible. If that's not working, how can we be sure where the segments are? It could send us anywhere.'

At last, the turning numbers settle. A coordinate, a place. Romana knows she doesn't need to look it up in the star charts. He knows. He always knows.

'Ashkellia,' says the Doctor. 'Interesting.'

'Really? In what way?'

He sighs, as if talking to an idiot. 'Because, as everybody knows, it's reputed to be one of the resting places of Valdemar. This is all starting to add up.'

'Not to me it isn't.'

'Well, of course not. You probably don't even know who Valdemar is.'

'But you're going to tell me.'

'On the way. We have to materialise whether it's the second segment or not. If for nothing else, for K-9's sake.'

Romana glances back at the machine. It sits, motionless, as if waiting for a command. She feels in need of some distraction therapy, some task to marshall her energies, as she was taught during the training she received on Gallifrey. One action always focuses her mind. 'I'd better pick some suitable clothes,' she says sternly. 'What sort of planet is Ashkellia? Not cold again, I hope.'

The Doctor seems distracted, barely listening. His eyes don't leave the coordinates. 'Cold? Oh no. Quite the opposite.'

Pelham, when she's not praying or trembling, watches through the portholes in the floor as the black shape below grows bigger. Luckily, the sensors are still working and Erik is very helpfully deconstructing just wherever it is that whatever it is that has them, is taking the bathyscape.

'Some kind of artificial stone construction. Too dense for any kind of clear reading on these sensors. Just tough.'

'It would have to be,' says Pelham, almost to herself, 'to have survived here without melting for a million years.'

Prahna, now without anything to do, can only get in the way. 'A million years?'

'That's my estimation as to when Valdemar was entombed by the Old Ones. They're called "Old Ones" for a reason, you see,' she says sweetly.

'You know, I never thought it was real, all this Valdemar stuff. It's just that Neville…'

'I'm glad I'm down here with you. So I can share in your life story.'

'Hush!' says Erik ('*Hush*'? Only Erik would actually say '*Hush*'.) 'I think it's opening up. The top… it's opening up.'

One good thing about whatever is now driving the bathyscape is that the ride is a lot smoother. Pelham can actually *see*. Whether or not she wants to see, is another matter.

The bathyscape drops into darkness, through the top of the construction that appears to have found them. Prahna activates the docking lights. They don't help much; the walls of the well are obsidian, black and smooth. It's hot still. Pelham, in her finery, feels the perspiration sticking the lace and silk to her back.

A bump, and they've hit some sort of ground. Pelham is now very definitely thinking of her nice old apartment in Antigua, purchased with the proceeds of her first Valdemar book. Gentle waves, white sand, blue sky. If only she hadn't made Valdemar out to be quite as terrible as she had.

Ears pop. All gulp. 'Airlock?' asks Erik.

Prahna gingerly touches at his controls, as if whatever possessed them is still inside, like it's contagious. 'Oxygen. Gravity too. Seems like these Old Ones breathed like we do.'

'Unless this is all being done for our benefit.' Pelham won't be optimistic. She refuses. They're all going to die.

'Well, um… shall we go outside then?' asks Erik. Keen, far too keen. If it weren't for his muscles, and tan, and those little glasses he wears that make him look so delicious…

They are looking at her. She is still nominally in charge. 'We don't have much choice, do we?'

Prahna, perhaps instinctively, breaks open a weapons pack. Pelham places a hand on his arm to stop him. 'I wouldn't. Unless you're thinking of using it on us if we're naughty.'

Prahna shrugs her off. 'I like to be prepared.'

Erik is squinting out into the blackness. 'Do you… do you really think this is the tomb? That Valdemar could still… you know?' Pelham shakes her head. She doesn't want to listen.

Erik is lost, gone off on one of his daydreams. 'The tomb of Valdemar,' he breathes. 'The Dark God. Captured and destroyed by the Old Ones after centuries of the biggest war in mythology, and buried here. After all the work we've done, Miranda. This is an historic moment. And all thanks to you, Miranda. You showed us the way.'

'We all have our cross to bear.'

Prahna opens the hatch. Chilled air relieves the travellers in their stuffy oven. The first fresh air they've breathed in months. 'Whoever installed the air conditioning, we should use them,' says Pelham.

'You could show a little more reverence, Miranda,' Erik snaps. He seems totally unafraid. Keen, far too keen.

'Just keep your eyes open,' says practical Prahna.

They are in a vast black cavern. Looking up, high above, Miranda sees their gigantic chain rising up to a small aperture, through which rage the gleaming gold storms of Ashkellia. Some kind of force field must be holding back the planet. She tries not to think how long it's all been operating. Heavy, heavy technology. Or magic.

In a way, it's all a bit of an anticlimax. Maybe it will be all right after all. Maybe Valdemar is just lying in some sarcophagus somewhere, smaller than you expected. Just bones, if anything. The mundane truth behind centuries of mythology. Behind her fanciful pseudo-factual stories.

Erik and Prahna are waving their torches around this cavernous nothing. Circular beams latch on to bumps and protuberances, natural or not they cannot tell.

Pelham feels the goose bumps lacing her arms, spinning a web on her skin. She shivers and the torches snap on to her like spotlights. She smiles. 'Come on then. If we're coming.'

Romana is wondering whether the TARDIS ever lands anywhere pleasant. It's cold in this dark tunnel. And what had he said?

It is thanks to him that she decided on this flimsy diaphanous collection of silks and drapes. She readjusts the silly costume jewellery coronet on her head. 'They like trifles and tit-bits and fancies and follies,' the Doctor had said. The twilight of the Second Empire, he'd said; discreet technology, fun. Highly aristocratic, he'd said, blend in with the surroundings, better to be one of those at the top... Opens more doors.

So how come he never wears anything except that ridiculous theatrical get-up? *Blend in?*

This know-it-all attitude is beginning to grate. Especially as they are already off-mission. She just hopes the Doctor's infamous curiosity doesn't get the better of him. As far as she is concerned, they need to find the source of this energy pulse, switch it off, repair K-9 and get back on track. What was that name he mentioned earlier? The one he presumed she is unfamiliar with; the one she is unfamiliar with. Valdemar? Who or what is that?

The Doctor is bounding out of the TARDIS, ready for the adventure. Romana expects to feel nervous, or wary or something. Not anticipation, excitement.

She hadn't been expecting this new life, back at the halls and lecture rooms of the Academy where she had spent most of her life slaving away for that triple first. Only when she graduated did she begin to wonder quite what the purpose of it all was. The serenity, the complacency had become familiar enough to be tiring. She wonders whether she had been bored.

The search for the first segment had been like a shock of cold water. Surely all their stop-offs weren't going to be like that? She is pleased with her own derring-do.

'K-9's still in shock,' says the Doctor. 'I think his system is trying to expel the new data from the energy burst. Exposure to the higher dimensions can do nasty things to the mind. Even metal minds.'

'Doctor,' says Romana impatiently. She isn't feeling particularly impatient but Doctor-baiting is good sport. 'It's cold.'

The Doctor licks a finger and raises it in the gloom. She sees the spittle gleaming on its tip fade out as the TARDIS door shuts. 'It is cold,' he affirms. 'Wind from the east.'

'I thought you said...'

'I know what you thought I said. Acid clouds, mean temperature in the low six hundreds. We're obviously inside an artificial structure. With very advanced air conditioning.'

Romana inspects a wall. She runs her elegant hand along its side. 'Artificial? This is igneous rock. Eroded. Which would make it...'

24

'Oh, at least a million years old. So it's a million-year-old artificial structure.'

'So how come the air conditioning is still functioning?'

'Look. Oh…' He is off down the tunnel. East, he said. 'Do I have to explain everything? You must learn to work things out for yourself. Come on, we're wasting time.'

Romana looks down at the smooth floor, aggrieved that he still treats her like a child. 'Oh yes, Doctor. Coming, Doctor,' she sniffs and strides haughtily after him.

The tunnel is short and ends in a crossroads. The Doctor peers into each road in turn. 'Isn't this always the way?' he says, perhaps affronted that the structure could do this to him. 'We really don't have the time.'

'If you'd brought the tracer like I'd suggested…'

'I don't need that. Anyway, it's a delicate machine, regenerating itself. And…'

'You don't trust it any more,' she realises.

'I don't trust it any more.' He turns and looks at Romana, for the first time since they left the TARDIS. He beams his smile at her. 'Good, Romana. Good. You're learning. Well done. You took the words right out of my mouth.'

The patronising… 'Thank you.' Romana curtseys and gives him her icy smile, perfected over months of dealing with ancient, similarly patronising Academy lecturers. 'So which way?'

The Doctor puts an arm around her shoulders. 'Now then, as a test for you. Which way?'

Romana, all politeness and sugar, shrugs him off. 'Wind from the east?'

He nods.

'Then I think east. At worst we may discover who did the air conditioning.'

There is a tremendous roar, a blast of cold energy, like the

25

bellow of some gigantic, incensed animal. The walls of the tunnel shudder as a gale hurls itself at them. Romana feels her flimsy coronet ripped from her head. Both she and the Doctor strain to keep their balance.

The roar subsides. The ringing in her ears remains.

'Very good,' says the Doctor, approvingly. 'East it is.'

Romana stays still. That roar was like... like nothing she has ever experienced. She is now extremely cold. 'What was that noise?'

The Doctor sniffs. 'I don't know. Let's find out.'

'It might be dangerous.'

'Oh, undoubtedly. These things often are. Try not to let it worry you. Shall we?'

Romana follows the Doctor then realises she is clutching his arm. She has discovered another character trait: she doesn't like walking down dark corridors towards hideous roaring noises.

Five minutes later, they reach the docking chamber of the tomb of Valdemar, where Miranda Pelham's bathyscape hangs from its chain. The Doctor identifies the make – a customised Star Probe Seven shell, with toughened uber-alloyed chain links – the fact that this device must have cost a fortune, and the inverse ratio of baroque design over efficiency. Romana wonders what the chain is attached to. The hatch is open but the occupants have gone.

Five minutes after that they hear the screaming. They race to help, back into the tunnel they have just left, and collide with Miranda Pelham. Her clothes scuffed and ripped, she is running clumsily back to the bathyscape, her face utterly white with fear. As she falls into the Doctor's arms, she faints dead away, the growls of the transformed Erik ricocheting up the tunnel after her.

Chapter Three

The Janua Foris is a mixture of confusion and uproar. All around the tavern, trappers howl and brag and shout. Many had arrived late and use this break to loudly demand the beginning of the story again. The very air seems thick with camr'ale.

'This don't make no sense!' shouts Ponch, unaware that he has had a further two camr'ales since the story commenced.

The old woman is giggling to herself. 'What is it that's confusing you, Ponch?' she asks.

'All of it! Big metal tubs swinging on chains, waves travelling back through time. Men turning into monsters. It's stupid.'

'Don't believe a word of it,' roars another good-humoured critic.

'And that way you tell it, all this "He says… she says", it ain't right. It should be "He said… she said". Like proper stories.'

The woman spreads her lined fingers. Ponch can see right up her sleeves, where the flesh hangs off her arms. He realises she is much older than anyone he has ever known. Maybe even thirty-five. 'I just tell it like it was,' she says. 'And what I didn't see, I make up. Using the best available secondary evidence of course.'

'We ain't got time to listen to stories. I thought it'd be short but that took ages.'

'And nothing happened. Just a load of folk talking.'

'Thought it'd be scarifyin'. Wouldn't frighten a child.'

Suddenly, from beneath the table, a white-faced Ofrin, reminiscent of Miranda Pelham in the story, emerges from beneath the table. He is shaking, looking around nervously. 'Get me a drink,' he gabbles. 'Christ, that put years on me. That thing with the dog and the eyes. I thought me heart was going to give out!'

He shivers, then stops. His tiny eyes swivel to the assembled company. All are watching him. 'What's up with you lot?' he growls, punching two nearby trappers into unconsciousness to reimpose his status.

Ponch finds himself staring at the 'book' on the table in front of him. Somehow, far beyond his befogged comprehension, there seems to be a face on the book. A woman. And beneath, strange scribbles. 'This is where stories end up. If you're lucky,' says the old woman, slyly.

Ponch squints at the face. A young face, beautiful, very much like…

'That's you,' he breathes. 'That's you, younger.'

The crowd gasp, theatrically. 'How's that then…?' Ofrin scorns.

'That's the story-teller,' says the woman. 'Many, many years ago. That is Miranda Pelham.'

'But it's you!'

The woman opens her mouth to reply, then seems to change her mind. She sits back and stares at Ponch, an amused glint in her eye.

'What I don't get,' says Ponch, 'is why you came here to tell us this.'

'Or how you got here.'

The woman smiles. 'None of these things are important. Perhaps I just mean to entertain you. I know of the reputation of the trappers, their brutality. Perhaps it's a survival tactic. Perhaps you will discover there is meaning after all. It's all a question of perception.' She turns suddenly to Ponch. 'How long do I have before the guild sleds arrive to take your furs?'

'End of the autumn. A few cycles.'

'Long enough.'

'For what?'

'For you to find out what I'm doing here. This is an

interactive story.'

'Uh?'

Miranda Pelham is unable to explain herself. The Doctor, much more worried than he has been letting on to Romana, carries her back to the bathyscape.

The growling is emanating from somewhere between them and the TARDIS. The Doctor isn't sure what has happened, but he knows growls when he hears them.

He lowers Pelham into a seat as Romana clangs the hatch shut. 'What now?' she asks.

Indeed. It's a quandary. Once again, events seem to have conspired to prevent his reunification with his ship. And poor old K-9. For a moment he feels irritated by this human woman. Why did she have to come here just at the wrong time and start messing about and causing all this trouble? Doesn't she realise what this delay might mean?

He sighs. Because she is human and that is what humans do.

'I don't mean to worry you, Doctor,' says Romana. 'But that growling is getting louder.'

'Hmm,' he replies. 'We need to go up. You'd think they'd have a telephone. Or a bell.' He looks at the crude operating controls. Brass levers and switches and round clock dials, a nostalgic façade for such powerful instrumentation. Shouldn't be too difficult.

'Doctor!' hisses Romana, just as Erik thumps on to the bathyscape. He bangs and pounds at its sides. Through the portholes the Doctor sees eyes grown over by matter resembling black coral, a face warped as if by tremendous gravity, a mind gone.

The man is bellowing, screaming. The sounds are odd, as if something has added tones to their range. The bathyscape rings and echoes with the noise and thumping.

'Please…' pleads Pelham, 'get us out of here.'

Without further ado, the Doctor hauls one lever back. It snaps into its new position with a clunk. There is a feeling of anticipation as the chain tautens. Somewhere up ahead, metal grinds.

He looks at a worried Romana and gives her his smile. 'Going up!' he says.

The bathyscape rocks as the chain yanks them aloft. The Doctor is ready, he has braced himself. Black rock speeds by. Romana and Pelham, on the other hand, are tumbling all over the place. Outside, Erik scrabbles and, by accident or design, grabs the hatch lock. The bathyscape begins to swing as its speed increases. Climbing over the women, the Doctor clamps a hand over the inner locking wheel on the hatch, just as the unfortunate creature starts to turn the latch.

He is surprised by the strength Erik is exerting. Like a man possessed.

'Help me, Romana!' the Doctor bellows, feeling the wheel start to turn. She is at his side in an instant. She feels cool next to him. Her slender fingers grip the wheel. Still, the shrieking creature outside is twisting. Through the glass in the hatch, the Doctor studies his adversary's face. The ears, nose and brow have been subsumed by the coral growing from the eyes. The skull is changing shape, becoming elongated. Only the large, slack, noisy mouth points to the original species. Its breath steams the window. The Doctor feels pity for the unfortunate man. He knows, with finality, that this process is irreversible.

Still, there are more pressing concerns. As the bathyscape is reeled in ever-faster to wherever it is heading, the creature's strength is intensifying. Wind generated by speed tries to haul it off. The wheel turns some more. Romana grits her teeth.

Then they are out into the red and gold sky. The grip releases. There is a final wail of despair and the Doctor turns away. He doesn't need to see; he knows precisely what the concentrated acid, the pressure and the heat will do to the creature's flesh. Something liquid drops like rain over the porthole.

'Erik…' moans Pelham, clutching the jewelled bangle on her wrist as if it were a life belt.

The vessel is swinging more freely now. The Doctor clumsily reaches for the leather hand-straps to keep himself upright. Romana is still gripping the wheel. She is struggling to remain detached. 'What affected him? Those were the same symptoms as K-9.'

The Doctor nods, nasty theories swirling inside his head. 'You know, I've got a feeling that someone here is trying to open the tomb of Valdemar.'

He looks at Pelham, who reacts to the name. 'How…' she stumbles, 'how did you know?'

'Because wherever there is trouble, I must always find it.'

Pelham is staring at him and Romana, as if aware of their presence for the first time.

'You're from the Protectorate…' she says.

'Oh no,' Romana replies instantly, 'we're travellers. This is the Doctor and I am Romanadvor– Romana. We arrived by accident.'

'That's impossible.'

That word again. If there is one thing the Doctor finds tiresome above all else, it is this re-explaining of himself that he always has to go through. He tries to use the word to his advantage, find out what's going on. 'What do you mean, impossible?' he snaps.

He is surprised when Pelham bites back. Not as stunned as he'd believed.

'Because this is Ashkellia and you mentioned Valdemar. Put those two together and the "accident" thing seems, shall we say, unlikely.'

'Mmm. Good point. How do you explain us then?'

'I think Hopkins sent you; you're New Protectorate agents.'

The Doctor considers this.

'I'm sorry but–' Romana starts. The Doctor cuts her off, instantly.

'New Protectorate agents. I suppose it's possible. If we were, would that be good or bad?'

Pelham eyes him suspiciously. 'Don't play games with me. I'm in enough trouble already. When we get to the palace, Neville isn't going to be best pleased. If you tell him you're Protectorate agents he will kill you. Eventually.'

'We're not New Protectorate agents,' says the Doctor cheerily.

'Which is what I tried to say from the off,' sniffs Romana. 'What is a New Protectorate agent anyway?'

Pelham starts to back away. 'You know, I have the feeling that perhaps I didn't escape from the tomb at all; that this is all some sort of hallucination and I'm still back there in the tunnels…'

The Doctor senses the cracks in her composure. She has been damaged by the experience. He has to know. 'What happened to your friends?'

Pelham is staring into space, trying to remember. Or trying to forget.

'I… Erik found a huge hall. A great gateway. It had to be the entrance to the crypt itself. We felt like something, someone, was guiding us. Like they wanted to be found. I was afraid, hanging back…' Her eyes clear momentarily. 'I told them not to, you understand? I know it's my fault but I tried to stop them. Together, Erik and Prahna, they opened the tomb. The light… the cracking noises and the light…'

'The energy wave?' asks Romana.

'Yes,' the Doctor says, feeling the weight of his words in his mouth. He looks at Pelham. 'You didn't get it open did you, not fully?'

'How… how do you know that?'

'Because if you had, the consequences would have been catastrophic. You would have released forces that are infinitely more powerful.'

'And they… started to scream,' says Pelham, disbelieving her own words. 'I ran to help and then… then they turned round. Prahna and Erik turned on him, attacked him, started to… I ran. I panicked. I've never been so afraid in my life.'

She lapses into silence. All the Doctor can hear is the grinding of the chains that haul them up and up.

'Where are we going anyway?' asks Romana. 'Who is pulling us up?'

Pelham smiles but with little humour. 'You may wish you had stayed in the tomb.'

'What do you know of Valdemar?' asks the Doctor abruptly. 'He would have been destroyed millennia before the birth of humanity.'

'Over a million years.' Her reply is muted. The Doctor hopes he is taking her mind off the horror she experienced in the cavern. 'And Valdemar is my job. I found him and I re-invented him.'

'Would someone mind explaining to me,' Romana asks patiently, 'just who this Valdemar is?'

The Doctor and Pelham begin to speak at once, both eager to tell their stories.

'Valdemar was a god…' says Pelham.

'Valdemar was a cancer…' says the Doctor.

And all the time the chain pulls and pulls… lifting them higher, to Paul Neville.

For the Doctor, memory is a hazy thing. He recalls events and names more clearly than he recalls himself. Who was the man who found the Daleks on Skaro, ready to emerge from their metal city and make war with the universe? Who was the man

33

who tricked the Great Intelligence, deep in the tunnels of London? Who was the man who solved the riddle of Peladon? He does not know.

Someone, it must have been him because he remembers, was once young. Centuries young.

He recalls the two students hooked up to the Matrix, their joint consciousnesses wired into headsets for the illegal terminal they had lashed-up, to prove that they could. Two students, in Prydonian robes. One dominant, clever, cunning. The other cautious, patient, thorough. Him.

At the Academy. Where his friend, the Time Lord who went bad and became the Master, revealed to him: Valdemar.

When the universe was young, younger than he, younger than even the range of a TARDIS, a race now known only as the Old Ones (a translation, but typical of the colourless, literal and long titles ascribed by the Time Lords. Old Ones was a name they gave to any long-dead, highly technologically advanced alien beings with incredible powers. As if they were afraid to give them real names) disappeared. Exterminated.

Why?

Valdemar.

The Doctor and the other student had travelled back, through the Matrix safeguards, tapping back through Gallifreyan history, through universal history.

Nothing was left of the Old Ones, except warnings.

They had released or created something, some black mass of life. Valdemar may have been the name of the first Old One, which it took for itself, or perhaps it was always called that. No one knew. For the two students, analogues of Valdemar portrayed it as a stain, blotting out stars, consuming planets, transforming races into servitors to sustain itself. Valdemar the Unstoppable, the Destructor, the universe at its mercy.

And then, somehow, the remnants of the Old Ones defeated

it. No record survived of how. It just stopped. Correlations from dozens of races' mythologies were processed by the Matrix, the result an aggregation of them all: Valdemar was killed and its body placed in a tomb. The tomb was sealed for ever under acid skies, lest Valdemar transcend death itself and return again to complete its destruction.

The students had emerged from the Matrix, the eyes of one them shining. 'The power.' he shouted joyously, 'Think of the power.'

The Doctor had stared at his friend and wondered just who, what kind of person, would gain so much unrestrained pleasure from such a nightmare.

Pelham, for her part, is finding life a little too much. She can't... won't remember what happened down there in the tomb... Erik and the other one, she has already forgotten his name. Her worst fears confirmed. Then these two strangers. The woman in a mishmash mélange of styles from the last two decades and the man with no recognisable style at all. Both talking gibberish. Is this some plot by Valdemar to drive the last remnants of sanity from her, an arcane revenge for all those stories she wrote about him?

They have to be from Hopkins, they have to be Hopkins's agents. There is no other sane explanation. Which, as it's true because it must be, means that more trouble awaits them in the palace. She feels the bump as the bathyscape is jostled by the core updraught. Suddenly their ascent, already speedy, becomes stomach churning. The updraught of gases pushes them on, threatening to loop the giant chain.

The Doctor is staring out of the porthole, eyes a-goggle, staring at the rushing coloured air pulsing upwards. 'You know Romana, I do believe I know where we're going. That is a core updraught. Superheated gases from the planet's core rising in a high-yield energy stream.'

Romana stops preening herself to rise and look upwards through the glass. 'I've seen it proposed as a theory, but never realised on any kind of scale.'

The Doctor turns to Pelham and suddenly she finds that her hand is in his, being warmly shaken up and down. 'Congratulations, Ms Pelham,' he beams. 'You've discovered the principle of atmospheric flotation, about six hundred years early. How did you do it?'

'I don't understand,' she stutters.

'How did you ensure stabilisation?' asks Romana curiously. Pelham believes the woman is serious. 'Wide-band streaming? Retro thrusters? Rotational spin?'.

'I haven't the faintest idea what you're talking about,' she replies, suspiciously. 'And to answer your question, we didn't do it – we found it.'

'Ahh. That explains a lot,' says the Doctor.

'Not to me it doesn't.'

'You knew the tomb was here didn't you?'

'We guessed.'

'You're some kind of historian? Archaeologist?'

'Novelist.'

'Really? That's interesting.'

'I'm glad you think so.'

'I can see the structure!' shrieks Romana.

Pelham cannot prevent herself staring into the Doctor's eyes. Despite their mirth and good humour they accuse, knowing she has secrets she should be imparting. 'You shouldn't have come here,' he says softly. 'You have no idea what you will unleash.'

'It's a palace!' Romana cries joyfully. 'A big golden palace, floating in the sky!'

The Doctor finally looks away, grinning again. Pelham

guesses they are seeing the gigantic, ludicrous thruster-nozzles, spinning furiously, keeping the baroque structure on an even keel. Home, she guesses. Home after what was on the surface of Ashkellia anyway.

Suddenly she feels cold, a trembling building up inside her. It's hot in here, hot and stale. Sweat on her brow, Erik turning round after the light...his eyes... gone...

'She's going into delayed shock,' Miranda Pelham hears Romana say as the rushing noise starts up, somewhere deep in her ears.

Soon their little craft, hauled up to the long crane arm, has been swallowed up by the bright searing glare of the palace.

The palace.

How to describe its bulbous ramparts, its smooth acid-dripping skin? The palace of the Old Ones, as big as a ship, spinning inexorably round in the magma heat, sending spraying sheets of smoking vaporous droplets out into the liquid sky...

'All right, all right,' says Ponch. 'How can a palace float, eh? In the sky? You must take us for mad.'

'Perhaps it's magic!' hisses Ofrin, eyes wide as a child.

'It's perfectly simple, so I believe,' says the woman. Difficult for Ponch to see her and the Miranda Pelham of the story as one and the same. Difficult for him to do anything as a critical mass of camr'ale has reached his brain and has commenced stuffing that organ with animal hides. 'This is how a floating palace works...' he hears.

Ponch gets up and staggers to the doorway, past snoring trappers who have already found the story too slow and demanding. He hauls the door open and shivers as the cruel wind grips him. He is sick, dizzy. It has been a long hard

37

summer out there. He had forgotten what camr'ale could do to a man.

As Ponch looks over at the Black Mountains, already tinged with the cold pink of the late summer sun, he thinks of those sleds, those gigantic sleds, featureless, metal-green, that will arrive over the slopes from who knows where and demand their tribute. He wonders for the first time who is inside, how do the sleds work, why must they take the trappers' furs?

The woman is working on him, he can feel it. This story, this daft story, it is something new, something different, a conglomeration of elements familiar yet strange. He does not know how a man can think of things that never were, have never had existence in the real world. Perhaps like Ofrin says, it's magic. Perhaps out there, somewhere, there is a realm where palaces float and bathyscapes can be pulled on seemingly limitless chains and men's eyes turn black...

Ponch eats some snow to wake himself up. He needs to know more. Not the story, that's for children, but what the story is doing for him.

He turns and walks back inside. The heat and the smoke are beyond belief. He feels these elements tear at his eyes. The woman, her husky voice rising, is completing her explanation. As Ponch reseats himself she is sitting back, that tiny smile playing over her cracked lips. 'So you see, gentlemen. The principles are simple...'

Ofrin and the others, he still can't get their names to come, lean back nodding to each other. 'Ahh...' says one.

'Like I said – magic.' Ofrin looks around in triumph.

The Doctor is not one to hang around. As soon as the telescopic crane has retracted and the bathyscape becomes still inside its cylindrical chamber, he is out and pacing the dimly-lit, functional docking airlock.

Frowning at her companion's lack of manners, Romana helps herself out through the hatch, her flimsy, gauze cloak catching on the handle. With a dismissive sigh, she unhooks herself. She turns and helps the shaken Miranda Pelham.

'Incredible,' says the Doctor. 'Humanity didn't build this. The dimensions are all wrong.'

'We found it on a sensor sweep,' Pelham says. Romana is trying the airlock hatch. She realises that she will soon tire of this constant orange and bronze.

'Just an accident. If we hadn't, we'd never have known about the tomb.'

The Doctor gives one wall a kick. 'It's aged well. Doesn't look a day over fifty thousand years.'

'It's aged incredibly well,' says Romana. 'How?'

'It's perfectly simple,' the Doctor explains. 'Self-maintaining, self-regenerating low-grade power status. Barring accidents or tampering there's no reason why it couldn't stay here for ever. It's not uncommon. Same principle as the city of the Exxilons. Mind you, it seems you haven't managed to get the power above minimum. That would get the lights brighter.'

Romana flashes him an icy smile. 'You're showing off, Doctor. If you really want to impress us, how about opening this door?'

'Oh, I'm sure someone will be here very soon to open it for us, eh Miranda? Someone very curious I expect. This expedition has cost somebody an awful lot of money and I'll bet it wasn't you.'

Pelham seems to have turned an odd shade of green.

Valdemar! Valdemar. The spring she had uncovered, the oil well she had drilled. Why had she chosen not to understand? Mess with monsters; they bite back. Her father had always told her that books would get her into trouble, and annoyingly he had been right. More than once. But this was the worst.

Valdemar. Finding him, finding *him* had been so simple. Almost as if he wanted to be found.

She had never heard of Valdemar, the fifteen-year-old Miranda Pelham bored beyond her years. That had been a different age, ancient history; it felt like a life lived by someone else, someone fictional. Before the civil war changed everything.

She had gone 'travelling' on her 'year out' round the sector. 'Year out' being a synonym for loudly and cheerily imposing yourself upon serfs and races on planets whose GPP was less than your annual allowance, demanding entertainment and 'native food' with a bunch of other like-minded, high-born, self-righteous, smug idiots, then going home and washing the filth of the planets' poverty out of your well-worn clothes before moving on to university.

Except Miranda Pelham had never gone home. She found Valdemar instead.

It was on the unlikely planet of Proxima 2 – that first of the settled worlds, now deeply, unfashionably familiar, little more than a stopover – that she discovered Valdemar.

She had been wandering the bazaars, her rucksack digging into her thin designer vest, looking for knick-knacks and a good novel. She was dying for something to read. Through crushing whitewashed hovels, dirty and bright in the sun. The shrieks of caged animals, the stink of slaves. All around, people were shouting, entreating her to come into their hovels and get ripped off for a rug.

The heat had been intense and her pale skin had marked her out as highborn as brightly as a flag. Her friends had gone drinking somewhere, under the official pretext of visiting some ancient native ruins in the mountains. They would be ruins when her companions finished with them. Pelham already knew she was starting to irritate these colleagues.

The thought of university was hanging over her like a middle-class eagle waiting to pounce. Thanks to her father's position as orthodontist to some minor high-born duchess, she had been accepted by some lowly provincial college somewhere at the back end of the empire for some tedious, drudging technical degree. Only the most noble were allowed to do anything interesting.

She was a voracious reader. Books had never really disappeared, despite numerous predictions heralding their imminent demise. People liked books, liked black print on white paper, liked holding something heavy in their hands, liked the fact that, unlike the digitised print that the serfs were exposed to, once type was on a page it was impossible to change it. Miranda didn't know all that she wanted but she knew she wanted books.

And then the parade, in the distance, through a maze of streets and alleyways. A procession like nothing she had ever seen. Despite the hoods, the racial mix was evident and surprising. Large wooden poles carried by colourful monks; humans, nu-apes, the lithe Kordszz and even a multi-limbed Centauri, its giant eye blinking moistly beneath its hood, under the hot Proximan sun.

Curious, jolted out of her boredom, Miranda followed. The monks, if monks they were, were oblivious to all around them. Oblivious despite the laws prohibiting religion in the empire. Mind, she hadn't seen a single militia soldier anywhere outside the spaceport.

Pushing her way through the begging, pinched serfs, Miranda watched as the parade halted outside what looked like a set of stone steps, then descended in single file down into something very, very black.

She remembers staring down those steps, afraid to follow. She remembers hearing the chants, unintelligible, nonsensical,

41

full of passion and ardour. They believed, they really believed. Only one word stood out. One alone: 'Valdemar! Valdemar! Valdemar!'

She had already left Proxima 2 when the news came in. A massacre, somewhere in the shanty towns of Proxima City. Hundreds butchered, a wave of carnage. It seemed the perpetrators had gone on a random spree, hacking away, carving flesh to suit some arcane, unimaginable purpose. And then the perpetrators doing the same to themselves. No one knew who these people were, although the racial mix was surprising. Only the black clothing marked them out. Undoubtedly something in the water, said the news liars, a sign of the times. Something that made them crazy. It happens.

She knew what made them crazy, she realised. It was Valdemar.

Miranda Pelham had stopped at the next spaceport, jumped ship and gone right back to Proxima 2.

There wasn't much evidence; the barest of clues. It didn't matter. Something had sparked in Miranda's brain; a creative force had been awakened. She was going to write the true story of Valdemar the legend, and the bits she didn't know, she would make up.

And she did it too. Didn't take long. Didn't sell particularly well, though at least the book wasn't banned by the high born. Not on most planets anyway. But only the über-noble still lived on Earth, and whatever they got up to probably had nothing to do with writing.

She made enough to never have to go to that university. To go and live on a *nice* planet with *nice* weather and get on with the writing she really wanted to do that no one wanted to publish.

For thirty years, that had seemed to be it. Contented, mildly bored, comfortable.

And then the high-born picked up on it all. What had that press thing said? What was it called? 'Valdemar, Miranda's mirror' or something.

Miranda Pelham, with her fables of ancient races and terrifying star gods, has tapped into a need amongst the children of the Elite. For the people who have everything, what is left but destruction? Pelham's stories of the all-consuming Valdemar are just the type of nihilistic violent fantasies that tap into the paranoid fears of those at the highest social echelons of the empire, especially in such conflict- and conspiracy-driven times. The opportunity to destroy reality itself is something an adolescent could only sigh longingly for. With Valdemar, they now have a literal image to hold up for themselves. A mirror, in which all their doubts about themselves and their status are reflected.

She had moved from comfortable to super-rich, from nobody to somebody. She even bought herself a share in an island on Earth. It seemed all over. Valdemar had made her, given her everything.

And then, inevitably, it fell apart.

First, civil war and the overthrow of the Elite. Second, Paul Neville.

Miranda Pelham looks up as Kampp, the butler, opens the door of the airlock for them. 'My dears,' he says, a lithe, sparkly-eyed man, 'How lovely.'

Miranda wishes the Doctor and Romana well. Once they've met Neville, she'll probably never see them again.

With a bow, Kampp ushers them out and along through the eye-breaking contours of this palace of the Old Ones. The Doctor whistles, still trying to get that tune. Romana's wincing reveals that she has not noticed how he is taking in everything as he walks. He looks first at Kampp's back, his silver livery, the muscles concealed beneath the effeminate, affected demeanour.

He sees the vast array of technology lying dormant: screens, power points, transmat-sensors. Sees the weird and unguessable aesthetics behind the curves; garish materials and colours that haven't aged a day in a million years.

Pelham feels the rough pull of gloved hands on her shoulders and is steered away by guards down a tributary corridor. If the Doctor sees that, he doesn't let on.

Kampp leads what is now a trio into a small shaft. The Doctor waits.

'Going up?' he quips.

'Going up,' Kampp replies.

The Doctor shrugs to Romana. 'Shouldn't be too much trouble to get the lights on. Then we'd better be on our way, lots to do.'

Kampp turns, his teeth white and apparently artificially sharpened. 'Oh no, Doctor, Mr Neville wouldn't hear of it. He is most anxious to meet you. Make yourselves at home.'

'Very kind of you, Mr Kampp,' Romana replies. The anti-grav kicks in, and they find themselves rising.

'Very good,' smiles the Doctor. 'I'm almost impressed. And what do you do here, Mr Kampp? Apart from ferrying guests around of course. Run errands? Laundry?'

If the barb strikes, Kampp does not let on. 'I am Mr Neville's high footman. A kind of ersatz administrator.'

'A kind of ersatz administrator, eh?' The Doctor's eyes are wide as he mouths the words. 'Jack of all trades.'

'I especially like medical work, Doctor,' the butler goes on. 'The kind that involves surgical instruments. You might say, it's a hobby of mine. I am told I have a certain talent in this area. A... relish. I like to think I am doing good. Giving something back.'

'You know, Mr Kampp, I believe you.'

'Where are we going?' asks Romana, once she has shuffled in closer to the Doctor.

44

'The guests are waiting for you,' sniffs Kampp, for once a note of… what is it?… disapproval in his voice. 'They should keep you entertained whilst we await the master.'

'The Master?'

'Mr Neville.'

A metal plate slides out beneath them and they feel the anti-grav lower them on to it. The lights are muted in the vast piazza that surrounds them.

The Doctor's first impression is of luxury, too much luxury. The air is thick with perfume and incense, the décor stuffed with exotic rugs and hangings and bowls and pictures, so much so it is impossible to gauge any details clearly.

'This way,' says Kampp.

There is laughter, there is movement and suddenly they all leap up in front of the trio, delighted grins on their faces. They are dressed as animals.

'Surpriiiise!' they all scream at once.

Chapter Four

From his makeshift control centre, Paul Neville, once the son of the mightiest planet-owners in the empire, is watching.

The palace is warm and the cloak he insists on wearing makes him even warmer. He likes the discomfort.

The screens unroll the pictures of the Doctor and Romana's entrance. Those children who think they are his guests welcome them in their way.

He feels a moment of unease. Surely it isn't possible that Hopkins has found him. He had been so careful, severed every link, right down to the pilot who had ferried them here, to Ashkellia. That pilot and his ship were now part of the atmosphere of this fearsome planet; pieces of them anyway. He doesn't need a starship now; he isn't going anywhere. Is it possible he has overlooked some factor, some clue as to his trail? No. Impossible. He has thought of everything.

He watches as Kampp slips away in grey monochrome to report to him, no doubt anxious to get on with the questioning of Pelham. What happened down there? He had barely been able to keep himself still when they found the tomb. At last, after all those years. He has to know, has to know what occurred. And where these strangers have popped up from.

For a moment, Neville allows himself to think of the future. Of the moment when, once again, the Dark One will return to this universe. When he himself will become one with his master. He thinks of the feeling of the cold vacuum of space rushing over him, of planets blotted out by his hand, Hopkins and his ilk screaming for ever, of the end of everything. His work, his lifetime's work. Yes, oh yes.

'Magus?' asks Kampp, fully aware of the folly of approaching him at the wrong moment. Neville unfolds his fists, balled inside his voluminous cloak.

'If it's… inconvenient…' Kampp purrs.

Neville swivels round in his padded chair. He hopes his eyes glitter beneath his hood.

'Who are they?' he demands.

Kampp shakes his head, hands clasped languidly behind his back. 'I don't know. Pelham picked them up down there. The other two, including our man, are apparently dead.'

'What happened?'

'I was just on my way to ask Pelham.' Kampp stifles a yawn. 'She seems… upset.'

'I have to know! Every detail, no matter how trivial. Can you do it?'

Kampp licks his lips. 'Oh yes, I can do it,' he says calmly. His eyes flick towards the screens. 'And them? Could they be the Protectorate? It would be interesting to ask them.'

Neville considers. 'We shall find that out. Let them reveal themselves. I want them watched. If it is Hopkins, they must not be allowed to contact him.'

'As you wish, Magus.'

'Go now, my servant. Find out what happened. Talk to Pelham.'

Kampp clicks his heels and bows. 'Mmm,' he says.

As for Romana, well, once the shock is over, she realises she is enjoying herself. She is relieved that these strange young people dressed up in their animal heads are actually pleased to see them. Nice to see the Doctor proved wrong for a change, no need for all that paranoia he carries around with him.

It seems that these people are guests at a masque, a dance. The animal costumes are part of the fun. She has had worse introductions… well, one worse introduction to the universe outside Gallifrey.

48

'Welcome, friends,' beams one particularly handsome young man. Blond and muscular and tanned, his head-dress an ornate, delicate lion. He wears an expensive, tan, furred suit. Cut to a style not that dissimilar to her own. Actually, she is pleased she nearly got it right.

'You're just in time for the games,' says the blond man. 'If you're hungry there's plenty of food. And wine…'

'Tenny…' whines an insipid-looking girl. Her hair hangs in pre-Raphaelite locks over her smooth, perfect face. A spotless gold-and-white dove costume curls over her head. She is almost supernaturally beautiful. 'Leave those boring people alone and dance with me.'

'Charming,' Romana sniffs. The Doctor just looks at the floor, as if waiting for this bit to be over.

'Be right there!' the lion called Tenny replies. He shrugs. 'Welcome anyway. You are…?'

Romana goes through the motions. It turns out the boy bears the implausible title of His Righteously Noble Lord Stanislaus, heir to the Canus system. First name Tenniel. 'And where are your parents?' Romana asks. Tenniel laughs and bounds away to the girl. From somewhere, music begins and the couple start to dance. Romana and the Doctor exchange bemused glances.

'Short attention spans, one supposes,' says Romana. 'Indicative of a highly-indulged upbringing and service-dependent culture.'

'In other words, aristocrats,' mutters the Doctor, clearly unimpressed. 'The same wherever you go.'

'Aren't they odd, Juno?' says one bovine young lady in unflattering yellow drapes and layers.

'Don't they look funny, Diana?' says what must be her twin, her costume the same but in red.

'I don't know, Doctor,' Romana tries. 'They seem harmless enough.'

The Doctor coughs, to get their attention. He coughs again. 'Excuse me. You do realise of course that you are all in terrible danger and must leave immediately.'

Nothing happens.

He tries again, 'I'm sorry to spoil the party but someone here is tampering with vast forces, probably... definitely, beyond your comprehension. You're all in terrible danger.'

Again, no one pays any attention. Romana watches, amused for some reason known only to herself.

The Doctor bellows, 'Oi!!'

At last, the guests stop and look. They all bear the same serene, self-confident expressions on their faces. There are thirty of them, Romana sees, none over twenty. What kind of madhouse have they stumbled into?

'Now,' the Doctor continues, 'I don't know why you're here and I'm sure it's terribly inconvenient but you should really make preparations to leave.'

'Leave?' asks Tenniel.

'Who does he think he is?' snaps the young woman in his arms.

'Yes, leave,' says the Doctor gravely. 'Young Miss Pelham has suffered a nasty accident down on the planet's surface and until I complete my investigation, for your own safety you should all...'

'Your investigation?' says the young woman again. 'Tenny, tell him.'

'Look here.' Tenniel is bashful, wanting to avoid confrontation. His voice is layered with the confidence of speech lessons. 'I don't know what all this is about but you're rather ruining the occasion. This is Hermia's birthday,' he indicates his dancing partner. 'If this is a joke, I'm afraid it's not being received as one.'

'A man, two men, are dead,' says Romana coolly.

This throws Tenniel briefly.'Dead?'

'Really,' says Hermia, 'I'm sure Mr Neville has everything under control. He said there would be danger and hazards and things like that.'

'As long as the danger and hazards and things like that happen to other people, that's all right, is it?' barks the Doctor, clearly unhappy about not being listened to.

'I'm bored with you,' the girl states baldly. 'Go away.'

'You're not even interested, are you?' Romana realises. 'Do you even know what's going on?'

'They may be agents,' says Hermia. 'Mr Neville told us to be on our guard.'

'Hermia,' Tenniel sighs, 'let's not ruin the party. I'm sure they mean no harm.'

Hermia pouts and flops down on to a ridiculously padded *chaise-longue*. 'The party's already ruined.' She points a finger at the Doctor. 'You ruined it. I shall call the guard and have you executed.'

'I assure you I'm only trying to help...' The Doctor keeps a hold of his temper.

'Oh, shut up.'

Romana feels very tempted to take this spoilt madam and drop her out of the airlock. She tries to remember her manners. 'Perhaps if we could come back later, after the party?'

'I don't know...' says Tenniel. 'What would Mr Neville say?'

There is a whine from the anti-grav shaft. Hurriedly, Tenniel nods and the music ceases.

From the shaft a man emerges. His dark purple robes seem like a black hole in this multicoloured, muted light. He moves slowly and with a royal bearing. Something about him suggests concealed power, quiet authority. Jewelled ringed fingers are all that can be glimpsed in the shadows.

As Romana watches, the hands lift and raise the hood from the head. The eyes are dark, black coins beneath thick grey eyebrows. The face is seamed, lined, wise; the effect heightened by the neat beard and cropped grey hair. He looks at the Doctor, then at her, and smiles.

'Good evening. I am Paul Neville.'

Leaving Romana at the party, much more her sort of thing than his, the Doctor allows this enigmatic hooded figure, who seems to be the only person who knows what is going on around here, to whisk him off on a tour of the palace.

'The guided tour,' says the Doctor, 'Do I need a ticket?'

Neville smiles. He is a charismatic, handsome man, the Doctor supposes. 'So, I hear you are a doctor?' he smiles beneath his stylish thatch of grey hair.

'Purely honorary, I assure you. And you?'

'A theurgist.'

'Ah. And what's that when it's at home?'

'"*Divinorum cultor et interpres*", a studious observer and expounder of divine things. I don't suppose you would understand.'

Oh really, the Doctor thinks. We'll see, shall we? He twirls his scarf as they walk, talking as if to himself. 'Oh, I think the principle is simple enough. To ascend before death through the created worlds to the condition of the angels.'

Neville smiles. 'Indeed, Doctor. As the philosophers once said, a theurgist's objective is "to walk to the skies".'

The Doctor returns the smile. The real question here is: who is interrogating whom?

'I've always found theurgy a rather simplistic concept.' And before Neville can react to this goading: 'Still, I'm sure you'll prove me wrong. How did you come to find Ashkellia?'

He's nearly got him, he can see it. Beneath the calm,

impassive face, the eyes are hot with anger. 'How did *you*?' Neville replies.

'Oh, I'm always stumbling into places I shouldn't.'

'That could be very dangerous.'

'Could it really? How?'

Neville strides into a large open-plan room, somewhere near the apex of the palace. The Doctor sees a large bank of impressive-looking computer consoles and feels the hum of power beneath his feet. 'Don't tell me, the kitchen?'

'The control room.'

'It depends rather on what you want to cook up. Why is the power off? Fuse box, is it? I always carry a thirteen amp if that's any help.'

Neville is still, like a sun. The Doctor orbits him, looking the dormant machinery up and down. He tries to take in as much as he can. No chairs. Perhaps the race that built the consoles didn't need any.

'I was rather hoping you could tell me,' Neville replies. 'The best efforts of my combined technical team have been unable to solve that particular riddle.'

The Doctor feels Neville's unblinking gaze upon him. He realises the real power in this place lies with this man. He has met enough sociopathic megalomaniacs before to know one when he sniffs one. 'These ancient alien races, they hide switches in the most unusual places. I suppose they were worried about burglars. Or squatters. Who are those peculiar children back there, anyway? Their lack of knowledge of the palace, of anything, astounds me.'

Neville idly waves a hand, dismissing the guests entirely. 'What they are, Doctor, is money. The last remnants of the old aristocracy. My own fortune was stripped and stolen by those Protectorate dogs and, alas, I am forced to pursue my vital academic archaeological studies under the patronage of these children. The sons and daughters of the Elite. There was nowhere for them to go, so their families decided to send them away with me. What they lack in intelligence they make up for in youth and beauty. They do not interfere.'

'And do they know what your real plans are?'

'Really, Doctor. I still don't know who sent you here. And you know, until the power is revived it could prove most difficult to return you from whence you came.'

The Doctor stops his orbit. The planet confronts the star. 'I thought it might,' he says softly. 'By the way, where's Pelham? In your sick-bay, I hope.'

'In a way, Doctor. In a way. What did happen in the tomb?'

'Tomb?'

'Come, come. We are practical men. You didn't just wander into the tomb of Valdemar by mistake.'

'You'd be surprised.'

Was that a twitch? Was he succeeding in irritating this Prospero of the palace into losing his temper and doing something appallingly dangerous?

'It took me six years and an entire fortune to locate the planet, let alone procure the bathyscape that would withstand the drop to the surface.'

'Well done, you're a very patient man. Let me tell you what I want, Mr Neville. I want to get back to my ship down in this tomb and I want to get on with the very important task I have been assigned. Now, what do you want? To get the power back on, is that it? You only have to ask.'

Neville is thrown. A little. 'I want the power back on.'

'Why?'

'That is my business, Doctor.' Neville looks up at the controls, the gigantic power relays embedded in the ceiling. The Doctor sees something like greed growing in the man. He presses again, trying to retain the advantage. 'You realise that would be a highly dangerous and foolish thing to do. Why do you want to disinter an alien corpse? What are you expecting to find?'

Neville stares at him. He isn't used to being crossed. 'Don't push me, Doctor.'

Stop. Stop there. The Doctor now has no doubt that as soon as Neville thinks he knows everything about him, when he has outlived his usefulness, the magician will kill him.

He stares back anyway, guileless, inquisitive. Neville returns his stare. They glare like this for far too long for their stares to be innocent.

'I forget my manners,' says Neville at last, dropping his gaze, the anger that's bottled inside him fermenting, growing. 'Let us withdraw for some refreshment. Before you return and begin work on restoring the power.'

'And what makes you think I can get the power back on? I'm flattered of course, but we've only just met.'

Neville smiles and indicates that the Doctor go back into the lift shaft. 'You'd better, Doctor. After all, this is a large and very strange structure. Without power I worry about the safety of your young companion, the lovely Romana, wandering around lost in the dark corridors. I worry. I really do.'

'Ah.' The Doctor tries to think, to gain time for himself. To weigh up the odds. The floor is marked with an odd bulbous relief pattern, like a three-dimensional mosaic. He looks up. 'Did someone mention refreshments? I could murder a cup of rosie.'

Unaware of her position as bargaining chip, Romana is getting used to life with the young. She had never realised that those with so little time behind them could be so desperate. They work so hard to amuse themselves, yet are amused so seldom. These pretty children are bored.

Romana wishes she could help. All she does, all she has ever done, is study. There was never much levity at the Academy. All leisure time was given up to a quite conscious development of mental and physical skills, from telepathic meditation to learning the traditional waltzes (days of studying the steps in yellowing, dusty old tomes – they'd called them the 'Foxtrots of Rassilon') and swimming. She hadn't minded the swimming.

The children don't know why they have come to this strange palace in the sky and they don't know what to do now they're here.

The only clue is the way they reacted when this Paul Neville walked in. They bowed, lowered their eyes in a highly ritualised manner. Clearly a man with a great hold over them. Even she had felt an aura about the cloaked figure, a self-possession that inspired respect. Wary respect. She hopes the Doctor is being careful.

She picks at another bunch of so-perfect-they-just-have-to-be-artificial Burgundy grapes and tastes them. Sadly, they are delicious.

Every step she and the Doctor are taking here seems to be moving them further and further away from their mission. There's no focus here, no answers, just more and more that's new until what they need to be doing, what they should be doing, is getting lost. As with the segment, she feels her mind is clutching at something just beyond her perception. She cannot allow herself to be drawn into this masquerade. The Key, she tries to concentrate, the Key is the focus.

'Romana! We must find you a costume,' chirps Tenniel, hauling her away from her wine and grapes with a surprisingly muscular grip. 'What animal would you like to be?'

'How about a cow?' sniffs Hermia, sulking in the background.

'Oh, I think I'm perfectly satisfied with being myself,' Romana replies, smiling the way she was taught. She wonders whether she has made a mistake. Don't contradict them, don't do anything to upset them and you'll be fine, she thinks, trying to remember the brief seminars on 'what to do when confronted with hyperactive, unstable, dangerously wealthy children'.

'Bor-ing!' yells the girl in yellow. 'Did she pick that herself?'

'Come on, I'll find you something.' Tenniel wraps a great hairy arm round her waist and lifts her up from the floor, fully prepared to carry her away.

'Do you mind?' she snaps. He doesn't let go.

'It's only a bit of fun! You've got to join in!'

Flailing, embarrassed, affronted, Romana yanks the lion's head over his face. Somewhere on his back, fabric tears. Tenniel lets go of Romana and slips. She holds her arms out to stop him but over he goes. His head bounces inside the mask as it hits the floor.

'Are you all right?' Romana asks. 'I apologise for hurting you. However, it has been a very trying day and I'm not in the mood for games.'

The only sound is a kind of muffled grunting from the lion. Tenniel writhes on the floor.

The other guests are looking at him, stunned. Well, that all went just about as badly as it could have gone. Wonderful. Triple first. At least the Doctor wasn't here to see it.

However, to Romana's bemusement, instead of sending for the guards, Hermia and the others begin to giggle. They point at their companion and shake along with his agony. 'Look at him! Tenny... "it's only a bit of fun"!'

'Doesn't he look stupid!'

'Like a little fish!'

Others have come to join in. Perfect specimens, aping his

movements, his pain. Within seconds it has become a new dance. A dark-ringleted boy whisks Romana around. She starts to feel sick. The room with its mad curves and colours, the music and shrieking and baying of the guests, the choking stench of the incense. She must pull herself free; she must clear her head of this whirling vertigo.

Only when the yellow girl commences kicking Tenniel with her pointed shoes does Romana realise this has all gone too far. With a nervous swallow, she decides she is going to have to *do* something. Remember, this is why you joined the Doctor, to *do* things.

Luckily, before she risks another confrontation, someone else joins the party.

The three girls stop laughing and turn. Tenniel stops shaking.

Into this decadence, this mayhem, comes a donkey, a baroque donkey, wreathed in paper flowers. Not a mask this time, a full head. And a tail. And hooves.

The donkey enters in a decidedly bipedal fashion and Romana realises that this must be yet another guest. It brays, and she feels that whoever is inside probably feels the same way about these people as she is beginning to.

Like a pack of wolves, the party-goers fall on the unfortunate creature. 'Hello ass!' shrieks an excited Hermia, eyes glittering with delight. They start to pull its ears and tail, as well as throwing kicks and punches. It falls, blindly.

Romana spins away, unable to watch. There is no forethought here, no planning. Just animals tearing at each other, with the slightest veneer - an excuse really - of civilisation to pretend this is still fun.

Surprising herself, she wades in. With a roughness she never believed she possessed, she pushes the others away and hauls the donkey to its hooves. She spots a merciful door and drags him through it, away from the curses and disappointed wails. She notes that no one has tried to follow.

'Let me get this off you,' she says when at last she finds a dark, cool corner. She wants to change her clothes; her flimsy garments are ruined.

With a heave, the donkey's head comes away. Flowers sprinkle the metal floor. Romana flings the head back along the corridor where it rolls and ends up half in shadow, eyes staring stonily back at them.

To Romana's surprise, instead of the gratitude she was expecting, the boy who is revealed pushes her away and squats by the curving wall, his head buried in his still-costumed arms. 'Leave me alone!' cries a cracked, high-pitched voice.

Romana takes several deep breaths. When she has calmed herself, she asks, 'Are you all right?'

This is the first boy here she has seen with ginger hair.

At her voice, he stiffens. He peeks a green-eyed glimpse at her and Romana realises she was wrong. This isn't a boy; it's a man.

'Who are you?' he asks.

Not again, thinks Romana. 'Did they damage you in any way?' she asks in return.

'D-damage?'

'Your friends. I think they lost themselves for a moment. I'm sure they didn't mean it.'

A smile. Pale, freckled skin. 'They're not my friends. I hate them and they hate me.'

The face is revealed and it is a boy after all. How could she have been so sure it was a man? Those eyes were mature, they knew.

Romana feels those eyes on her now, and the sensation is not pleasant, as if they'd popped out of their sockets and are crawling over her. The boy's face is a ruin, almost a model of the misery of puberty. Huge red pustules swarm across it and its surface swims in its own grease. The bright, carrot-coloured hair contrasts poorly with skin so pale it seems green, or at least bruised. Then the boy flushes red, his breathing increasing as he weighs her up with an equal lack of forgiveness.

For all these obvious signals, however, something is wrong. Romana senses someone, another person, beneath the adolescent exterior. It is like he is the victim of plastic surgery gone drastically wrong. This person is not a child; she cannot help but know that.

His breathing reminds her that they are hunched close together in the corner of a darkened corridor. 'Who are you?' she asks, pulling her clothes in, covering herself up.

Arrogant now, proud he has been asked a question, the boy/man stands up. Romana understands that his manner is a front; she could crack him like a glass window. 'I'm Huvan,' he says, too brashly.

'That… that's a nice name,' she replies, wondering how not to offend him.

'No, it's not. I hate that too.'

'Oh. Is there anything you like?' Try to keep the irritation out of your voice, Romana.

Huvan smiles, his teeth looking sour and repellent. Romana tries not to let her repugnance prejudice this youth. 'Oh yes,' he says. 'Oh yes.'

She understands what he means. Change of subject, she thinks. 'I'm sure those people in there don't really hate you,' she says, for want of anything else.

'Yes, they do. They just pick on me all the time. Said I had to wear this costume.' He hauls off his false hooves.

'Do you do everything they say?'

He seems unsure. She is on uneven ground once again. 'Of

course not, don't be stupid.'

'I'm sorry.'

Romana flinches as she realises Huvan is thinking about placing a freckled hand on her arm. He spots the flinch and the hand jerks away. Why did she flinch?

'No, *I'm* sorry,' he says charmlessly. 'Thanks, I s'pose, for helping me. You didn't have to. They won't follow me, they're not allowed out of the piazza.'

'That's all right. I'd had more than enough of their fun and games. Do you stay here, in the palace?'

Huvan looks round. 'Yes. Mr Neville brought me. He's my master.'

'Master?'

'I was sold to him, as a kid. Not like those others, they think they're using him but they're wrong. I'm special, you see. Mr Neville needs me.'

'Really?'

Huvan winks, as if letting her in on a secret. 'That's right. Come back to my room...'

He stops talking and blushes. 'I mean, to talk.'

'Of course. What else?'

He giggles, trying to hold the sound in. 'Nothing. Just to talk. I'm going to tell you my life story. It's really interesting. Interesting and sad. You may not believe it, but I am a very sad man.'

Romana is having trouble following these illogical thought processes. There is something strange about this boy. Still, if he can shed some light on what is actually going on in this place... and what else has she got to do...

'Great!' she says, brightly. She doesn't mean it. Something about him has unsettled her. 'Lead on.' She tries to remain enthusiastic.

Huvan leads her along corridors, up walkways, and up in the

anti-grav lift. They seem to be heading somewhere very remote inside this labyrinth. Romana realises she had forgotten they were floating high up in Ashkellia's atmosphere. The palace's stabilisers are incredibly efficient. Could it really be a million years old?

Finally, secretively, Huvan ushers her into a large bedchamber. The walls are a clumsily brush-stroked black. 'It chose this room. The palace. It reflects my state of mind.'

'It?' asks Romana.

'The palace,' he replies loftily. 'It knows me. Knows what I need.'

Clothing is strewn everywhere, none of it clean. Paper and books lie in scruffy piles over the floor and tables. The bed is a ruin. She daren't even look at the sheets. 'Sit down. If you want,' says Huvan, vaguely gesturing her to a padded chair.

Romana walks to it and lifts a bundle of paper out of the seat.

'You can read that. I won't mind. I don't let just anyone read it. In fact, I'd kill anybody else who tried to, but I don't mind you looking at my work.' Huvan is coy now, flopping down on the bed.

She eyes the bundle. It is scrawled with messy writing. 'Thank you, what is it?'

'A poem. I only write poetry.'

'How nice. What inspires you?'

Huvan smiles at her. 'Love.'

Something crawls at the back of Romana's mind. A warning. 'I see,' she says, starting to realise why he is being so friendly to her. She has read about adolescence and what it does to human males. She feels a sudden need to find the Doctor. Huvan is too unpredictable, as if something in him is fighting to free itself.

Except, realistically, there is no way out; not without upsetting him. And she doesn't feel ready to risk that.

Trying to keep the reluctance out of her body language, she sits back and reads, aware of Huvan's sweaty gaze, a gaze that never leaves her.

Back at the Academy, Romana's specialities lay in science and technical disciplines. Her knowledge of the appreciation of Gallifreyan poetry, she would admit, is at best functional. It isn't really her thing. But she knows when a poem is bad.

And this is poor. As poetry goes, it's down there with the Sontaran battle odes.

'Long ago when Love was real...' it begins, and Romana knows this is the worst thing she will ever read.

'It's eighty pages long. It's tragic,' says Huvan triumphantly.

Romana sighs.

When the deed is done, when Romana has got through the endless repetitions of self-pitying misery, of relentlessly pompous, self-important, total-recall verse, of lonely, desperate lack of insight, she forces a smile on to her face. 'It's very good.'

'It's how I feel. The pain of existence. No one else understands. I seem to have been born with an extra-special sensitivity. If I didn't have poetry I'd... I'd kill myself.'

'You're lucky, Huvan,' she says, keeping a straight face. 'You have a gift.'

'I know,' he replies modestly. 'And now, I also have something else,' he says. 'I'll tell you a secret.'

Please don't, Romana thinks to herself. I can live without whatever it is, I'm sure.

'I'm going to write a poem about you,' he tells her.

The smile is there, fixed in place. She hopes her eyes aren't telling a different story. 'I am honoured, Huvan, but please don't bother, not on my account.'

'It's no bother. I want to... I must!'

Romana stands up. 'Don't go!' Huvan barks, all confidence gone. 'Please...'

'Huvan, I… I need to know why you are here.'

'It's my room.'

'No, why you are here in the palace. All of you. Some very powerful forces are at work and the Doc– *I* think you could be in danger.' Why doesn't she want to mention the Doctor? Does she think the boy could harm him?

'Don't be frightened, Romana,' he says. To her, his voice sounds like curdled milk. 'I'll protect you. Anyway, there's nothing to be afraid of. Everything is going to be all right. We're going to have the power.'

'Power?'

'That's what Mr Neville calls it. Those others, those idiots, they think he's going to make them rich again and get all their planets back.'

'But he's not?'

Huvan looks around, as if worried that perhaps Neville is listening. 'Oh no. He's just using them. It's me. I'm the special one. I'm going to get it all and then they'll be sorry.'

'I don't know what you mean, Huvan.' Romana is worried. Very worried. Just what is this Mr Neville going to do? She recalls Pelham and the bathyscape. 'He's going to open the tomb of Valdemar, isn't he? Why? What does he expect to find?'

Huvan smiles. He is keeping a secret from her, and very pleased with himself he is too. 'That is not dead which can eternal lie,' he says cryptically. 'Waiting for me…'

'Huvan!'

Instantly, the boy is back with her. That feverish stare running up and down her body. 'Don't worry Romana, nothing will happen to you.'

'I'm sorry to say this, Huvan, but you're young. I mean, how do you know Mr Neville isn't trying to trick you too?'

Huvan snorts. For once his arrogance overcomes his awe. Something is definitely out of kilter with this boy. Adolescence is one thing, but Romana is beginning to think he is much more hysterical than is normal even for that.

'Young? What do you know? Do you think I'm some sort of kid?'

He is up off the bed, advancing towards her. Romana backs away. Indeed, he shows distinct signs of a deep-rooted ego-deficiency complex. Huvan barks at her, eyes wide and red-rimmed. 'How old do you think I am? Eh?'

'I wouldn't like to say. You're obviously mature for your years...'

'How many years?'

Romana feels the cold, black-painted wall against her back. 'I don't know–fifteen, sixteen...'

He is glaring right into her face. She feels the hot, lemon breath on her lips. 'I am thirty-four years old,' he states, ever so proud of himself.

65

Chapter Five

In the morning, Ponch does not feel well. In fact, he feels like someone has been kicking him repeatedly in the head. Perhaps someone did, he can't remember. That godless cam'rale, scourge of the Black Mountains. There should be a law, except there aren't any laws.

He finds himself in a corner of the Janua Foris, wrapped in a blanket. He stands, head drumming, and walks out into the morning. The dry cold air helps him feel a little better as he coughs out the wreckage from last night. The feeble sun is brightening, filtered through the watery sky.

Already the fights have started, out in the tundra, where the ruins of last year's township lie like some charcoal skeleton. Fights about furs, fights about money-let's face it, fights about anything they can think of.

They have a season before the guild sleds appear, twinkling on the horizon. Ponch has always feared these gigantic metal slugs, their annual crawl over the mountains. Their huge metal hands that grab at the precious furs, greedily bundling them deep inside themselves, as if their mysterious masters can no longer wait; they must have them now. NOW!

He wonders who they are, these guild procurers. What they look like, how they live. He has never wondered this before.

The woman! Miranda Pelham (for Ponch is sure it is she).

How could he forget?

Ponch rushes back through the growing streets, past the trappers who eye him with suspicion. Many grasp their fur bundles close to themselves, as if he's going to steal them.

He races into the inn to find it empty. There is no one around. The fog in his head is bright with the tips of icebergs-nuggets of the story Pelham was telling.

He can't believe he missed the end, it had only just got started.

It is not the trimmings of the story that have worked on Ponch – the funny Doctor, the floating golden palace, the silly lovers in their draperies. It is something else, something he can't quite place or remember. He feels that, somehow, the woman made it clear that the events on Ashkellia (and it's amazing how real that name is to him, more real than his own world, which he never knew even had a name) are related to events in his life, here in this frozen waste. He feels he is undergoing some test, some mystery he must solve. He feels compelled to prove himself worthy.

She is nowhere to be found. He looks and looks but finds no trace that she was ever here. He feels aggrieved, he has better; things to be doing, work on his furs that must be completed. This inertia towards the tasks he has performed for his whole life cannot be allowed. He will die if he comes in below quota.

Ponch sits in the snow and thinks about the story. His head reminds him it was his own fault he missed the end. What a fool!

'Something on your mind?' asks the woman. She is there, sitting next to him, laboured breath falling in droplets from her mouth. In the light she appears almost see-through, ethereal as the ghosts reputed to haunt the foothills he is staring at. Her white furs and the snow contrast with the brown seams of her face.

'I never heard the end,' he says mournfully.

The woman smiles, at her own private joke. 'I never got to the end. Perhaps there is no end.'

'I thought…'

'The story is for you, Ponch. For your ears. It ends when you end it.'

Miranda Pelham raises an arm and points at the sun. 'I am old, Ponch. This sun, also. I sometimes believe this is the last sun.'

He tries to listen, understanding some, the rest dangling just out of his reach. She continues.

'Centuries ago, philosophers and scientists often thought about the end of all things. The physical universe, time itself, ceasing to be.'

'You mean dying?'

'I mean ending, Ponch. The way a story ends, complete, all thematic possibilities explored and exhausted. Universal heat death, some said, and you never know, they may even have been right. I sit here in the cold and think. The last humans, light years and millennia from home. Humanity's end.'

'I don't understand.'

She places a hand on his. The flesh is withered but surprisingly warm. Ponch is entranced by her eyes. 'It doesn't matter. Understanding is incomplete. It's part of the answer, perhaps most of it, but governed by the conscious. And the conscious is such a small thing. The story of the Doctor and the tomb of Valdemar, I think you already know some of why I tell it. I can see it in you, Ponch.'

Quite simply, Ponch doesn't have the faintest idea of what she is going on about. There's no need for the complications. Part of him just wants to kill her and get them out of the way.

At last, at last, he manages, 'Why does it all have to be so difficult? When we speak to each other, the trappers, we speak plain. What happened, what will happen. Why can't you tell me like that?'

'Why not? Fair enough, my way irritates the hell out of some but whoever wanted things to be easy? I might also answer that some of what I say cannot be told easily. That you must make your own meaning. When the time comes, and you are ready, you will understand.'

'If it's a story, you should have more fighting and killing. Otherwise it's just not interesting. What sort of answer is that?'

'The one I'm giving. Now, do you want to know what happened to the Doctor or not? The arrival of Hopkins, the opening of the tomb, the death of…'

'Don't tell me! I don't know those bits!'

Pelham stands and offers Ponch her arm. The effort makes her wince. 'I forget where I am sometimes. Let's go somewhere, away from all this noise.'

The Doctor sometimes wonders if it is fate that keeps tripping him up. This whole situation is becoming far too complicated. His options are shrinking alarmingly. He has to see things in the widest possible perspective.

Only one thing matters, and that is the Key to Time. The stability of the universe is at stake; he had thought he understood that. So how has he managed to get himself tangled up in this mess?

His instincts tell him to stay and sort out this tomb of Valdemar business. This Paul Neville, this so-called theurgist, judging by the brief time he has known him, is obviously very dangerous.

Under normal circumstances he would have felt compelled to stay. However, these are definitely not normal circumstances. The time is coming when he is probably going to have to leave this situation as minimally damaged as he can risk.

The Key to Time has to take precedent. Time is running out for the universe; the White Guardian's voice rings in his memory.

All right, Doctor. What is the right move? How much time would he waste by acting on his instincts?

The easiest course of action is, obviously, to get back to the TARDIS with Romana and leave, hoping the situation will resolve itself. It's a nice idea. Because so many of the situations in his travels would always have resolved themselves for the best without him. Wouldn't they?

It is important–no, imperative–to discover Neville's motives. Why has he gone to such effort and expense? When the Doctor knows this, he will be able to choose the correct path. After all, it's not the end of the universe, is it?

To discover Neville's motives he will have to find Pelham. Romana seems to have gone missing, certainly no accident, so he will have to do this himself.

His brain whirring, filtering the important from the unimportant, the Doctor sonic-screwdrivers the door of the room where Neville has locked him, and saunters off into the depths of the palace.

He chooses, at random, an ornate door. Inside is a bewilderingly large hall full of ferns and creepers, emerging from a range of outsize pots, colonnades and what are unmistakably tables. Or perhaps one table, large and curving, constructed to some inconceivably arcane design. The walls contain a thousand round holes, each filled with shining brass cylinders; the floor is a chequered mosaic that sends the eye looping back on itself. The design is vaguely fifteenth-century Venetian... vaguely. The Doctor whistles. He has never seen a library like it. He wonders about the fine for a late return.

'Doctor, I knew you would find your way here eventually. Everybody does. The palace seems to send everyone to their most appropriate destination.'

Paul Neville, still draped in his ridiculous conjuror's outfit. All he needs now is a pointed hat with stars and moons. 'Far be it for me to go against the majority,' the Doctor replies, wondering what devices Neville is using to track him.

He lies down on the table, expansively puts his hands behind his head and stares up at the high, faraway ceiling. Let Neville come to him to find out what he wants. A something burnt bronzed glows up above to capture his attention. He feels the hum of the palace stabilisers through the warmth of the table.

'Interesting architecture,' he muses.

'Fascinating,' comes the booming, echoing reply. 'The Old Ones. So similar to us in so many ways, yet so much remains defiantly beyond our understanding.'

'I don't know, I'm sure a good painter and decorator could knock something up for you in no time.'

Footsteps, a sharp staccato on the floor. The Doctor relaxes his muscles. He needs to be ready. 'Your flippancy does you credit, Doctor. A lesser man might take you for a gabbling idiot.'

'But not you.'

'No, Doctor. Not me. You know as well as I do that the information stored here in this library contains knowledge a million years old. A data-storage repository that spans millennia. It staggers the mind.'

Neville's shrouded face looms over him. The Doctor sees the greed there and smiles. 'Now, you know you're only allowed four books at once.'

'Sit up when you speak to me.'

Shrugging, as if disappointed, the Doctor obeys. 'You really think your little cult could hope to activate this archive? Those nice people downstairs?'

Neville looks around and the Doctor can feel his frustration, his anger. 'It will be done.'

'Why, Mr Neville? Why do you want to know?'

'How can you understand? The years I have spent finding this palace, the countless setbacks and failures. Now, I have the secrets in my grasp and yet this final step, this last simple process, I am unable to achieve. To have victory snatched from me at the last... Understand this, Doctor. I would give anything, anything at all to bring this palace to full life once more.'

'I asked why, Neville.'

Neville raises his arms. He spins, taking in the whole hall. 'The Old Ones were a mighty race, Doctor. Proud, inquisitive, philanthropic. A rule that spread halfway across the universe. Nothing could stop them, nothing! Yet one day, they simply disappeared, never to return. What could have done that to them? What immeasurable force could make that happen?'

There is a pause as Neville's words ring round the empty hall. 'Valdemar,' the theurgist affirms simply.

'Valdemar is a myth,' says the Doctor gently. 'There is nothing here for you.'

'NO!' Neville smashes his fist down on to the table. He brings his temper under control. 'No, Doctor. The evidence is too conclusive. Pelham found everything. Her work proved conclusively that Valdemar was real.'

'And what do you get out of all of this?'

Neville's innocent expression must have taken a supreme effort to manufacture. The Doctor could almost believe it was real. 'Me, Doctor? Knowledge, of course. Knowledge to take back to the New Protectorate. With one gesture, I will have accelerated the progress of humanity by ten thousand years. Once I return with the secret sciences of the Old Ones, they can hardly refuse to restore my titles and lands, can they? That is all I humbly ask, Doctor. Is that too much?'

The Doctor shakes his head, not believing a word. 'Of course not,' he replies. 'A noble cause, if I may say so.'

'As for Pelham, it pleases me that I should have restored the reputation of a great visionary, the woman who rediscovered Valdemar.'

'Indeed. I wonder if she knows how honoured she is.'

* * *

Assuming he could, the Doctor would have found Miranda Pelham in what has become Kampp's dungeon. An appropriate word, despite the lack of chains, ankle-deep water and mouldy bread. Dungeon – yes, she thinks. Or how about torture chamber?

Her nerves still ring from the 'interrogation'. She told Kampp everything, immediately; there was no other choice.

Well, not quite everything.

After so many sessions over so many years under Kampp's care and attention, Pelham has worked out a method of keeping her sanity intact. 'You have done this before,' she tells herself, as she waits for the needles and the shocks and the metal. 'It does end. No matter how long it lasts, it will end.'

And it does. Kampp is always faintly disappointed when he realises she has told him everything he wants to know. It is not for the gathering of information that he does what he does best. That is of no importance to him whatsoever.

Miranda hates Kampp and often dreams of situations where their roles are reversed and she is given the opportunity to revisit the many occasions upon which she has been taken to him. And, she knows without hesitation, get this straight – whoever said that the interrogator and the interrogatee develop a unique and personal bond can join him when the time comes.

She finds herself thinking about the Doctor and Romana. Who the hell are they, where did they come from and what are they doing here? If they're New Protectorate they sure don't act like it. Apart from anything else, they have no idea who Neville is. It is inconceivable that Hopkins would send them here without that most basic of information.

Furthermore, how did they get into the tomb? Unless they've got some kind of fancy ship that defies all known laws of physics, there's no way they could have got there. They can't have followed the bathyscape; they would have to have known the location in advance. And Hopkins could never have found the tomb. She herself had only found it when Neville's scans had chanced upon the mineral anomalies.

No, there is only one thing they can be and that is a rival expedition. Which means there is someone else out there, with her knowledge and after the same thing.

She realises she is frightened. Sick and frightened. Not just of more of Kampp's handiwork, although that is daunting enough. No, Kampp is a known quantity, a sick dream.

She is frightened because events are out of control. Coming to a head. Events she sparked off nearly thirty years ago. Birds coming home to roost and all that.

Miranda sighs and leans back in her chair. The straps are beginning to chafe her wrists. She eyes the bangle that sits placidly, uselessly, in a plastic tray with her other personal belongings and jewellery.

Christ, it's impossible to know anything these days.

And Romana? Where is she in this summation of the first day's activities?

There's not much more to say than has already been said.

After a great deal of polite pleading, only starting to verge on the hysterical, she finally gets away from the poet. Unbelievably relieved, she wanders the corridors until a kindly armed guard emerges from the shadows and silently escorts her to her own room.

Where she is in for a shock. She walks in to find her own room from the TARDIS. The exact same room, up to and including that huge wardrobe filled with clothes from all corners of the universe. For a moment she reels, falling on to her own bed. The ornate sheets even smell the same. This place, it seems like a dream to her, like a fragment of her own consciousness.

Her shock at Huvan's revelation is considerable. A thirty-four-year-old adolescent? Genetic tampering on such a thorough scale is monstrous. The kind of biological, chemical and radiation-led tampering that is morally, utterly repugnant. Surely the Daleks had proved…

No matter. It had been done. The question was why? Why take a fifteen-year-old boy and restructure his metabolism to trap him indefinitely in the misery of adolescence? What possible motive could there be behind that, unless someone wished to cultivate a perverse taste for bad poetry?

Romana's sense of moral decencies prevents her pursuing this line of inquiry. Unlike the Doctor, she is incapable of projecting herself into the mind of her opponent.

Oh, she can play the victim well enough. She can empathise with Huvan himself, his feverish sufferings, his hormonal imbalances, his decades of stretched-out misery. This is not a problem.

What Romana lacks are the resources to imagine how degraded, how cynical, how unfeeling the perpetrator of Huvan's agony must be. Perhaps later, when travelling the universe has ingrained itself into her, these faculties will develop, but now, now all she can think of is to find the Doctor and ask his advice. She knows he will understand her feelings all too well.

Reluctant to confront the mad lovers in the piazza, she wanders the corridors, dodging guards, poking her head into empty, incomprehensible rooms. Unfortunately, somewhere in the upper floors, when she is thinking of simply giving up and going back to bed, Paul Neville steps out from the shadows in front of her and holds out a hand.

Watching from his control centre, Neville had considered sending Kampp to fetch Romana, but thought better of it. He didn't want to frighten the lady and his butler tends to get over-excited when it comes to the opposite sex. However, Neville doesn't want her interfering with Huvan, putting ideas into that idiot's head.

The Magus has expressed an interest in the Doctor and Romana. These people intrigue him. Neville is surprised when that deep, resonant voice tells him to allow them limited freedom, to see what occurs. It is all part of the great plan.

Whether or not they are Hopkins's lackeys does not concern the Magus. Neville tries to explain that there could be danger in this freedom, that people are looking for him and the Doctor and Romana may find a way to communicate with them. The Magus cuts him off. Neville's master wants the power of his palace restored and believes their visitors are capable of doing it.

Neville has listened to the Magus long enough to know not to argue with him. He wearily accedes to all demands. The logic of his mentor's words is inescapable.

It has been a long journey getting here and Neville has no intention of rushing it now. The Old Ones were clever enough to set traps and already two men have been lost on what was obviously a stupid mission. And perhaps Romana is important.

So he goes himself.

Romana is startled to see him. 'Looking for something?' he asks kindly. 'Don't tell me, your friend the Doctor.'

'Well, Mr Neville, yes.' She looks around, blinking. She is afraid of him. Good. An advantage.

'Let me escort you. I've just left him in the library.'

She does not want him to, but agrees. 'Thank you. You are most kind.'

He offers a hand. Elegantly, very elegantly, she takes it. He leads her.

'I understand you have met my protégé, Huvan,' he states.

'Indeed. An interesting boy. Man.'

Neville gives her his sincere, amused glance. 'I can only apologise as to the quality of the poetry. However, be reassured that although you were obliged to be privy to but one of his tragic epics, I have been audience to them all. On numerous occasions.'

Romana is amused. He has got through. She tries not to speak, and fails. 'My condolences,' she says, no doubt considering herself wicked. He knows he is good, very good.

'However,' she continues, 'it is not in my nature to mock those who cannot help the way they behave.'

Ah. She is obviously less delicate than she appears. He bows, acknowledging his mistake. 'My apologies, Romana. You clearly disapprove of my little experiment. But before you judge too harshly, you should be fully conversant with the facts of the matter.'

'I am conversant, as you put it, with the fact that you have violated a young man's genetic structure in such a manner as to cause considerable damage to both body and mind. On many civilised worlds, this would be considered a grave moral crime.'

She lets go of his hand, clearly ready to take him on. He stops, all contrition. 'Of course, and you would be correct in your thinking. It was a heinous act. I am a man fully aware of the crimes he has committed. If there had been any method other than the one I was forced to use, I would have used it. Alas, I was young and the disease too advanced.'

'Disease?'

'A most unfortunate syndrome – Baylock's palsy. Rare but undeniably fatal.'

'Baylock's palsy?' She is sceptical.

'Baylock's palsy. Premature ageing. Those afflicted never live a year beyond puberty. He was a serf, one of my family's people. The treatment was expensive and in its infancy. I took

78

it upon myself to do what I could. Believe me, his family were only too relieved.'

Forget that image of those greedy peasant parents grabbing at the pittance he paid them, shoving the screeching child into his carriage, dancing with joy as he drove away. You are telling a lie, it didn't happen. If you're saying it's true, it is a lie.

'Really,' Romana says, but she is uneasy.

'I'm sure you wish to find your friend,' he continues, easily. 'You know, one of these days you really are going to have to tell me who you are.'

Romana smiles back. 'One of these days. Am I a prisoner here?'

'Oh no. I have no claim on this palace. I am merely a tenant. The real owners, well, who knows...?'

'Indeed, the riddle of Valdemar and the disappearance of the Old Ones is one of the ten great mysteries of the universe,' says Romana. 'Number six as I recall, from those on my planet who were obsessed with lists.'

'You want the Doctor.'

'Please.'

'You realise, of course, that this palace is nothing more than the control centre of a jumped-up particle accelerator,' says Romana after Neville has left her and the Doctor together in the library. It is evening now, not that it makes much difference on Ashkellia, but somehow the dim palace lights have dimmed even further. Shadows loom large in this repository of the Old Ones.

The Doctor grunts. He has been tinkering with one of the data-storage cylinders. Slowly, he lowers it on to the carved table. Oh dear. Romana realises she has made a big mistake.

'Of course I know,' he replies, patiently. 'Now, undoubtedly, so do they.'

79

'Ah. Sorry.' She tries to spot the recording devices. 'Which is why Neville was so helpful in bringing me here. How do you think he is observing us?'

'It doesn't matter. Nano-bugs, cameras, telepathy for all I know.'

'I'm sorry Doctor.' She is still painfully aware of the gap between intelligence (the understanding of the purpose of the palace) and experience (knowing when to keep one's mouth shut).

'Don't worry. He would have worked it out in the end.'

Romana paces the huge hall. 'But applied on such a scale. Even Gallifrey... What could they possibly have hoped to achieve? These Old Ones.'

The Doctor's face is in shadow, but she could swear the lines on his face had deepened. He seems older, old as his years. 'To breach the higher dimensions,' he says.

Romana is shocked. Really shocked. 'But... but that's impossible. The whole idea, that's ludicrous.'

The Doctor laughs, but without humour. 'Why are you so upset? Because the Old Ones did it? Or that they achieved an engineering miracle not even the Time Lords could manage?'

'The experiment was closed down. The Dimensional Ethics Committee...'

'Banned any such experimentation. I know. The consequences would have been appalling.' The Doctor sits back in his chair, furiously twiddling his thumbs. To Romana, it was as if he had been there, as if the experiment had been taken from him. A personal insult.

'Why, Doctor?' she asks. 'What would happen if the higher dimensions were breached?' She is on familiar ground – the debate, the discussion of evidence.

'Reality would begin to change,' he muses, looking up at the data cylinders lining the walls. 'Or more strictly, appear to change. The higher dimensions *are* reality, just a greater reality than we can perceive. Even Time Lords, with their occasional insights into the fourth and fifth dimensions, aren't immune to their effects. You recall that poor man inside the tomb?'

Romana shudders. She remembers all right. 'And K-9?'

'The mind and body adapt to exposure to the higher dimensions. Organs in the brain, dormant for centuries, begin to grow. The eyes...'

'Yes, I know about the eyes.'

'Ah!' He is suddenly awake. The air pops with the sound of snapping fingers. His own wide eyes gleam in the dying light. 'Of course! How could I have been so stupid?'

'I don't know. What are you talking about?'

'Telepathy. Nano-whatever, cameras, telepathy, that's what I said, isn't it? Don't you see?'

'No. What's all this got to do with Valdemar?'

'Telepathy! That's what this has got to do with Valdemar.'

Romana frowns at him. She thinks she understands what he means. She remembers a rather fanciful paper on this very subject at the Academy. 'Doctor, that was only supposition.'

'Supposition? Superstition? It's fact and the Time Lords knew it! Valdemar. Of course. It has to be.'

'That certain individual forms of life are more adapted to perceive the higher dimensions? It's a childish conceit. Like the idea that certain privileged families could control and master some universal force...'

'It's undemocratic, I'll grant you. But I think it's true. The Old Ones must have had great quantities of psychic energy. Enough even to instil their computers with that knowledge.'

'Doctor. This is speculation.'

'Is it really?' He is up and pacing now. 'Even on minimal power, the sensors could interpret your psychic energy and re-create an environment you felt a deep empathy towards.'

81

'My room?'

'What else would you call it? Magic?'

Romana doesn't want to be convinced. She doesn't want to believe she is trapped inside a giant living computer that can read her mind. '"It knows", Huvan said. A frightening thought.'

The Doctor spreads out his arms. 'Frightening, indeed. Imagine. A million years ago, the Old Ones breached the higher dimensions. The effect would have been catastrophic. But not for everyone. Certain individuals, perhaps only one, were sufficiently psychically evolved to control its influence. To shape reality to its own ends. With that kind of power, it could do anything. And in the end, millennia later, when even the universe itself has changed beyond recognition, the memories of this time still live on.'

'Valdemar,' breathes Romana.

'This palace is only a fragment,' says the Doctor. 'An echo. If it can do what it does now, what would it be capable of when operating on full power?'

The words ring round the hall. Together, they look up at the library. It seems to have provided them with knowledge after all.

'We can't allow that,' Romana says.

'No,' the Doctor replies, somewhat evasively. 'No. Of course not.' He keeps himself impassive, not allowing his face to betray his real thoughts.

Up in his control room, Paul Neville rubs his hands with glee. His fingers dance over the video-disc controls. The Doctor's words are repeated once more. 'No. No. Of course not.'

It is time to begin work.

Night falls in the palace . Its battered metal skin is still assailed by the same liquid storms; the stabilisers still spin and fire; the updraught from the core still holds it aloft. However, deep inside, self-maintaining sensors understand and respond to the needs of its latest occupants and perform operations, relevant to their biological clocks.

In a way, the palace becomes even more fairy-like at night. We pass over the sleeping bodies of the young nobles, exhausted from yet another day of frolics. They dream of money and ease and love. We move to Huvan, muttering and flinching in his sleep from the thousand dark blows and slashes from the creatures living inside his mind.

We see Pelham, who has been released from her bonds by the terrifying Kampp, and escorted to a comfortable cell. She will be summoned in the morning. She dreams of her golden past, the success she never appreciated, the greed that brought her here. Of Robert Hopkins and his threats. Mercifully, memories of her treatment at the butler's hands, as well as the experience in the tomb, are overridden by these pleasanter scenes.

Neville sleeps at his console, like a grey spider in its lair, the spying machines still bobbing and floating. It's obvious what he dreams of – power. Limitless power. And Valdemar.

Finally, we see the Doctor and Romana, doing whatever Time Lords do that passes for sleep. They are trapped here, they know it. The weight of the universe presses down on them; the need to get moving, to get on with their mission. As yet, they feel themselves unable to proceed. Worse still, unable to perceive those factors larger than themselves that would allow them to know which decision would ultimately prove correct. What do they do? Escape and continue with the Key to Time? Or stay and prevent the worst, the unimaginable, from happening again, as it did a million years ago?

Sweet dreams, Doctor.

Chapter Six

You see, you have to see, the thing is – the Doctor is so very, very wrong.

All this talk of higher dimensions and particle accelerators, that's the typical kind of pseudo-rationalisation so beloved of our new lords and masters in the Protectorate.

He lacks the true knowledge, the true perception of what is and what isn't.

Valdemar cannot be tidily explained away, much as they would like him to be. Valdemar is aeons old, almost as old as time itself, so how can this Doctor arrogantly spout that he knows better, that he can reduce the Dark God to such principles? It is the mouse saying to the cat that he cannot exist because he is not just a big mouse, carrying on these protestations as it is consumed.

The truth can only be discovered through dedication, through exploration and, of course, through faith. Not the diluted, whining materialism of the New Protectorate, faith is an absolute belief that there is something more, something greater than this grubby life. One just needs the right eyes.

Perhaps if the Doctor had suffered, the way the small bundle of life energy known to the universe as Paul Neville has suffered...Paul Neville. A name given to this bundle by other bundles. Quite accidental, quite random.

Of course, nothing is random, or accidental. Neville was not born the eldest son of two of the richest and most powerful planet-owners in the empire for nothing. Oh no, there was meaning there, a predestination. This was always known.

Neville has a memory. He recalls events perfectly. His upbringing on the private moon, its atmosphere and gravity terraformed to provide just the right effect. The parents had been ostentatious, something Neville disliked. Their home was a re-creation of the famous Alton Towers, that apex of twenty-first century culture. Their Alton Towers, however, was large, much larger than the original. Ninety-five kilometres larger.

Neville remembers long summers and skeletal rides; ornamental fountains that stretched to the horizon; the indolence of the duke and duchess.

He himself preferred science. Oh yes, science. He gave it a go. Let the Doctor and his sceptics mock, but Neville tried their way. Determined to create something, something that would aid him in his destiny.

For a moment, emotion breaks in. Neville had a pet, a dog, its pampered life extended through genetic manipulation. Neville remembers – he extended that life span himself with surgery, to see what he could achieve. And more, so much more.

Neville remembers the horror on his parents' faces when he introduced the dog (what was its name again – Pinch? Punch?) to the court, clad in its own fine doublet and hose, and it opened its augmented mouth and politely introduced itself with a languid bow.

Alas, speech did not suit the creature. Despite the modifications to its brain, it lacked some spiritual component in its canine nature and failed to adjust to its new life. The new perceptions, the human perception, drove the creature mad.

The dog... Oh, there was some unpleasantness with servants, a death perhaps; he was only eleven at the time... and it had to be exterminated. Neville remembers this was the first hunt he was allowed to attend; that and the dog's blood on his face when it was eventually cornered.

Soon after, he knew science was a dead end. The life of the spirit was what consumed him now. Could life be altered spiritually? Was life any more than just living?

He gained entrance to the most prestigious arcane university on Earth, despite the parents' disapproval and, in fact, refusal. Oh yes, that particular turning-point.

When the shells of the duke and duchess were found poisoned in their private herb garden, no one could understand how this could have happened. The duke was an idiot; three centuries of noble breeding left no doubt about that, but the duchess, she knew everything she needed to know. Maybe it was a suicide pact, in the face of the impending revolts on their major planets. Even in his idiocy, the duke was rumoured to have extra-natural clairvoyance; perhaps he had forseen the day Hopkins would come and take his planets, wealth and lands off him.

It had been interesting to Neville. To watch as the spirits left his parents' physical trappings; their bewildered pleadings. At that moment, Neville realised he could breathe in those spirits and make himself stronger; compound his sense of self. They lived in him now, occasionally making their voices heard.

The human Neville left university having learned little – officially anyway. He already knew he was greater than anything his professors could teach him. He needed more. Oh, he had learned the usual arcane arts, even added to his store of scientific and medical knowledge, but he sensed a greater truth, beyond theurgy, beyond even him.

By this time, Neville had a reputation. He was a visionary, a fanatic, one who saw. His first group gathered around him. He remembers those days with amusement, children practising useless ritual – the candles, the evocations, the chalk circles. Neville likes to think of these times as groundwork. They were a masterpiece of style over content. The engine contained the parts but there was no power to drive it.

And then, there came the revolution. He remembers the slogan: 'The oppressed masses of this evil empire will no longer tolerate centuries of idle cruelty.' Dull, unimaginative, long-winded, like the revolution itself.

Neville, the young Neville, his hair already greying with the knowledge of a generation, was on Europa at the time, wandering the universe, looking for that which he needed, when the word came. His home, that moon with its palace, had been scorched. An Immolator Six capsule fired into the atmosphere from Robert Hopkins's own personal starship.

Robert Hopkins, Chief Prosecutor to the New Protectorate, second only to the Virgin Lady High Protector herself. Hopkins, an ugly man, who refused even basic plastic surgery to improve his appearance. Austere, and driven by a desire matching Neville's own.

It was Hopkins's aim, it was stated, his goal, to bring in the arch-necromancer himself, the Duke of the Second Quadrant, Paul Neville. Bring him back to Earth and personally behead him in front of his mistress. Oh, after a lengthy and just trial of course.

As for Neville, the news did not trouble him. The loss of his fortune was again predestined. He would make his way, armed only with his dark knowledge.

When he was twenty-eight, hiding in the slums of Sao Paulo city, Paul Neville read *The Tomb of the Dark God*, by some unknown, dipsy, utopian author, Miranda Pelham. The book changed his life.

Of course it was New Age nonsense. Of course it was crude and contained a fraction of the knowledge Neville needed. Yet something was planted in him: a seed, an idea. Enough to put him on the right path. He knew he had to meet Miranda Pelham.

How the times had changed. She still lived in luxury, in her own permanent time-share on a Caribbean island. He, who once would have commanded millions, was forced to travel incognito in the storage bays of hovercraft, his entire collection of books and magical equipment stuffed into an ageing sack.

Avoiding the New Protectorate guards at the dock, he walked to her beach hut. The apparent wealth there made him sneer. What could match the wealth he had grown up with?

Already, the island's calm was dissipating. Troops were arriving. Property would be seized to house corrupt protectorate officials, who preached poverty but ended up as greedy as those they had overthrown.

Neville found Miranda Pelham on a sun lounger, sipping cocktails. He could not imagine anyone more ignorant.

She was no longer young, no longer the aspirant. Her hair was dyed platinum blonde, her skin a deep brown. Time had done its work. Neville threw back the black cowl covering his head and introduced himself. 'I believe you,' he stated simply.

Pelham, for all her faults, had been thorough. Neville had been right to track her down. Amused by him then, she had no idea of the extent and importancce of the knowledge she had collated.

'What do you want?' she asked constantly, as night after night he studied the documents, the transcripts from a hundred planets and races, all traced with painstaking accuracy. All boiled down to the single root myth, the story of Valdemar.

A dark god from the beginning of time, released by the Old Ones to cut a deadly swathe through the universe. Finally trapped and buried in its tomb beneath a raging ocean, asleep and dissipated perhaps, but not truly dead. All the legends narrowed in to this one single termination. It had to be true. To Neville that was as clear as the sun shining.

Now he understood his destiny. His life was preordained, dreamed into existence by a sleeping god an eternity away. Only him, no one else. He was Valdemar's chosen son. He had looked up from the parchments, up in the warm inky night to the full moon of Terra. He seemed to see a face up there on

89

that orb, a dark face, revealing itself to him at last. Pelham was sleeping in the next room, unaware of the significance of the moment.

When the soldiers came, he and Pelham were ready. Even she had been forced to comprehend that she was about to lose everything.

On the night itself, they climbed into the motorboat and raced away from her burning home. Shots and cries came from the beach, the joy of destruction.

After an eternity they found refuge with some of the last remaining Elite, in a far-flung corner of the disintegrating empire.

Here, they planned. Pelham was sceptical... Perhaps she still is. Neville, however, was very persuasive.

His first major realisation was that he needed a psychic. All the legends spoke of Valdemar as being a force, a black shadow, an entity that needed life to contain its essence. All the legends spoke of this... this possession. The Centauri called it 'Stoodlhoo', the Xanir 'Prah-Tah-Cah', the Ogrons with their lumpy language simply 'The Getting Into'.

Which is where Huvan is so necessary. More proof of the Doctor's misunderstanding. You call Huvan a coincidence?

He comes from a half-remembered project from Neville's university days, when he was still dabbling in science. Neville had been at home, randomly screening subjects for psychic potential. Even as a twelve-year-old, Huvan was off the scale. Neville was guided even then by his dark master – the experiments, drugs and surgery to stall the boy's adolescence, to prolong forever the time when psychic potential reaches its maximum, the body in a constant state of war with itself. It was worth the emotional turmoil, worth the tantrums and fevers of puberty, for now, twenty years later, Huvan is the most powerful psychic force in the galaxy. Neville is glad he had not had the brat killed.

Neville now had a host for the master; the hardest work was over. All that remained was to find the resting place, the tomb beneath the sea.

He and Pelham wasted three years scouring planets with high percentages of water until Neville realised that perhaps the legend described a different type of sea. He was running out of funds and so his enforced patronage by fellow displaced Elite families began. He and Pelham created a fanciful story of wealth and power to encourage this patronage. It helped that the author still possessed a reputation amongst these decadent idiots.

These years of searching and begging and constant failure seem a blur to Neville – so many setbacks, so many near misses.

For Hopkins was still hounding him, determined to bring him in. He became Neville's nemesis. They met once, at a starport on Centauri. An elaborate trap, set in motion by an impoverished Elite governor, desperate to retain the last leavings of his wealth.

Neville remembers the encounter, in the doorway of the orbital shuttle, the soldiers running. Hopkins's twisted face, slavering with anticipation, then disappointed as Neville operated his transmat-bracelet. Hopkins's face fading away, never tiring, disbelieving.

Since then the clumsy fool has not even been close. Neville has outsmarted him all the way.

And now Ashkellia, that nowhere in the middle of nowhere, further even than the outer colonies, at the very limit of travelled space. Ashkellia, the tomb of Valdemar, and the Doctor. Spread your sedition, Doctor. Send your girl to stir up trouble amongst my lackeys. Nothing happens here without my knowledge, without my seeing it happen. Do all those things.

But you will re-power this palace.

Do you understand? This is no amateurish expedition stumbling by accident across an ancient burial site. This has all been foreseen; dreamed of centuries ago by a creature so powerful, it could die and design its own resurrection through me. *Through me!*

The time is right, Doctor and all you others, the Time is Right. The Stars are Right.

Romana raises her arms and dives. Below, a benevolent face looks up. It is good to feel herself stretch through the air, those brief fragile moments of sensuality before she impacts. The mosaic face dissolves into a thousand fragments.

The water is cool and clear, exactly what she needs. Rather than rising, she thrusts forward with strong strokes to the end of the stone pool. She feels she has somehow transcended herself; it has been a long time since she last swam. She has become a new kind of creature, one for whom only motion matters. She twists and starts out for the other end once more, springing away from the mosaic tiles. The pool is circular, like so much here, and perfect. No thought, just action; the silent void of water.

Five minutes later, Romana surfaces with a gasp of simple, joyous laughter. She shakes her head and gulps in the warm air. She settles back and floats, looking up at the blurred, shadowed ceiling high above. The mixture of scents from the jasmine plants around the pool do not quite overpower that clean refreshing smell of fresh water. Heaven. Absolute heaven.

'I thought you were never coming back up.' A voice, changing everything. 'You must have the lungs of a Birostrop.'

For a moment, Romana cannot place the voice. She swivels her head and sees the golden-maned man watching her. Stanislaus. Tenniel Stanislaus.

'I've never seen this pool before. The palace must have created it just for you. It's nice.'

Not as stupid as he looks, thinks Romana, strangely embarrassed that she has been observed revealing her emotions. And dressed as she is in this flimsy white one-piece.

'Why don't you dive in?' she says, trying to keep her voice even. Even though the Doctor has asked her to mix with these people, she is reticent. Why, she does not know. Perhaps Stanislaus is the one sane person amongst them, a kind of lever into the hearts and minds of the others. Perhaps some maturity is lurking there after all.

'All right!' He grins enthusiastically and hits the water like a bomb.

Romana hauls herself out of the pool. Stanislaus has been attempting to prove his own breath-holding abilities and surfaces yet again, lips turning blue with cyanosis.

'I think you'd better come and have some breakfast,' says Romana. 'Before you drown.'

Stanislaus grins feebly, blinking away tears of effort. Romana walks to the cane table, laid as it is with amphorae and fresh fruit. Water follows her on the stone-flagged floor. She sits and pours herself a drink. Stanislaus follows, dabbing at himself with a towel.

'I must say,' Romana says as she pours for him, 'this palace can be extremely civilised.'

'It's your taste, Romana. You know how to pick and choose what you want. *We* want everything now, all the time.'

'You must learn to manage your imagination.'

'Easier said than done. This palace can give you anything you wish for.'

Romana smiles. 'Careful what you wish for… And what about Paul Neville?'

'What about him?'

'What does he wish for?'

Stanislaus screws up his face and thinks. Romana winces at the effort this must take. 'He is going to give us back what the New Protectorate took.'

'How?'

'Valdemar.'

'And what has he told you Valdemar is?'

'Who are you?'

'I am Romana.'

They stare at each other. His eyes are blue, piercing blue. The water is drying on them. 'I need to get dressed,' says Romana. 'And no doubt the lovely Hermia awaits.'

Stanislaus whoops. Playfully, he flicks his towel at her.

'Yes,' she says calmly. 'Don't do that again.'

She stands, relishing his discomfort. 'And I wouldn't believe everything Paul Neville told you either,' she continues. 'Do you know the old saying, "There's no such thing as a free lunch"?'

'No.'

'If you want something, the usual method is to work for it. What Neville is offering you has a price. You just don't know it yet. Goodbye.'

And with that she leaves for her room. 'Wait! Wait...' His yells end when she closes the pool-room door.

Unfortunately, Romana does not make it to her room, not yet anyway. Someone is lurking in the shadows of the corridor. Feeling distinctly underdressed, she has a good idea who this lurker might be.

She will have to brazen it out. 'Huvan!' she snaps, turning to face him. 'I would rather you didn't follow me around.'

He is sheepish, genuinely ashamed. 'I'm sorry,' he says, 'I couldn't help it.' He steps out of the shadows. What is he wearing? A black T-shirt with some kind of poorly printed motif emblazoned on the front, a crude joke involving the unintelligible word 'smeg' that is neither funny nor interesting. Tight black jeans and white shoes. And when did he last wash that ginger hair? Honestly, does Neville make him wear these things? Is it some form of punishment?

'Huvan,' she sighs. 'What do you want from me?' If only she had brought that towel with her, anything to shield herself from that stare.

'I... I...' he stammers, 'I... just want to... protect you...'

'Oh, grow up!' Romana snaps, tired of these adolescent rantings. 'Stop mooching around after me!'

She tries to walk away but something stops her. Something not herself. Her hearts suddenly pound in her chest. The power, magic, whatever it is, forces her to turn and face Huvan once more. He is smiling in the shadows.

'I saw you in there, I saw you speaking to him. Don't do it again.'

Romana stays silent. How is he doing this?

He continues. 'Don't worry. I could never hurt you. Ever.'

The force is gone and so is he. Rage bubbles inside her. How dare he possess her in this way!

Before her temper is brought back under control, before she goes off looking for the boy and regrets what she says, she stomps back to her room and locks the door, sick of Huvan, sick of being watched.

The morning ritual. Just the thing to get you going, a spot of black magic before breakfast.

The Doctor follows the acolytes into what he remembers as the large piazza where the young ones held their masque. It is all very different now. These children, they know not what they do.

He conceals himself behind some purple drapes put up especially for the occasion. Whether or not Neville already knows he is here is not the point. One has to keep up the traditions.

The ex-masquers, in their black robes, shuffle up to a small raised dais that emerges from the floor. They raise their arms, chanting words that seem to the Doctor harsh and cobwebbed with age. Words from another aeon.

The Doctor feels a cold draught whip round the piazza. Now, is that atmospheric control or something else?

Paul Neville enters in the full regalia – cloak, staff, beard.

'Valdemar!' he bellows. The acolytes kneel and murmur the appropriate responses.

Actually, the rest of the cabal is rather dull. The Doctor watches but with no particular interest. A mishmash of occult rituals common the galaxy over to groups with nothing better to do. All designed with one aim in mind, to get the psychic juices flowing. He vaguely recalls a church, back on Earth, twentieth century. The Master and the trouble he caused. Forget it; a different age, a different Doctor.

The Doctor supposes this mumbo-jumbo might actually do it; it might convince the palace to switch itself on. He doubts it though. For the real work to be done, for the whole thing to get going, Neville would need the power of a genuine psychic prodigy, and he has seen no evidence of one here. In fact, these decadent children would have trouble pulling a rabbit from a hat.

'Ah!' Realisation hits him. He claps his hand over his mouth. The murmuring continues. He has thought of a way out.

His thinking has been flawed. What would be so wrong about restoring the power to the palace? There's nothing Neville could do without a psychic key to utilise that power. All right, the lights would come on and there would be a lot of beeping, but without the psychic control of the Old Ones, the palace would just idle, turning over like an engine in neutral.

Restoring power is not without its risks, the Doctor admits, but once he has the Key to Time fully reassembled, he could always come back and close it down again. For once, he would have to leave a job temporarily unfinished. But the stability of the entire universe was at stake. He couldn't be expected to be in two places at once.

The Doctor nods to himself. Very well. Get the power on, find Romana and get on with the mission. There seems to be no other way.

That's not to say he has to make it easy for Neville…

The chanting has reached its inevitable shouting climax. Neville is on his knees, sweat pouring out of his robes, screaming for his master. 'Valdemar! VALDEMAR!'

The drapes by the entrance rustle in the cold wind. The Doctor hasn't bothered to stay for the end.

He waits for Neville in the control room of the Old Ones. He has draped himself over one of the baroque instrument panels, scarf dangling. He appears completely calm, just waiting. He pops a jelly baby into his mouth.

A sound, in the doorway. The Doctor grins. 'Knock, knock,' he says. 'Hello Paul.'

Neville's eyes glitter from his exertions. 'You wanted to see me?'

'Yes, I did want to see you.' The Doctor leaps up. 'Yes, I did. How was the black mass? Very strenuous, I should imagine. If you want to go around raising demons and the like, I'd make sure you have a vigorous warm-up beforehand.'

'I take it you wanted to see me for something more important than this nonsense.'

'How about I get the power back on for you?'

Neville hides his surprise. 'You can do it?'

'Of course I can do it! The question is, do you really want it done?'

'What does that mean?'

'Restoring the power won't get you what you want. You should know that.'

Neville is staring up at the controls. He is bunching his fists.

The Doctor grabs those fists. He stares into Neville's face. 'Nothing for nothing, Paul. This is a negotiation.'

Neville pulls away. 'I would do anything. Anything.'

'Now that's not a very good opening gambit, is it?' The Doctor is casual again. 'I mean, the essence of negotiation is that we slowly reach an agreement, bargaining our way to…'

'Shut up. What do you want?'

The Doctor considers. 'Return myself and Romana to the tomb. Release Pelham from wherever you're keeping her.'

'Is that all?' Neville laughs, genuinely amused. 'You give me the universe and that is all you want? I am not an idiot, Doctor. What is down there?'

'Just my ship. I promise not to interfere with whatever you want to do.'

Neville considers.

Why is the Doctor feeling hot all of a sudden? Why can't he get that line out of his mind: 'Had I as many souls as there be stars, I'd give them all for Mephistophilis'? *Faustus*, Act One, Scene Three. Don't think about it.

'You don't believe I will be able to use the power, do you?'

'That's not for me to say.'

'You think I don't know what I'm doing?'

'Do you want this bargain or not? Because I'm tired of listening to you.'

Neville smiles, his perfect teeth shining. 'Doctor. How can I refuse?'

The Doctor hears a rushing sound in his ears. Why is his conscience acting up? It isn't fair, why should such a choice be left to him? He forces himself to think of the Key; the consequences of failure should he not collect all six segments. He thinks of the end of the universe.

It is as if he is no longer in control of his actions. It's not possession or anything like that; he has come to this conclusion logically. Rather, it is as if someone has fed this intention into his mind; cut off any pathways to alternative actions; guiding him inexorably towards that which he knows he has to do. As if he has been hoodwinked.

What he is doing is right; he can't put his finger on any flaws, any way out of the necessity to restore the power.

'Doctor, do it,' says a panting Neville. 'Do it now.'

Feeling like the victim of some arcane confidence trick, the structure of which he is unable to comprehend, the Doctor snaps his fingers and the power comes on.

Something happens. All around the palace lights and sounds, operating from instruments previously hidden or ignored, suddenly emerge like a new morning. In the piazza, the lazy cultists are astounded by the sudden shifting of their architecture. Nothing stays still, even the floor is moving as if working its way through some carefully rehearsed ballet. Hermia, Stanislaus and the others clutch at the trundling furniture, certain that all their suspicions are well-founded. The palace is full of devils.

Romana sees her room begin to grow, the wood of the wardrobe expanding and darkening, as if previously only sketched in. Her bed, in fact everything, becomes more defined, though she had never realised it lacked that definition.

Huvan claps his hands and laughs. The music in his head, that sweet noise that has lodged itself in there ever since his arrival, swells and layers. He feels in tune with the palace. His poetry rises from its squalid piles, the scribbled sheets hanging frozen in front of him. Huvan yells like an ape. He did this. He has made it happen.

He has never been so happy.

In the control room, Neville is lost in his rapture. He is weeping as he stares at the returning life. Somewhere deep inside the palace, great cogs are turning. Neville touches this, feels that, watches the swells and transformations of the magic of the Old Ones. 'It's alive!' he roars. 'IT'S ALIVE!'

As for the Doctor, he just looks, his usually animated face stern and unmoving. He is perhaps the only still object within this palace, a centre, a void.

He watches Neville's rapture with but one thought in his mind. What have I done? What have I done?

Deep down beneath the skin of Ashkellia, a great spin is beginning. Particles, invisible microscopic particles, are charging up ready for their planet-spanning marathon. Machinery a million years old and more prepares itself to begin work again, after all this time.

Inside the pyramid, the tomb of Valdemar comes to life.

The great gateway to the tomb, huge as a tower block, lights up. Bolts and locks slide into place. A pattern appears, apparently growing from the metal. The image is that of a five-pointed star.

The door shakes. It rattles, and blows of indescribable force hammer into it. Something is pounding, a force that has lain dormant for a million years. Dormant no longer.

Chapter Seven

At last, the changing ceases. The palace seems brighter, more focused than before. All feel the difference, as if they had just awakened from a strange, elusive dream.

The Doctor sits and waits for Neville to go back on his word.

Once the theurgist has got over his excitement, he calls for Kampp. The unimpressed, impassive butler takes the Doctor by the arm.

'You wanted to see Pelham, Doctor,' says Neville. 'Off you go.'

The Doctor nods. 'And Romana? I don't suppose you're going to let her go, either?'

Neville scratches his beard, eager for this to be over. 'She has her uses. It seems my young ward, Huvan, has taken rather a liking to her.'

'This way, please,' says Kampp silkily, pulling the Doctor's arm just a little too firmly.

'Look, I've got work to do,' says Ponch, 'and I think I've guessed what this is all about. Is there a Valdemar there or not? Why don't you just tell me?'

The woman scowls. 'You can't stop me mid-flow. You're destroying all the cumulative tension. I get enough stick as it is. If it's not my plots that are too complicated, it's my characters. Now they'll have an excuse to attack my style as well. Trying to be clever but no content, that's what they'll say. Hell, we live in a godless age. Can't you give a girl a chance?'

'Girl?'

'Shut up.'

Footsteps in the snow behind them. Ponch whirls around, ready for an attack. It is Ofrin. He yells. 'You gonna help me

with these hides or do I have to knock your brains out?'
Particles of ice crystallise in his great beard.

'All right, all right, I'm coming.'

Ofrin blinks and spots Pelham. 'You? Where did you get to... last night?'

'Good morning.' She turns, obviously in some great arthritic pain. Ponch is surprised to notice she has turned paler since they sat down.

'Great ending by the way,' Ofrin says softly to the woman. 'Lots of fighting and that's what we all want, innit? Ponch!' he bellows again.

'All right, all right, I'm coming. So, the ending's about fighting?'

'Perhaps.' The woman looks at the snow. 'Perhaps it changes depending on who hears it.'

'Eh?'

'I think you should stay for the end. I don't think I've got long left. If I don't tell it now, I may never tell it again.'

'Ponch, don't you dare.'

Ponch turns to the bearded giant. He has never stood up to Ofrin in his life. 'I'll be there soon. I've got to hear this.'

Ofrin starts to growl. Ponch has already said enough to get himself killed. He will have to fight.

'Leave us, Ofrin. Ponch will be along shortly.' The woman is staring at the giant, kindly but unblinkingly.

'But I... the work...' Ofrin stutters.

'This *is* work.'

As Ponch watches, he sees Ofrin flap at his own face as if bothered by a snow-fly. The big man's eyes, almost hidden in his hair, screw up as if grappling with some insoluble problem. 'It won't take too long,' says Pelham.

Ofrin nods. As if he has forgotten something, he turns and clomps back to the growing settlement, muttering angrily.

Ponch is impressed.

'Right,' says Pelham, settling on to the tundra bank again. 'No more interruptions.'

'I'm sorry, Doctor. Mind you, you've only got yourself to blame.'

He looks around at his new surroundings, new but so, so familiar. The bare metal room, the locked door. Only the padded, restraining chairs separate this from the hundreds of other cells he has been locked into. And Miranda Pelham, tired and bruised, strapped next to him.

'I thought something was up,' she says, 'despite my rather limited view of the world at the moment. What happened? How did you get the power back on?'

The Doctor is not listening; he is thinking through all the possible permutations of escape.

'Doctor?' she insists, breaking his concentration.

'Do you have to ask so many questions? You're worse than Romana.'

'Oh, I'm sorry,' she snaps, sarcastically. 'I've been stuck in here for a day now, without a word to anyone. Typical that when Neville finally sends me someone, he doesn't want to talk. Anyway, I thought that your Romana seemed very intelligent.'

The Doctor ponders. 'Hmm, she started well...'

'Doctor. The power?' He realises Pelham, for all her seeming innocence, knows a thing or two about interview techniques. She isn't going to let go.

'It's perfectly simple. The power was never off.'

'I don't understand.'

'Let me put it this way. When a person is asleep, they're still alive, aren't they? Everything is still switched on; otherwise, they'd be dead. Sleep is simply a different form of consciousness. I was an alarm clock, telepathically speaking.'

'So you gave Neville exactly what he wanted. And ended up here.'

'Oh, I expected Neville to go back on his word,' the Doctor replies, indifferently. 'They always do.'

'Then why the hell did you switch the palace on?'

The Doctor cannot answer. He doesn't know. Or maybe 'it seemed a good idea at the time'. 'Don't worry, there's nothing he can use here,' he says, avoiding the question. 'Oh, the quality of the catering will probably improve, but it won't help him with Valdemar. I must get back to the TARDIS. At any cost. No, I don't think he can do any particular harm.'

Pelham shakes her head. 'If you had known anything about Neville…'

'If I had…! All right, tell me about Neville. That's obviously why he has put me in here with you.'

'OK,' she says. 'We've got nothing else to do. It all started…'

'No, no,' he replies, irritated, 'the short version. I need to be out of here, very quickly. He plans to reawaken Valdemar, doesn't he? Why?'

'Revenge, power; to regain those possessions and lands lost to him. It's a good story, I fell for it myself. And not just me. It's ten years since Neville became the Magus of the cult of Valdemar. From my little book, and a club of a handful of nutters, the cult has become the most powerful magical organisation in the New Protectorate.'

The Doctor turns to look at Pelham. He wonders at her motives. She isn't stupid, she isn't easily swayed, so why is she here?

'I was afraid.' She supplies an answer for him. Her bright blue eyes darken for a moment. To the Doctor she seems, for the first time, old. 'He was fanatical, ruthless, charismatic. I fell for him, I guess. I lost everything in the revolution and hanging around with him seemed a good idea at the time. I was thirty-five years old. Old being the operative word. You know, back in the old days, a long way back, all you got was about thirty-five years. Now, all you get is about a hundred.'

The Doctor hears the tremor in her voice. Miranda Pelham is afraid of her own mortality.

'Valdemar was my life's work,' she continues. 'I may never have believed it but Neville is good, very good. If there was some chance, any at all… Somehow he managed to raise all this funding and I really didn't have anything better to do. Like you, however, I'm starting to regret that decision.'

Pelham sneaks a glance at the Doctor and he realises there is something she's not telling him. 'And it was as simple as that?' he asks, probing. 'Really?'

'Really.' She keeps her face straight. 'What about you? I still don't know anything about you. You could be Valdemar himself for all I know.'

At last, the first restraint comes loose. The leather snaps apart and the Doctor raises his freed right arm. 'I might, at that,' he says mysteriously. When she flinches he gives her his disarming smile. 'Shall we go?'

'How did you do that?'

He unwraps himself from the remaining restraints. Distracted, he replies, 'You know, if I spent less time answering questions and more time getting on with the job, I'd never get into half the trouble I do get into.' He moves to unravel her restraints.

'One thing, Doctor. You said Neville couldn't use the power of the palace. How can you be so sure?'

'Who said I was sure? I'm taking a chance and I don't like it. However, Valdemar is not what he thinks it is. Whatever is down there in that tomb, it's not some sleeping all-powerful god. For Neville to achieve anything, he would need a highly disciplined psychic controller. A telepath of unbelievable sensitivity. And that, Miss Pelham, only occurs naturally in the human race about, ooh, once every thousand years. The chances of Neville having one on board are negligible. Obviously, if that were the case, the danger to the universe would be… ah, there we are.'

Most of the restraints are off but Pelham does not move. In fact, as she lies there her strong face drains of colour. She stares at him and he wonders whether she is going to be sick.

'What? Come on, come on, chop chop.'

Her mouth moves but the words don't emerge. He puts an ear to her lips and feels warm breath trickling into his head. 'Tell me,' he says.

'You…' The words are whispered. 'You haven't met Huvan, then?'

'Huvan? I've heard the name.' He goes cold just as the cell door is opened. He barely hears Kampp enter the room.

'Time enough, Doctor,' the butler purrs.

He feels light, gorgeous. The pain, the black dog that hounds him, biting at his confidence, ruining his life, has gone.

Huvan doesn't like to admit it, but he feels good. Life is not the empty black hole it has always been. He wouldn't do it in public, he wouldn't want anyone to know, but he can't help smiling.

It must be the Lady Romana. It has to be. She walked into his life like an angel, out from the tomb. He couldn't breathe when he saw her; that's how he knew. And now he cannot bear to be in the room with her, so certain is he that he will mess everything up. She brings meaning to him. Oh, that's good; that's a good line. Better write it down now before he forgets.

Huvan sits up. He scribbles on the yellowed paper, not realising that the pencil is six feet away, writing on its own, stabbing through the air over his table. He just wants to get the line committed; he is already sixty-three lines into his 'Ode to Romana', the work he will present to her when it is done. Isn't it amazing how a man can write the truth about his feelings, when speech is so ugly and stunted? Visions of her gratitude overwhelm his imagination. She will fall to her knees, tears in her eyes.

Even the palace has changed since she arrived. Huvan knows there is a presence here, something he cannot explain, something not even the Magus can explain, he bets.

All his life he has known he is special. The Magus tells him often enough, has worked on him enough. Huvan remembers the endless operations, painful operations; so much a part of his growing up; they became normal, even attractive. Every time he resurfaced on the operating table, Neville's face was there, reassuring him it was all for his own good, that he would have died without these messy procedures.

Huvan is afraid of nothing, he is certain of that. Nothing except Hopkins, the creature that would destroy them all. And even he has paled, a childhood nightmare.

Inevitably, work on the poem is disrupted by more rewarding musings. This new lightness he feels has not served to help him forgive. He thinks about Hermia, that blonde witch, the one he would have given his life to. Until Romana. How mistaken he had been. Smiling contentedly, Huvan settles back on to his bed. The pencil drops to the floor with a wooden plunk. Time to go over the retribution, the punishments; those deceptive blue eyes, that flawless skin, those caustic snarls she gave him when all he wanted to do was be nice...

The door opens and breaks into his fantasies. The Magus himself.

Instantly, Huvan is up and on his feet.

'Relax, my boy,' says Neville, in that brown, warm voice of his. 'I trust you are well.'

How can Huvan explain his new self? How can speech describe what he is becoming? And it is all thanks to the Magus, of that there can be no doubt.

'You do not need to speak,' says Neville. 'I can see.'

'What's happening to me?' asks Huvan.

'Are you in discomfort? Pain?'

'No. The opposite, Magus. I feel… born again.'

The older man smiles. 'Good. That is good. I have rekindled the power of this palace. Can you feel its blood running around us, in the air, beneath our feet? This is your time Huvan, you have much reason to be happy. At last, the universe will understand what you are, what I have made you. We live in exciting times.'

Huvan likes it when the Magus talks like this. 'What… what…' he asks, stumbling over the words, 'what is it you want me to do?'

Neville shakes his head. Modestly, he says, 'We are past what I want, Huvan. You must seize this time. This is your moment.'

Huvan considers. 'Yes, but what do I have to do?'

'Wait. Just wait. Tonight, I will arrange a meeting of the full cabal.'

'Will those others be there? I don't…'

'Have no fear. From tonight you will be feared, respected, even loved.'

And now Huvan can't keep that smile hidden. 'Really? Me? I've been waiting so long, so long. Will Romana be there?'

Neville frowns. 'Romana? Ah. I see. I think that can be arranged. You have a special… feeling for her?'

Huvan turns away. 'No, it's just…'

'Look at me!'

The barked command ruins everything. Huvan feels tears

welling up. He recalls what the Magus can do to him when he is angry. He obeys the order.

'Never lie to me again,' the Magus says, a fury barely contained within him. 'Never forget he to whom you owe your life.'

'I didn't mean anything.'

'You have feelings for Romana?'

Huvan nods. 'Feelings' – such a superficial word for what he really means.

Oddly, the Magus is not angry. His voice has returned to those soothing familiar tones. 'Then, of course, she shall attend.'

He turns to leave. Huvan cannot let it go at this, even in his fear. 'What's going to happen, Magus?'

Neville does not turn back, but Huvan can see he is shaking with excitement. 'My boy. For twenty-two long years I have nurtured you, raised you with more care than I would my own son. Let me tell you what will happen tonight. The final moment is upon us. The time has come to resurrect the Dark One.'

The party has started again, perhaps it never ends. Unaware of Huvan's, and for that matter, Neville's intentions, Romana has been wandering the palace, avoiding the occasional leather-clad guard, trying to find the Doctor. Because he is apparently nowhere, she has in her desperation reluctantly decided to appeal to the foppish nobles.

When the power came on, she knew the Doctor had done it. For whatever reasons, he has given Neville exactly what he wanted. Now they have nothing to bargain with. Unless the bargain has already been made. Either way, she has to find him.

The piazza in which the children fritter the days away has grown into a minor palace of its own. Thick with green ferns and chequered marble flagstones, new additions include ornate noisy fountains and cold, unblinking statues of athletes. Steam rises from the numberless stone pools in which she finds Stanislaus and the others.

'Romana,' he shrieks with delight, blond hair plastering his forehead. The beautiful Hermia, flushed and somewhat less delighted to see her, brushes the strands back. Somewhere in this balmy decadence, the others are laughing and running.

'I need to speak to you,' Romana says, realising she will have to be direct.

'Really,' yawns Hermia. 'Will it take long?'

'Hermia!' Stanislaus reprimands, without conviction. 'Join us, please.' He invites Romana into their water.

'No, thank you.'

Hermia pouts. She drinks from a sparkling goblet.

'I'm not sure the Magus would like us to talk to you. In fact, I think he would probably be very angry. Why can't you just leave us alone?'

For a moment, Romana is irked. Who does this brat think she is? She restrains herself. 'Fine, I would prefer to conduct my conversation with intelligent life forms, so feel free to find something more deserving of your attention any time.' An icy smile forces its way on to her lips. Hermia blushes.

At least Stanislaus is listening. Listening intently. Now, how to phrase this? 'I can't find my companion,' she tries. 'I was wondering if you might know where Neville would put him.'

'Tenny, no!' snaps Hermia, without a second thought. Mind you, Romana muses, a first thought is trouble enough.

'What makes you think he would have put your companion anywhere?' asks Stanislaus, but not unreasonably.

Hermia is making a face. 'That funny-looking old man with the hair. I thought he looked odd. Not normal at all. Ugly. We shouldn't allow ugly things in here.'

'Believe it or not, Hermia, he is trying to help you,' offers Romana.

'The only person who wants to help us is the Magus,' Hermia says triumphantly. 'Why don't you just go away?'

Romana is unable to hold herself in any more. Putting her hands on her hips in best fishwife fashion, she starts on Hermia. 'You really think I would have come asking you people for help if I had any, and I mean any, alternative? I don't know the palace, I've only just arrived.' She turns to go, sick of the whole preening lot of them. 'I'm sorry to have inconvenienced you.' Almost a snarl but not quite; her composure has been developed over centuries.

Just as she starts off, Stanislaus rises from the pool, his toga unleashing a cascade of water. 'Wait! Of course I'll help…'

'Tenny!'

'Oh, shut up!' he shouts suddenly. 'I'm bored with you.' Romana tries to conceal her surprise. Stanislaus gestures to the scattered mass of revellers, the palace, everything. 'In fact, I'm bored with the whole thing. Come on Romana, let's find this friend of yours.'

Energetically, Stanislaus grabs a towel and as they walk to the double doors, he dries his golden hair. That done, he turns and flings the towel at Hermia, whose angry tears are already being attended to by the next golden-haired youth.

Humans, Romana muses; what does the Doctor see in them?

Miranda Pelham has also had enough of passivity. She is sick and tired of being locked up and tied down. It's time to give something back. And take her mind off the black dread that threatens to drill into her sanity.

Thanks to the Doctor's distractions, Kampp never realised she had nearly been freed. Pelham works away at the other leather straps until she can free herself completely. Try not to

111

take any notice of your beating heart, she tells herself. Even a born coward can act when they have to. She'd read it somewhere.

How to get out of a cell. It was so easy for fictional characters; they just clutched their stomachs and pretended to be ill. Yeah, right. Like that would fool a child.

Short of suddenly developing amazing locksmith abilities, the only alternative was to wait until some really thick guard with a muscle-wasting disease opened the door and bent over to allow himself to be knocked out. That should do the trick.

A weapon. Hmm.

Pelham paces the cell. A weapon.

There aren't any. Unless she can pull a two-ton chair out of its moorings and hold it over her head until this mythical guard arrives. What else? Karate? Death pinch?

It will have to be the old-fashioned punch on the nose then run like hell.

Pelham sits and thinks. This isn't going to work.

Like others in the palace, this switching-the-power-on thing has opened up a new perspective in her mind. Why did she agree to come here with Neville? Of course he was going to try and raise Valdemar, like the Doctor says. For a so-called writer, she is painfully unobservant. Or perhaps she just chose not to know, to limit her own perception.

Not for the first, or last, time she rubs the bangle on her wrist. It is making her arm sore.

And then, once the thought is lodged, she is tempted. Ever so tempted to use it. I can't, she thinks, he'll kill me. This still is not the worst.

What can she do? What the hell is she going to do?

When the cell door finally does open, Pelham is caught by surprise. This isn't how it works in the books, she breathes, as she dives back into the chair and replaces the restraining straps.

Neville flicks a switch on his console. Kampp's face fills the screen. 'Magus?' asks the butler.

'How is the Doctor?'

'Recovering.' Kampp's lip curls, his best attempt at a genuine smile. 'I've just returned him to Pelham. Don't worry, there isn't any permanent damage.'

'What did you find out?'

A dark shadow crosses Kampp's brow. Upset? 'Hardly anything. Except that he knows a lot more than he's letting on. And I'm convinced he's not one of Hopkins's men.'

'I'll keep monitoring him. He seems to like talking to Pelham. Anyway, we have a new challenge. Stanislaus.'

'Oh. Interesting.' The voice has an unmistakable lilt of anticipation.

'He was always the most problematic,' says Neville. 'Now he is with Romana, looking for the Doctor.'

'And what would you like me to do? Discipline him?'

'Whatever you fancy. Just don't harm the girl. I need her.'

Kampp shakes his head, as if dismissing Romana entirely. 'Have no fear. Stanislaus, eh? I've had my eye on him. I feel a long session coming on. Thank you, Mr Neville.'

'Just get it done. Before the cabal.'

Neville flicks the switch and Kampp disappears. He leans back and looks at his robes, rubbing his chin thoughtfully. Soon, very soon now, magus.

On an impulse, Neville leans forward and re-signals Kampp.

'Yes, Magus?' asks the butler; just a trace of impatience there.

'I've changed my mind,' says Neville. 'Kill the Doctor. Do it now.'

* * *

He has started to see things, pictures. He cannot tell if they are real or not. Of course, he sees Romana.

Huvan finds himself unsurprised by these developments. It is as if he has always known he could do it, an itch in his mind he has only now decided to scratch. He visualises this new thing, the light that shines in his head, on the back and to the left. If he looks into that light there is a slight painful tug and then everything is released. It is like touching a fresh gap left by an extracted tooth, it makes him feel sick but it is fascinating.

She seems to be with that oaf Stanislaus. They are searching for the Doctor, dodging Neville's guards. He could have helped them, told them exactly where all the guards were, told them where the Doctor is for that matter.

They are going the wrong way. Huvan giggles to himself. He is laughing at the blond boy, the one who was almost worse than the others. For a start, he was always with Hermia, touching her, cooing to her. His pitiful attempts at niceness. Sheer hypocrisy, barely concealing the hate within. How Huvan longs to bring the whole place down on all of them. And soon he will be able to do it too. This new thing in him, it's growing.

'Which way now?' asks an exasperated Romana.

'How should I know?' shrugs Stanislaus. 'I've never been out of our quarters before. It's cooler.'

'This is going to take all day.'

Stanislaus looks back the way he came. To Romana, he certainly looks the part of the rescuing hero, like something from a myth. If only he had brains to go with it. She realises she is now doing exactly what she did before, wandering aimlessly through this shifting maze. Only now there are two of them. With Neville no doubt watching their every move.

'I guess,' says Stanislaus, 'I guess the cells would be on the lowest level. That's where my father always had his cells.'

'What happened to your father?'

'He died in them. Hopkins put him there and left him to starve.'

'Hopkins?'

'You know, the finder-general.' Stanislaus yanks open another door, ready for battle. 'Ha!'

'Actually, I don't know. And that's a cupboard.'

Suddenly, Romana feels a buzzing in her ear, like a wasp. She shakes her head, clapping a hand to it. Stanislaus is there at her side in an instant. 'What is it?' he asks, manfully.

The buzzing hurts. Romana slaps her ear. 'Tinnitus?' she asks herself, disbelieving. She feels the commencement of a headache. And something else. 'We're going the wrong way,' she murmurs, suddenly certain. 'I can see the Doctor. He's two floors below. There's an anti-grav lift, second turning on the right.'

'I'm impressed,' says Stanislaus. He looks it.

Romana is too worried to notice. 'How could I know that?'

'Never mind.' Stanislaus slaps her arm, 'Let's go!' He dashes for the lift.

'Er…Tenniel,' says Romana, coughing. She points. 'This is right.'

Valrus, a high cult guard and one of Paul Neville's personal retinue, has them in his sights. He keeps to the shadows behind them as they walk.

He doesn't like this palace, doesn't like the miles of empty corridors and shifting rooms, but like the others he is thrilled at the prospect of being a part of the Dark One's rebirth. Neville has made it clear to him that he, and the others, will be rewarded in the life to come.

He keeps delaying his shot. Bring down the man, said Kampp, but the girl must not be harmed.

They had simply drifted down past him in the anti-grav lift. Lucky for him he was looking. Word was they were in the upper levels, totally lost. Well, they seemed to know where they were going now. He had followed, waiting until he saw where they stepped out.

It is quiet in the palace, too quiet. It's like a vacuum, like space. Bright space. The others had said, when they first arrived, that you'd need a thousand men to search it properly. If someone or something wanted to stay hidden, no one could find them. It was like the whole place went on for ever. The three months in that cramped ship to get here had felt bad, but you knew where everything was. You could *see* everything.

Valrus follows the couple into the darker world of the palace's lowest level. They are definitely heading for the cells. Where Kampp will be waiting for them.

He will have to fire soon, otherwise the butler will grab all the glory. The thought of that creepy lithe toad makes Valrus shudder. There is something wrong with Kampp, they all feel it, something unwholesome. He enjoys his work a little too much.

Ah, they've stopped. Just standing in the corridor. The man looks round, probably suspicious. Valrus keeps quiet (too quiet). It will have to be now (this palace, so much room, God knows what could have hidden itself. Take a thousand men to find it). Valrus raises his pistol. As quiet as if the universe has stopped. He aims directly at the nobleman's back. Bring him down; then make sure with a head shot. No mistake. Quiet.

Except a noise, some noise, breaks his concentration. Just a little noise. Line it up… in the centre of the back…

It is breathing. Just behind him. Someone is standing behind him. His hand wavers (so much empty space. Anything could be in here) and he turns.

Before he can shriek, before he can even look up at its face, that which has been hiding in the palace for so long is on him.

'Did you hear something?' Stanislaus asks suddenly. They have stopped, Romana trying to shift this buzzing in her head.

'No, and nor did you,' she replies, irritably. Something is throbbing, right behind her eye.

Stanislaus is looking back the way they came. 'I could swear…'

She grabs his hand, tired of him. He has the attention span of a child.

When they reach the cells, and it's funny how she can be so certain these are the cells, they find Kampp waiting for them. The odd thing is, he's asleep, lying across the doorway, his arms wrapped round himself.

'This is the one we want,' Romana says.

'How do you know all this?' Stanislaus asks suspiciously, staring down at the supine butler. 'It has to be some kind of trick.'

'Does it really matter?' snaps Romana, by way of reply. She just wants to get the door open. There appears to be a simple electronic pad welded into it. So, it's only just become a cell. She needs something for her headache.

'How do you open it?' he asks. Romana had rather hoped he wouldn't.

'You need the correct number sequence. And before you ask, that is something I don't know.'

'So what do we do?'

Romana points down at the butler. 'We're going to have to wake him up.'

However, before she can reach down, she hears a musical chime, then a click, and the door to the cell slides open.

'There's something going on here,' says Stanislaus. 'This is too easy. We're being watched, I know it.'

117

Despite her mounting irritation, despite her headache, she knows he is right. Somehow, someone is guiding them, helping them. Neville? The palace itself? Only one man will know the answer. 'Come on.'

Romana leads the way, only to see a small, dimly lit room where two restraining chairs sit empty. 'What?' she asks, just as the hand claps over her mouth.

Somewhere in the distance, Stanislaus shouts. Romana struggles. She tries to keep calm, tries to remember her training but her head, her head is pounding.

A figure moves in front of her. A smiling figure. She realises the hand over her mouth is small and feminine. A ring scrapes one of her teeth as the fingers relax.

'Sorry,' says Miranda Pelham from behind.

The figure continues to smile and Romana feels her headache disappear completely. 'Doctor!' She almost cries with relief.

'I'm terribly sorry. We thought you were the guard. Miranda here was all for knocking you out and everything. Hello Romana, how are you?' He holds out that little paper bag.

Chapter Eight

There is something in the air, something new. He can feel it.

The human Neville is donning his robes for the meeting of those fools in the cabal. Their last. After tonight he will have no further need for these children.

He rolls his neck to relax the muscles, hearing the tendons crack. The robes of the Magus, this being who he will soon become *in toto*, are warm and welcoming as he slips them over his body. Soon, he is certain, he will no longer be Magus in name only. He looks forward to the time when the weak and transient Neville is gone completely and has become the new, true acolyte of Valdemar. The vessel. He is sick and tired of humanity.

The Magus talks to him. Roars at him to Become. Sometimes, the Neville-being feels he will burst with the noise. He must change or be destroyed. The Magus will not compromise.

The human Neville places the hood over his head and lights the candle in the chalice. He can feel the Magus straining for release, pleading angrily for him to hurry; feels the greater being's muscles and sinews straining for rebirth. The human Neville tries to placate the voice – it must understand that to rush now would be fatal. This final ceremony must proceed according to the ritual that Neville spent a decade piecing together.

A frenzied beeping from the console breaks his concentration. The still-mortal part of Neville's conscious mind, that part he is attempting to dissipate, recognises it as a call from Kampp. No doubt with details of the Doctor's slow demise. Neville ignores the signal. This is the time, the ultimate fulfilment. The moment to bind the strands of a lifetime. He thinks of all those lives on all those planets, the cult members who gave up everything for him, for the promise of the resurrection. Do they now look up at the stars and understand, feel how close the moment is? The human Neville sniffs. Who cares?

As the human Neville moves gracefully down the wide marble stairs that eventually lead to the piazza, he is completely focused, staring at the candle, ready for the ritual.

'Master. Magus,' comes a small, frightened voice. Huvan, sitting on the steps, dressed in the white robe, waiting for him. If only the boy knew, if he had only half an inkling of his historical importance. The Magus will remember him with honour. As he is consumed.

Not yet, not yet. The human fragment still controls, just. Huvan, for all his years, has the mind of a child and must be treated as such. The human Neville can barely look at that oily, pitted face.

Attempting to retain his concentration, the human Neville arches a silver eyebrow beneath the hood.

'Are you prepared? Is there anything you need, Huvan?' He remembers to use that caring, fatherly tone that voice-tests revealed worked most effectively on the boy's psyche.

'I don't know. I don't know anything.' Huvan looks away. He is embarrassed. The human Neville understands the boy is seeking attention, needing to be told once again just how important he will become. Inwardly, the human Neville sighs.

'Let's sit down. Share your troubles. You want to talk about it?' He realises that the fact that Huvan responds so well to this pseudo-therapy jargon, known as op-rick, is merely one of the inconveniences that make him really hate this little sod.

'I'm worried,' says Huvan. 'What if I mess everything up? What if it all goes wrong? I don't think I could handle rejection again.'

'You have to believe in yourself.' The human Neville can recite this as slickly as he can speak the ritual passages. 'Give yourself respect. You are a human being; you have a right to be heard. Listen to your own inner voice. It doesn't matter what others think.'

'What if they laugh at me? What if nothing happens?'

'It will, Huvan. It will. You must just believe in your own worth. You have a great gift, a special gift…'

This goes on for another twenty minutes until every avenue, every possible permutation of doubt, every paranoid barrier has been overwhelmed. Huvan is at last finally filled up with the pompous praise and agrees to do his best. He spends the next ten minutes apologising before skipping his way down the stairs, making the human Neville late for his own black mass.

Once Neville has descended the stairs, he is enraged to find that his servitors are not ready. They are dashing around, half-dressed, covering the tables with the starred black cloths, arranging the pentagrams, lighting the candles.

'What is happening here?' he bellows, unable to believe this farce.

One of them, Hermia in fact, her teeth chattering in panic, drops to her knees. 'We weren't sure what to do,' she moans. 'Tennie… I mean Brother Stanislaus… has disappeared. He's the only one who knows the rituals. Please forgive us!'

The others drop to their knees in contrition but the human Neville is too angry. He walks round each in turn, kicking them over. 'You mean he was the only one who could be bothered to learn. I knew I should have left you on Palma station and brought the inner circle. You're useless! I should destroy you all!'

This provokes much wailing and entreating him to spare their lives. At this point Huvan enters, and the human Neville allows him to put in a few choice kicks of his own. 'Now get this mess sorted out!' he yells.

At last, they begin. The human Neville takes a deep breath. He ushers the group to kneel at a large, black-draped stone table. Huvan sits opposite him, next to Hermia, staring furtively at the black cloth. 'Take each other's hands,' Neville orders. The cabal obeys. If Hermia is unhappy with Huvan's sweaty palm, she does not show it.

'The spirits of the Old Ones are all around.' The Magus is with him, clearer now, directing operations. Eager; willing the human Neville on. 'They would prevent our communion with the Dark One. Concentrate, concentrate and join with me in the hymn of rebirth.'

He starts up the low chanting, the notes alien to the human tongue. It took the human Neville five years to master the phonetics.

It ends, as always, with the one word, the one true word. 'Valdemar, Valdemar, Valdemar!'

Suddenly, Huvan moans. He looks around, eyes wide. 'I can't do it! I don't know what to do!'

'Huvan!' the human Neville barks at the boy.

'Magus, help me. What shall I do? I feel nothing. I did before but now there's nothing. You made this happen, you're all laughing at me! Where's Romana?'

He stands, ready to run, unable to cope with what is expected of him.

Romana. All is not lost. The human Neville speaks, quickly, to sustain what is left of the moment. 'She is in the arms of another, Huvan. Look, you know this is the truth.'

Huvan falters. He looks around, almost through the walls of the palace. 'No, she can't…'

'Romana has already betrayed you. She is with your enemy, she is with the traitor Stanislaus!'

Hermia pulls away from Huvan. 'No, Magus, no! That's not true!'

'Open your pretty mouth again and I shall tear out your tongue,' he hisses. Hermia sits down, instantly. Neville's voice has changed. 'Huvan, tell me you know this to be true!'

The human Neville is lost, gone. He feels a rushing in his ears, the blood rising, and then the Magus is all that is.

'It's true, it's all true!' screams Huvan.

A sound, something like thunder, blasts round the palace. The lights flash furiously. A wind whips at the robes of the cabal, sending its members shrinking under its force. Hermia screeches in fear. Only Huvan is calm, unmoving, his eyes rolled back into their sockets so that nothing can be seen but the whites.

'VALDEMAR!' roars the Magus.

The noise, the lights, the wind all cease. The air is thick with electric tension. The Magus is still, black eyes glittering beneath the hood.

'Er, sorry to interrupt you,' comes a voice from the stairwell. The cabal, as one, jumps. The tension has gone. The Magus starts to slip, a begging pleading Neville unwillingly returning.

It is the Doctor, alive. He sits and plays with a yo-yo, staring intently at it as he tries to master a trick. As if he has only just become aware of his audience, he looks up and smiles. 'Oh please,' he says smoothly, 'don't let me interrupt. It all looks ever so interesting and you were having such a nice time.'

'Doctor!' bellows Neville.

The Doctor had been wondering why Neville had kept him alive. After all, he had got the power back on, had refused to talk and was no longer of any value. A man in Neville's position… well, surely he had to kill him, it was just a matter of time. Which was why the Doctor and Pelham had been forced to set up their rather implausible escape plan. The one that involved hitting whomsoever it was that came into the cell. Unfortunately, it had turned out to be their would-be rescuers.

The Doctor was certain that the man, Stanislaus, would recover from what was only a tiny bump on the head. He was strong, had youth on his side and all that.

The upshot of it was, they were free. Of course, his first instinct had been to dash for the TARDIS, the last vestige of his original intentions.

Finding Kampp curled up and asleep outside the cell, his bag of instruments by his side, had half-convinced him otherwise. The dead guard on the way to the anti-grav lift had fully convinced him. You don't die of fright in an empty corridor.

There was nothing they could do to wake Kampp. He was just there, a dead weight, like a cat. Pelham was all for using the opportunity to repay some old debts, using the butler's own instruments, but he and Romana managed to persuade her to restrain herself.

He couldn't leave. He knew it, had known it the moment the cell door opened on the sleeping Kampp. It just wasn't in him to walk away from a situation, especially one of his own making. The Key to Time would have to wait. If he felt guilty, he would have to make amends.

There is an odd tingle in the palace, a pressure, as if the place is about to suffer an internal thunderstorm. He notices his hair has become even more static-prone than usual. Something is about to happen and Neville has to be behind it.

'What are we going to do?' Romana had asked, as he finished inspecting the guard.

'You know Neville's going to blame us for this,' said Pelham.

The Doctor had closed the guard's tortured eyes. 'There's more than a dead guard to worry about,' he murmured softly.

'Huh?' grunted Stanislaus. Young, but stupid. Keep him in the background.

'Huvan,' said Romana.

'Huvan,' he repeated. 'The psychic catalyst.' He turned to Pelham. 'Why didn't you tell me?'

'Me?' She pointed at her own chest, realising she was getting the blame for something. 'I didn't know. It wasn't me who turned the power on.'

'It doesn't matter,' the Doctor said, carefully avoiding that particular issue. 'What does matter is that Neville is much more organised and dangerous than I suspected. I have to get to him and prevent Huvan opening the gateway.'

'Gateway?' asked Romana.

'The gateway to the higher dimensions. What Neville calls Valdemar.'

He remembers starting to run, leaving the others behind, desperate to get to Neville and stop him.

'You will die for this intrusion!' Neville has completely lost control. The cabal quake, helpless under their master's extreme and seemingly infinite rage.

The Doctor, however, seems unmoved. 'That seems a little harsh. A simple telling off would have been more than sufficient. Better still, how about a sign saying, "Keep Out – Dead God Awakening"? Hmm?'

Neville's eyes threaten to burst from beneath his hood. He raises a threatening finger. 'You dare… you dare…'

The Doctor ignores him. He speaks instead to the cowering nobles. 'You know, there are dozens of ways to reawaken a sleeping deity, much less draining. I heard of one case…'

'Shut up!'

'You realise, of course, that Romana would describe Mr Neville here as a paranoid schizophrenic with an almighty inferiority complex. Cross that with an unchallenged, over-privileged upbringing and you end up with a very unstable personality…'

'You will die, Doctor, slowly.'

'Whose threats go on far too long. It gets boring. Don't you think it gets boring?'

He directs this question at Hermia, a smile on his face. She, confused and frightened, looks in turn at her Magus.

'You realise, of course, he's completely mad. And worse than mad, he's wrong,' the Doctor continues.

Neville produces a pistol from his robes. He raises it to the Doctor who quips, 'Now that is a variation on the magic wand I've not seen before. Abracadabra.'

And he has gone, just as Neville fires. The bullet sings into the far wall, where the damage it causes is sealed and repaired within seconds. Neville looks round, aiming left and right.

'Here! Here!' shrieks Hermia, pointing under the table right next to her.

A curly head pops up. 'Now you see it…'

Neville aims and fires. Hermia stops screaming. Neville is still as he observes the girl topple back out of her seat. She hits the ground like a broken doll, the gun's roar still ringing round the piazza. The Doctor stands, his face worn and grim, all that cheeky energy draining from him.

'Who do you think you are?' he mutters, looking down at the dead girl. Neville smiles and raises the gun once more.

'Stop!' Romana yells. She and Stanislaus dash down the stairs. Neville turns and aims at them. As if possessed, the gun leaps from his fingers. He is as surprised as anyone.

The Doctor leaps across the table, kicking over candles, and throws himself on the robed lunatic. Both topple to the ground. The cabal leap up, as if galvanised into manic action. Romana and Stanislaus find themselves in the middle of a panic.

Only one person is still, absolutely still, and with a cold shock Romana realises just who has been their secret helper all this time. He probably doesn't know it himself.

Huvan is oblivious to the mayhem around him. He just stares, his mouth moving to its own silent messages.

'Doctor,' says Romana, unable to take her eyes off the boy. 'Doctor!'

Abruptly, the noise ceases. The cabal responds as if to a signal, falling mute and turning to Huvan. The Doctor stands, releasing the cataleptic Neville. Huvan has become the focus, not just of the living but of everything.

Like a puppet, the boy looks around. How he can see, none can tell, as there are no pupils in his eyes. The mouth continues to move slowly, almost in a parody of speech. The red of his mouth is like an obscene flashing light. Blood streams from the pustules on his face. 'Release me,' comes a voice like gravel from his throat. 'Or I will kill you all.'

Romana has one horrible thought, one nightmare realisation. The Doctor is wrong. Valdemar is real. Valdemar lives!

She is disturbed to find that the boy seems to be staring at her. 'Doctor,' she says, slowly. The cold wind is back, sending goose bumps rising up her bare arms.

Huvan stands and smiles. The grimace is a death mask. The boy does not stop at standing. He starts to rise from the ground.

'There is no Valdemar,' the Doctor states. 'Don't believe it.'

'Come with me,' says the dark, supremely resonant voice. Huvan forms the syllables of her name. 'Romana...'

She looks around, unsure of her next action. The Doctor steps in front of her. 'I'm sorry,' he says, 'she's all booked up. Come down from there.'

Huvan raises an arm, as if to strike. Romana flinches; what does he want from her?

'No!' yells Stanislaus all of a sudden, and leaps heroically on to the stone table. 'Leave her alone!'

There is a deep throaty chuckle, a small movement from the floating boy and Tenniel Stanislaus explodes. Literally explodes.

As the pieces fall, Romana sees Huvan's pupils return and, with an expression of terrible suffering, the boy seems to deflate and collapse noisily to the floor.

Heat returns to the hall.

Romana looks at the Doctor, who seems stunned, too stunned to move. Pieces of Stanislaus sizzle everywhere.

A rustle from the drapes by the stone stairwell. Miranda Pelham pulls aside the curtain. 'Is it over?' she asks, like a frightened mouse.

Outside the palace, in the never-ending acid storms, Ashkellia is shrieking. Night falls as the planet spins. The clouds bubble and froth and the surface far below quakes. The palace stabilisers jet and smoke with the effort of retaining stability.

Something is moving under the planet's surface, a charging rumbling monster of unbelievable proportions. It is as if some gigantic force is fighting for its freedom, tearing at the bonds that hold it down.

Kampp, awake at last after his phantom sleep, is conducting an autopsy on the dead guard. His hands shake as the palace rocks. Just what can be occurring up there?

Neville has ignored his messages, informing him of the Doctor's escape and the murder of one of his men.

Honestly, the Magus is impossible at times. All that spiritual nonsense, why do people bother? Kampp has always had other preoccupations, flesh being prominent amongst them. Flesh and blood and mortality – the true canvas of the artist. So why do his hands shake so?

Apparently there has been some sort of disturbance with the children of the rich. That young, ugly protégé Huvan. He has disappeared and so has Neville.

He is not worried about the genetically altered boy. Kampp has always had a deep distaste for ugliness; to work on Huvan would be a duty, not a pleasure. However, when Neville is lost too, it is time to worry.

It is undoubtedly the work of the strangers. Once again the guards are out searching for them.

As far as the butler is concerned, Neville should have let him loose on them as soon as they arrived. Pelham too, she always had a smart mouth. He would like to have worked on her long ago, held up that flapping tongue for her to see.

Kampp cannot stop his hands shaking. His sleek moustache itches. He stares down at the corpse in front of him, the sculptor's block of stone ready for the shaping. He feels odd, like time is standing still. He cannot account for his sleep, was not even aware that he had fallen asleep. He remembers the order to kill the Doctor, preparing the instruments and receptacles, walking to the cell. And then he was on the floor outside, with something like a sticky black stain on his head. The guards running towards him, panicked, one of their own struck down.

Kampp attempts to cut into the flesh. Something distracts his attention, something at the edge of his vision. He tries again. His hand trembles, he cannot hold the cutter still.

For some reason, he cannot take his sleek eyes off the guard's face. That expression... what did he see? What did he see? He feels a certain envy that something could have engendered such fear. It was a professional job, whatever it was.

This autopsy is personal; Kampp needs to know what killed the guard. He is never averse to learning new tricks.

At last, he gets his hand under control. He lowers the cutter to the guard's white chest. With his left hand he smooths the skin. It is warm beneath the glove. He draws a red line with the cutter.

Again, that thing, whatever it is, distracts him. Kampp blinks, as if a light is behind his eyes. What is wrong with him?

The guard's body should not be warm. Kampp spreads his hand, just to check. Impossible. And now it starts to glow, as if lit from inside. The contours of the body seem to warp and change, to expand into shapes he knows are impossible. Something is crawling into his own eyes. The light burns, burns right into the pain centres of his brain. Something in his head strains for release, a white-hot scorching needle. It pumps through his eyes. Screeching, Kampp drops the cutter. Blinded, he reaches for his eye sockets.

'Oh, you beauty,' he purrs, impressed, as his mind is flooded.

The Doctor is racing to the library of the Old Ones, with Miranda Pelham in tow.

'That was unpleasant,' she huffs and puffs after him.

'It's going to get a lot more unpleasant if we don't do something about it,' he barks back, skidding into the vast repository.

'What exactly are we looking for?' Pelham asks, as she looks up at the thousands of brass cylinders on the wall. 'And how the hell are we going to find it?' She leans against the long table, trying to get her breath back.

The Doctor rubs his chin. 'It's a question of knowing the referencing system. Once you know what you're looking for, the library itself should find it for you.'

'Simple as that?'

'Simple as that,' he affirms.

Pelham is finding the palace a cold and unwholesome place.

For the first time, she is realising just how alien and ancient it all is. 'What about Huvan? That was a dirty trick of yours, making Romana look after him. God knows what he'll do to her.'

The Doctor is marching along the rows of cylinders, looking for something she can only guess at. 'He's developed some kind of emotional attachment to her…'

Pelham gives him a wry smile. 'Emotional. Yeah, right. Not the adjective I would have employed.'

'She is our only chance of containing him.'

'You mean Valdemar.'

The Doctor stops and faces her. 'There is no Valdemar. The sooner you realise that, the bigger your chances of staying alive.'

'But he spoke. We saw him!'

'No, we saw Huvan flexing his psychic muscles. He has presumably been indoctrinated into believing in Valdemar. He has absolute faith that this is a fact. I'm sure Neville saw to that when he brought him up. Now his psychic powers have been awakened, the strain on his mind is too much for him to comprehend. His subconscious has converted this new power into something he can understand. To keep his sanity.'

'Ahh…'

'You understand now?'

'No. Not really.'

'Never mind. I think I do.' The Doctor has found a tiny socket, no more than a screw hole, in the wall. He points at it and stares wide-eyed at Pelham. 'Do you know what this is?' he asks.

'Why don't you tell me?' Pelham is saturated with information. She doesn't think she can take in any more.

'It's a library ticket. A fail-safe in case of problems with the telepathic circuits.'

'Really? How does it work?'

The Doctor shrugs. 'I suppose I could try sticking my finger in it.'

'Isn't that awfully dangerous?'

'Oh no, I'm always sticking things in places I shouldn't.' He jams in a digit. He smiles. 'Aaaahhhh!' he bellows. Somewhere in the wall, something electronic fizzes. Pelham makes to haul him back but he waves her away, his face creased in agony.

'I think that's right, yes. Should see something now.'

The library comes to life. Pelham looks up to see previously hidden cogs and wheels and slats and slots churning and moving. The cylinders are filing themselves along discreet, oiled pipes. The noise is relentless and echoing. She claps her hands to her head.

The Doctor removes his finger from the socket. He licks the digit, as though it had been burned. 'That should do it,' he says smugly.

'Do what?'

'Help us to find the psychic inhibitor that we need to suppress the effects of the higher dimensions.'

'You know,' Pelham sighs. 'I wish I hadn't asked.'

Two cylinders pop out of pipes to settle next to them. Pelham sees they are like vacuum flasks, with ornately decorated heads. Exactly what the library of Valdemar should look like, she thinks.

'Come on,' says the Doctor, picking up the cylinders.

She places a gentle, restraining arm on his shoulder, determined to stop him. 'Look, give me an idea, at least. If I just know what to look for, two of us will find it more quickly than one.'

He thinks about it. She really believes he would rather get on with it on his own. However, reason gets the better of him and he offers her a seat, dropping the cylinders on to the floor with a clang. 'Whoops,' he smiles sheepishly.

'Who is Valdemar?' she asks, directly, with the uncomfortable feeling that everything she has ever done with her life is about to be cruelly swept aside. 'Be gentle.'

The Doctor toys with the lid of one of the cylinders. He is having trouble getting it open. 'Valdemar is an experiment,' he says. 'The product of fantastically complicated trans-dimensional physics. The Old Ones were phenomenally advanced and that was the end of them. Why can't I get this lid off? It's perfectly simple.'

'Perhaps you're doing the wrong thing. Perhaps it's not supposed to come off. If Valdemar isn't in the tomb, what is?'

'Nothing. The tomb is a gateway. You see, this planet, the whole of Ashkellia, is a gigantic particle accelerator. You know what a particle accelerator is?'

'No.'

'Designed to smash a hole into the fabric of reality.'

'I said no, I didn't understand.'

The Doctor is not listening. He places the cylinder on the table and glares at it. 'Good. To punch a hole into the higher dimensions, you need an awfully big fist. An unbelievably muscular fist, in fact. Even my lot never really got to grips with it.'

'Your... lot?'

'Too dangerous, you see. Three-dimensional life...' He sits up and looks at her, thinking something through, '...even four-and five-dimensional life, is unable to perceive the higher dimensions. We lack the necessary sensory apparatus. I mean, there are theories that suggest that these organs lie dormant in the brain but... ah!'

He snaps his fingers.

'What?' asks Pelham.

'Telepathy! Perhaps that explains telepathy and why only certain people are rumoured to have the gift. Perhaps the sensory organs in some individuals are better developed. I suppose it's possible that telepathy, in fact all psychic phenomena, are utilisations of the forces of the higher dimensions.'

'So what happens if we get exposed to these higher dimensions without these extra organ things?'

'You've seen it, in the tomb. The man who attacked us.'

Pelham remembers. She realises, guiltily, that she has not thought about Erik at all.

'In both a mental and physical way, exposure to the higher dimensions drives us mad.' He is concentrating fully on the cylinder in his hand.

'I can understand that. About being driven mad. So this particle accelerator thing kicked it all off. If it's all so dangerous, why did they do it?'

'Curiosity. Insatiable curiosity. There was nothing left for them to learn. They were an ambitious species and they didn't know when to stop. Millennia ago, the Old Ones must have punched a hole in reality. That hole grew and grew until it threatened to swamp the universe we inhabit. A shadow, spreading like a cancer, breaking down the barriers between dimensions. It consumed the Old Ones, it must have consumed nearly everything.'

At last, Pelham is beginning to see. 'Which explains the myth. So, Valdemar was just a hole in space.'

'What? Just a hole! Not just space either. Time, thought, imagination, everything. Every life form it encountered experienced total perception. The results must have been catastrophic.'

Pelham can imagine the catastrophe. Her imagination is salivating. She thinks of whole planets, whole star systems consumed by this plague. 'I see, I see.' Something hits her. She turns, but the Doctor seems to be humming at the cylinder. 'So what stopped it?' she asks.

'Mmm… look, I think I'm on to something here. I think the cylinder reacts to telepathic communion. Half of what I just told you, I didn't tell you, you understand. It told you through me. What did I say?'

'I'm asking you… it a question. What stopped the spread?'

The Doctor pauses. He stares at the deceptive-looking object in his hands. 'It doesn't know. Perhaps we need a different cylinder. Somehow they found a way. The Old Ones found a way.'

'And got themselves wiped out in the process. Doctor, what the hell are we doing here?'

He hurls the object across the library. 'Finding a neural inhibitor!' He bellows up at the gallery. 'Where are you? Show yourself. You know it's all your fault! A million years ago you found a way. Somehow you sealed up the gateway. Tell me! Tell me now!'

Pelham shies away from him. A cold thought has just entered her brain. The way he's acting, his obsession. He's just like Paul Neville.

He turns to her. 'We'll have to search the cylinders one by one. This is going to take a while.'

Pelham picks up the second cylinder. She stares at it, desperate to calm the Doctor down. 'OK, OK,' she says. 'We'll find it. Just stop shouting.'

'Stay calm? Stay calm?' He is astonished by her scolding. For a moment, Pelham thinks he going to start on her again. Instead, he sags in realisation, looking so sorry for himself that she can't help giggling. 'Was I shouting? I'm terribly sorry. It must be the cylinder. It must leave some sort of psychic residue in the mind.'

Pelham nods sarcastically. 'Oh yeah? I think you just had a tantrum and you're trying to make excuses.'

'You know, I think you might be right. Come on!'

Laughing, Pelham stands and starts to help the Doctor pull the cylinders out of the walls.

Chapter Nine

There is someone living inside his head. This, he has long suspected. His mind stings, rings from the blasts of the ritual. If he opens his eyes, he can see little but a red haze, and odd floating dots. He prefers to keep them closed, and look with his mind.

Sometimes he hears music, out amongst the stars. The man in his head, the dark man with Neville's face, tells him this is the music that binds the stars together. Like invisible strings, oscillating strands of white sound.

The dark man has opened up so much to him, taken him out of that body he hates. This is what he has waited for all his life.

He hardly remembers the golden-haired boy, cannot recall at all what he did to him. Only that overwhelming flood, that tide that came from within. Had been hiding inside him for so long. He felt his mind slip away, that white-out he used to get when absorbed in composing his poems, when the muse descended, but a thousand times more powerful. There is so much passion in him, so much energy. Scores to be settled.

The someone inside his head is laughing, egging him on. This must be Valdemar, he realises, come for him.

'Huvan?' comes a distant voice, from his old life. He tries to hang on to the music but it is fading, fading fast. He wants to cry out, shut out the voice. He doesn't want to return to their fragmented, incomplete world. He can no longer live separately from the whole.

'Huvan?'

Yet there is something in that voice, something he remembers. The sound of that word, once his name, spoken in such a manner. He is drawn back, chasing the bait.

The lights and the music and the man in his head fade away.

The dark man licks his lips in anticipation of when he will return.

Huvan opens his eyes.

Romana is not thrilled to be following the Doctor's orders.

'No,' she had stated categorically. 'Ask me anything, but not that.'

They had been standing in the ruins of the cabal. Shock had them rooted to the spot until the Doctor realised Neville had disappeared.

Huvan had slumped forward, apparently unconscious, over the table. The rest of the pathetic coven had scattered.

The Doctor had run to the boy, hauling his head back. He pulled open his eyelids, revealing the dark retinas within. 'The psychic energy running through him must have burned out a mental fuse. He's lucky to be alive. Poor soul.'

'Poor?' Pelham had shrieked, clutching the drapes. 'He was going to kill us all!'

'We haven't much time,' said the Doctor. 'If he wakes up and I'm not ready, he may well kill us all. We need a way to keep him calm. Find someone he can trust.'

He looked up at Romana and she could see it, could sense that vile idea germinating in his mind.

'Romana...'

'No,' she stated categorically. 'Ask me anything, but not that.'

And now, here she is, back in Huvan's room, paper and other less savoury items strewn all over it. Gingerly, she drops a cold compress on to his head. Over and over in her mind she revisits the image of Stanislaus coming apart. She has never seen anything like that, not even when the Sontarans were strutting through the Academy, no one daring to halt them in their atrocities.

She wonders how much the Doctor has seen, has witnessed through his many lives. What had it been like for him, the first time? She feels like she has entered a war, a war where unimaginable realities must be sublimated, dealt with, taken for granted. The idea that she might become blasé sickens Romana.

Mind you, the idea that she now has to return Huvan's pathetic crush is equally appalling. She is certain the Doctor had the ghost of a smile on his lips when he suggested it, and Pelham turned away completely. Five minutes ago, this was the child, claiming to be an ageless dark god back from the dead, who turned an innocent young man inside out. Now, she is supposed to simper and fuss over him. As far as Romana is concerned, this is melodrama of the lowest of the low-brow.

'Huvan?' she forces herself. Lighten the pitch, add a few sobs of concern, ignore the fact that perhaps it is an emotion more primeval than repulsion that is making her tremble. That for once the Doctor might have underestimated his opponent.

'Huvan?'

The boy's eyelids flicker. He groans. 'Romana?' he utters. 'Don't leave me…' He goes on to deliver a speech so bathetic, so choked with childish self-absorption, so stuffed with cack-handed adolescent craving, that she can only assume he has rehearsed it.

'Hush now, Huvan. Yes, I feel the same.' Come on Romanadvoratelundar, at least try and sound sincere. 'You must come back to me. You must tell me what happened to you.'

Huvan is awake. He looks up with glistening eyes. 'I don't know. I felt… live, like I was being electrocuted. But it was nice. I didn't do anything wrong, did I? Was I… was I all right?'

He grips her arms. Romana smooths his pitted forehead. Well, if you're going to do it, you've got to do it properly. She gazes into his eyes, those eyes so recently altered, and shamelessly says, 'Huvan, you were marvellous.'

And the coven? And the guards? Just what is the upshot of Valdemar's apparent return?

Let's start with the lower levels and work up. And that's not just for show, for as the night outside gets darker, the palace itself is continuing its emergence as a character. The scattered tenants hear all sorts of strange far-off (and not so far-off) noises, not all of them mechanical. Lights appear in the distance, glowing balls that dance and bobble, inviting you to chase, to follow. The lifts become erratic, sometimes not working at all. Nobody uses them any more; they are sticking to their own levels.

Down in his artist's studio, Kampp rises to his feet. Black, coral-like scale has grown over the sockets of his eyes like the shiny carapace of a beetle. Ignoring the body of the dead guard (who remains dead, whatever you might think was going to happen), he staggers out into the corridors, looking for someone. He comes across the duty guard – a dull-witted, heavy man called Srohan, deemed fit only to act as jailer and night-watchman down here.

This slow-wittedness manifests itself in his sleepy failure to recognise the alterations crawling all over the advancing Kampp. Instead, fatally, he leaps to his feet and salutes, just as the butler is on him. In time-honoured fashion, Srohan doesn't even have time to scream.

And then there are two of them.

At about the same time, probably and correctly on the stroke of midnight, the scattered children of the cabal cower in their quarters. The palace is no longer their playground. Through Huvan, a boy they have tormented without cessation since they met him, Valdemar has returned. With the deaths of their two friends, they understand the extent to which Paul Neville has betrayed them.

The twins Diana and Juno, the two bovine ladies in yellow and red from the masque, particular playmates of Huvan's, have hidden themselves in their plush apartment and blocked the doors with furniture. Like Srohan, they are not overly burdened with intelligence or sense, such needless qualities bred out of them over the centuries. They have been frightened out of their wits by the day's proceedings. They curse their dispossessed parents for sending them here with Neville, conveniently forgetting it was they themselves who staged the tantrums and sulks until they got their own way (Hermia had said it would all be a blast. One supposes that for her, it was).

'No one is getting through that door,' says Diana, taking her red-handled lady's pistol from the cabinet.

'No one,' replies her sister, taking the equivalent yellow handle.

'You're getting fat,' says Diana.

'So are you,' says Juno.

Now only Neville remains in this précis of the night's proceedings. Shocked beyond all reason by the display of Valdemar's power via Huvan, and the overwhelming success of his plans, he has spent the last few hours communing with the Dark One, praying for guidance.

It is the Doctor who upsets him the most. How has Valdemar allowed him to live? It was his interference that prevented Neville's final transformation. He had been so close, so close to Becoming. He would have got away from himself, yes, if it hadn't been for the Doctor and those meddling kids...

The Magus releases the answer. The human Neville is not worthy of Becoming. He has not completed the tasks Valdemar has set for him. The Doctor is his responsibility. And the Doctor is still alive. There is work to be done.

Neville returns from his meditations. He opens his eyes and stands. He needs to find some guards.

The night wears itself out. Morning triggers the palace to light up the Doctor and Pelham still at work in the library. Well, the Doctor anyway. Pelham has fallen asleep.

Even the Doctor is reaching a point where fatigue is overriding efficiency. He could swear he has read this knowledge cylinder before. He senses that the palace is in some way to blame for this. It has done something to time, slowed him down, given itself a chance to grow. The night seems over much too quickly.

And then, as he thinks about this, the solution pops into his brain. He hadn't read this cylinder before after all.

It shows him the dormant organs of the human brain, collected and dissected by the Old Ones when man was merely an unthinking brute, little more than the ape he grew out of. Yes, the Old Ones visited then. They knew the Earth.

The organ is located inside the hypothalamus; a mere stub in a mass of newer, better-developed cells and synapses. It is a vestige of a time when all life was connected, without the barrier of consciousness and self-awareness, to the complete and synchronous universe. Before there came a severance somewhere along the line, for some evolutionary reason, and life moved outside the whole.

No wonder the Old Ones were so curious about the higher dimensions, no wonder they risked everything. They had discovered so much, the interconnection of everything. And they rushed like lemmings to re-attain it, not caring what they might lose. Only their experiment turned back on itself.

Instead of reaching into the higher dimensions, the higher dimensions reached into them.

There had to be a way that they had protected themselves, there had to be something.

Now that the Doctor has learned the cylinder's tricks he forces it to reveal its secrets. What did you do? he asks. What did the first explorers do to protect themselves from madness and transformation when they opened the gateway? Tell me, relic of the Old Ones, give it up!

Miranda Pelham wakes to find the Doctor sprawled over the table, his face utterly white, his right hand clasped around one of the knowledge cylinders. His hat is jammed on to those vibrant curls. For a moment, nothing registers but the disappointing revelation that sleep is over. Then the panic hits her.

'Doctor!' she shrieks.

To her intense relief, he jumps awake. 'Search the plastic factories, Brigadier!' he yells, much to her confusion. He turns and laughs. 'I found it, Miranda. I found it!'

Still, she doesn't understand. She just wants to get out of here. But she is glad he's glad. 'Great. Now what do we do?'

'We go to the control room and find the neural-inhibition vaccine the Old Ones left there for us.'

'I remember, I remember… a man, he was following you. You and Tenn… Stanislaus. I didn't like it.' Huvan is clutching her, like a drowning man. Romana concentrates on a spot on the wall. Remove oneself from the physical proceedings, rise above them.

'Really?' she replies. 'What did you do?'

'I don't know how I saw him. I could do anything. He tried to kill you. I stopped him, made him stop himself.'

'How?' She tries to remember when this might have happened, or whether Huvan is lying again. The guard. The guard they found in the corridor.

Huvan chuckles. Romana feels his mirth shaking her. 'He was afraid, I knew that. He thought something was in the palace. He was right, but he created it out of himself.'

'That was clever of you. And what was it he created?'

'Big.'

The anti-grav lifts don't seem safe, she doesn't trust them. In fact, she doesn't trust anyone or anything. And that includes this Doctor. Somehow, using this strange pencil-like sonic device, he unscrews a panel Pelham hadn't even guessed was in the ceiling.

This guy is impressive.

Once off, the panel reveals an upward-leading shaft and a set of pipes that maybe a small mouse could scale. 'Doctor, I'm forty-two, not twelve.'

'Breathe in,' he offers. Smart arse.

At least he goes first. The climb isn't as bad as she'd thought. The squeeze only hurts if she does something silly like breathe, or attempt to move any of the limbs of her body. It isn't so much a climb as a corkscrew, arms up, fingers brushing the underside of his battered shoes. Get me out of this alive, Doctor, Pelham promises, and I'll get you a new pair. Ten. A hundred.

One of the other really nice advantages of this climb is this – it gives her plenty of opportunity to think about the nightmare in that black magic room. It was one thing to write about Valdemar. It had even seemed a sensible rationalisation to agree to come here with Neville to reopen the tomb. It was quite another to come face to face with the Dark God she had equated with the destructive power of the big bang. Yes, she could really have done without that. And knowing that it was all her fault.

In the next life, Miranda, she promises herself, you'll write a romance. OK?

Just as she is going to die of claustrophobia, there is light at the end of the shaft. Pelham hears a clanging noise and scrapes her head on the Doctor's shoe. 'Sorry,' he says in what sounds suspiciously like a stage whisper.

'I take it we're there,' she snaps.

Much more lithely than she expected, the Doctor is out and helping her clamber awkwardly from the shaft. They are right inside the cavernous control room. Pelham has only been here once but she is pretty sure that the corridor where they were before was not immediately underneath it. Someone's been mucking around with the geography of the palace. Is it alive? she wonders. Does it actually know what we're thinking?

She hugs herself, afraid to admit how scared she really is.

The Doctor is orientating himself. The consoles and controls hum with an energy that this place never possessed before. Pelham thinks about the Old Ones, imagines the control room full of them, whatever they looked like. A million years ago, panicking, perhaps realising that their day was passing, that they were making way for history.

Were they afraid, like she is afraid? Or did they think they could seal Valdemar up and walk away?

Pelham looks at the Doctor's back, as he performs some arcane task with one of the consoles. The way his arms and legs blur as he moves, suggests to her that the Old Ones were possessed with more than the standard allocation of limbs.

She realises she doesn't believe the Doctor. She knows Valdemar is real. Real and waiting.

The Doctor turns, holding two long clear vials like champagne flutes. The contents look appetising – vomit suspended in transparent liquid plastic. 'Nice of them to leave some,' the Doctor says.

'What the hell is that?' Pelham asks, feeling nauseous. 'What do we do with it, dare I ask?'

'Eat me. Drink me,' the Doctor replies cryptically.

'Alice had cake, not liquid garbage.'

'There's no other way. The effects of the higher dimensions have already taken root. We need to keep clear heads.'

'There are only two portions.'

'We'll take one between us. I'll analyse the other and try and synthesise more.'

'That'll take time.'

'We'd best be starting then, hadn't we?' He snaps the top from the first vial. Immediately a stench, an odour, spreads through the room like something crawled in there and died. Pelham finds herself instinctively backing away. 'Uh-uh,' she waves her arms. 'No way. I'm not drinking that. The Old Ones, they weren't human. Maybe that stuff sorted them out but how do you know that for us it isn't poison?'

The Doctor sniffs. 'Good point,' he says reasonably. 'I know, I'll drink some. If I drop dead it's probably best not to use it.' He up-ends the vial. Slowly, the ooze trickles out and drops into his mouth.

Pelham watches. For a moment, the Doctor is still. He seems to be thinking about what he has ingested. 'I think the effects will probably be immedia–' He stops talking.

'Doctor?' she asks. Christ, what the hell has he done? 'Doctor?'

His eyes bulge. Slowly he raises a hand to his throat. Some kind of noise, a cross between a gargle and a choke, emerges from inside him. His eyes start to water.

Suddenly, he bunches his fists and bends over. He drops to his knees and begins to pound the floor. Oh God, thinks Pelham, it was a poison, it was a poison after all.

She is just about to move to his aid when he raises a trembling hand. His face is red, very red. However, despite the watering eyes and laboured breathing, he stands again.

'Yes,' he announces. 'I think you'll find it's probably not that nice.'

'Oh, Doctor!' she sighs and moves to embrace him. Instead, he holds out the vial. That stops her. She glares at it, like it was a spider.

'Has anything happened?' she asks, suspiciously.

The Doctor looks around. His tongue is hanging out. 'Mmm. The effects are subtle but yes, it's definitely done something. Your turn.'

'Do I have to?'

'It's too late to just say no.'

Cringing, as if the sample is alive, Pelham takes the vial. She closes her eyes and breathes deeply. With a quick movement, she up-ends the whole lot into her gullet.

Ten minutes later, once the Doctor has helped her down from the ceiling, and stopped her screaming, she starts to feel she might actually live. She gulps in air, trying to stem the torrent streaming from her eyes.

'Did…' she coughs the words out, 'did I scream much?'

He smiles. 'A little. And some interesting new words I was unfamiliar with until now. How are you feeling?'

Pelham looks around. The stuff was so foul, she'd completely forgotten that it was supposed to do something.

Yes. Yes, there is a change. Subtle, like he said. Not so much in the way things look, but rather the way she sees them, as if certain filters and lenses have been removed from her mind.

'It may take some getting used to,' says the Doctor.

It is as if the palace has been put into perspective. It no longer seems a magical, fairy-tale structure, full of mystery. She can see it as it really is, a rather dank, rather ordinary space station, old and tatty. This control room, once so alien and unknowable, is actually bare and functional; the baroque décor, once so impressive, is actually nothing more than a few tatty plants and some chipped stone tiles. The air is warm and stale. The palace machinery thumps and bumps deep below them, creaking and inefficient.

'How odd,' she remarks. 'To think this all seemed so strange.'

'Indeed,' the Doctor replies. 'We just couldn't see how things really are.' He looks down at the remaining vial. 'Hmm, unless this isn't how things really are, and we just think it seems that way.'

'Yeah, OK, Doctor. Let's not go down that road. You've got enough to do as it is.'

Yet, she can't shake off this new feeling. Even Neville seems nothing more than a tired, desperate and rather moth-eaten old man.

She turns to the entrance. For some reason she is hungry. Too late, she registers Neville standing right behind her, his face cold and impassive. He smacks her across the face. She feels the blow, feels the red tide and the sting and then the stone of the floor crashing into her mind.

Romana is getting seriously close to breaking point. She has been alternately cooing and praising this idiot boy for hours now. Isn't it time the Doctor came and gave her something else to do?

Huvan is pacing his bedroom. There is a red flush in his face that to Romana looks conspicuously like the first sign of madness. 'I can see so much,' he crows. 'I can do anything, destroy this palace if I feel like it. I feel so happy, Romana. I don't care about anyone else, just you and me. I feel like we're the last two people in the universe, that everyone else is dead.'

'Right, yes. I feel the same way too… of course. Er… Huvan,

do you… would you mind if I went to find the Doctor? I'm sure he's in some kind of trouble.'

An angry expression crosses Huvan's face. 'No! Why do you want to go? Do you hate me, is that it? Just like all the others!'

'No, no,' she replies, putting an extra-special layer of saccharine sadness in there for good measure. 'How could you think that? Listen to me. If we are to become… to get to know each other… then we must learn trust. I have to trust you and you have to trust me.'

She isn't sure whether he is falling for it. He screws up his face. 'You wouldn't lie to me, would you?' The stare is penetrating. Can he actually read her mind?

It's time for desperate measures. He's a child. A psychotic child perhaps, but still a child. In for a penny…

'Huvan,' she states. 'Don't push me. If you want me to like you, you've got to earn the right. I'm not some object. You don't own me.'

He's starting to get angry. Keep going, keep going…

'Now, I know you're a sensitive, mature man. We are both adults. Let's not rush things. I like you, you know I do, but we must allow each other room. The Doctor is my friend and I am going to him.'

She hasn't got anything else to say. She can only wait. Huvan's lower lip begins to tremble. 'All right, all right, go. But you will come back, won't you?'

Steeling herself, Romana takes his hand. 'Of course I will.'

She keeps her eyes on him as she opens the door. There, outside, freedom and fresh air. 'Goodbye, Huvan.' She smiles sweetly and walks out.

Closing the bedroom door, Romana leans against it and sags. She exhales for a very long time. Sorry, Doctor, I just couldn't go through with it any longer.

There is movement in the corridor. A corridor that seems

suddenly full of shadows. 'Who's that?' she asks. Her heart sinks. She recognises the slinky black suit of Kampp and, behind him, a guard. Romana raises her hands. Even this seems a relief after Huvan. 'All right, all right. I'll come quietly.'

Kampp hisses and lunges at her, black eyes glistening. She sees his gloved fingers heading for her throat and leaps back. Kampp arches himself up to strike her and Romana opens the door hard into him, its leading edge catching his head. Rattled, the butler staggers back. Behind him, the fat guard is also preparing to attack.

Romana leaps back into the bedroom, hurling the door shut and hurriedly slamming its bolts.

Huvan leaps up, sheer joy on his face. 'You came back!'

Romana starts piling the furniture on to the door. 'I couldn't stay away,' she mutters.

The Doctor regards Neville and his guards. With the vaccine or whatever it is running through him, he has penetrated the illusions created by the higher dimensions.

He is surprised at how strongly the liquid has affected him: without its protection the men in front of him are well advanced in their condition.

Organic black fronds grow from their eyes; their skin is coarse and leathery, their heads beginning to elongate like in a distorted photograph. They do not realise what they are becoming. Except perhaps Neville; yes, perhaps he does know.

'Give me that, Doctor,' Neville orders, indicating the remaining vial.

Sighing theatrically, only too aware of the rifles trained on him, the Doctor does as he is told. 'This is your only protection. I wouldn't drop it if I were you.'

Neville inspects the grainy liquid within. 'Really, Doctor? Protection against what?'

'The infiltration and transformation of your mind. Without this fluid, your brain won't be able to cope with the shock of regrowing receptors for the higher dimensions. Already your physical forms are changing. Very soon you'll either die or go mad. In your case, madder.'

Neville looks up and smiles. 'Always the wit, eh, Doctor?'

'Not always. Sometimes I use simple sarcasm, sometimes…'

'Silence!' Neville mutters to himself, trying to gain time, trying not to let on how important this liquid is to him.

'You did ask…'

Neville breaks the vial open. He begins to tip the liquid on to the floor. The Doctor attempts to remain impassive as the drops burst on the stone tiles. 'You see, Doctor,' (drip) 'you see how the Magus deals with these pathetic tricks'. (Drip) 'The Old Ones were fools to resist Valdemar. He is unstoppable, immortal.'

The Doctor tries the guards, without much hope. 'This is your salvation he's pouring away. If you let him do it, he'll kill you all.'

(Drip)

'These are specially selected men, Doctor. The high guard have pledged their lives to the rebirth of Valdemar. They know the rewards that await them.'

'Interesting career decision. What are the holidays like? The standard twenty-eight days or…?'

The Doctor leaps for Neville, but feels the butts of the guards' rifles on him before he even gets close. They knock his legs out from under him. He struggles, but there are three of them, grinding him into the floor. He gets a snail's-eye view of the control room.

'Turn him over,' says Neville. Hands obey. Neville is looming over him.

'Hello.' The Doctor blows a section of scarf away from his mouth and smiles.

Neville straightens his robes. Slowly, thoughtfully, he picks up the almost empty vial. His bejewelled hands stroke its ancient length. Then, with great deliberation, he smashes it into the ground. The glass shatters, sending up a spray of shards.

'There, Doctor. There's your precious "protection". What do you say to that?'

The Doctor considers. The ground is covered with a glass frost. 'Well, I would say you're an idiot, but then again you probably know that already.'

There is another pause. 'Something I said?' asks the Doctor.

'Bring him,' Neville orders. 'And the woman.'

'Where are we going now? More gloating?'

'Oh no, Doctor,' says Neville. 'No more gloating. In fact, for you and Ms Pelham, no more anything.'

He leads the Doctor and Pelham back into the hall where the nobles so recently played their games and held their masques. There is nothing now but the detritus of the black magic rituals. Even Hermia and the remains of Stanislaus lie where they fell.

As Neville leads his group into the entrance hallway, the nobles emerge from hiding. The Doctor, holding up the groggy Pelham, hears a snuffling. He immediately thinks of an animal, then watches as cloaked figures shuffle into the hallway from the shadows.

The guards, shaky for all Neville's boasting, turn their guns on these beautiful ones. The figures snort and jerk. The Doctor only gets glimpses – leathery hooves growing out of what once were hands, bristly snouts instead of noses, thick, yellow teeth.

'Magus, help us!' snorts one creature. 'Help us!'

They fall to their knees, metamorphosing hands clasped together, pleading for mercy.

Neville stops. He appears to ponder on their condition for a moment. 'Oh, for heaven's sake. Guards,' he orders. 'Kill them.'

Once the dust has settled and the noise has died away, the Doctor removes his hands from his ears. The bodies lie in their shrouds, their deformities hidden from sight. The guards are smiling, pleased to have been of service. Cartridges eject from stocks.

He glares at Paul Neville, disgust overwhelming him. 'How many more, Neville, how many more will you kill for your ridiculous delusion?'

'Just two,' Neville replies. 'Put them in the airlock.'

'Neville!' implores Pelham. 'We're partners!' She pushes herself away from the Doctor, trying to distance herself from him.

Neville looks at her with disdain. 'Partners? A vain, attention-seeking hack like you? You're joking.'

The guards herd them to the circular hatch. Beyond, through the glass of the porthole, sits the bathyscape. Neville spins the hatch lock. 'You are about to get a unique view of the palace, a view that no one has experienced in over a million years. It should be interesting, if a little brief.'

The hatch is opened. The guards push the pair towards the airlock. Neville watches, amused. 'Should you wish to beg, I should do it now.'

The Doctor tries for the last time. 'Neville. I'm trying to help you. All I've wanted to do since I got here is help you. You're making a terrible mistake. The higher dimensions are inimical to all life. All. Including yours and all your followers.'

Neville is smiling, barely listening. 'It is time to open the tomb of Valdemar, Doctor, time for the Dark One to live again. He is awake now. I can hear his voice. He is everywhere. Such a pity you will not be here to witness the glory.'

'Neville!'

The guards push them into the airlock and the Doctor can only watch through the porthole as Neville locks them out. He sees him mouth a command. Presumably, to open the floor hatch to the outside and the corrosive clouds waiting for them.

'Any bright ideas, Doctor?' asks Pelham, anxiously jumping from foot to foot, unconsciously toying with that bangle on her wrist.

'Hundreds, but none of them work.'

'Well, we've got to do something.'

There is a terrible grating sound. The temperature drops and the Doctor feels his ears pop. 'They're lowering the pressure. We've got about ten seconds.' He looks around. There's got to be something, some way out. There always is.

The grating noise increases from worrying to deafening. Pelham looks at him, her face drained of all colour. 'Is this the worst thing?' she moans.

'I think so,' he nods. There just isn't enough time.

The floor begins to move, sickeningly quickly. Maybe there isn't a way out of this one after all. There's a first time for everything. He is surprised when Pelham suddenly leaps at him, arms open. 'Hold me,' she cries.

The floor opens up and they plummet, straight down into the acid clouds.

Part Two

'But how is it that this lives in thy mind?
What sees thou else in the dark backward and abysm of time?'
The Tempest

Chapter Ten

Robert Hopkins is in his cabin, running over the latest ship's-efficiency statistics when the call comes.

If any member of the crew, or anyone at all for that matter, had been unwise enough suggest that what Hopkins was doing was meditating, they would have regretted that suggestion quickly enough. Meditating, however, is essentially what he is doing.

There is something reassuring in the cold lists of percentages that run in neat orderly lines down the white pages. Hopkins finds that studying them concentrates the mind and body wonderfully, and each time he emerges from this task he feels his muscles are less stiff, his mind less cluttered than when he began.

Checking the ship's efficiency is as good a way of passing the time as any, and passing the time is all they are doing here for the moment.

They have been in orbit around Ashkellia for exactly twelve days, six hours and eighteen minutes. Hopkins keeps a timepiece by his cot to keep him aware of this fact.

When the alarm goes off, he is jerked out of his studies. It can only mean one thing.

He feels himself begin to shake in the flashing of the red emergency lights. His breath emerges in short jumps. Got him, he thinks. Got him!

He must compose himself. Already the boots of his crewmen are hammering along the decks of the ship. His ship.

Hopkins unfolds his leather battledress and fits it neatly over his white, hairless skin. His skin has always been utterly smooth, up to and including his head. A hereditary disease introduced accidentally into his family through genetic manipulation by those who were once his masters. He only has to look in the mirror to give himself a thousand reasons to go on, to persist in bringing them to justice. Him, the son of generations of bookkeepers and clerks to the Elite.

He closes the ship's log, marking the page with a thick bookmark. He will have to finish this later. The pride he is feeling is because he knows what is happening has nothing to do with fate, or destiny, or any of that phoney mysticism so beloved of the Elite. It is down to hard work and persistence. Nothing but. Groaning and straining, he pulls on his tight knee-length boots.

The footsteps have become knocks at his cabin door. Hopkins pulls on the steel helmet. He is ready.

Once open, the doorway reveals the bare access route to the bridge. It is lined with his lieutenants. They snap to attention, saluting. He looks up at them (they are all far taller than he) and struts past, triumph unconcealed on his face.

'So, he is here, Carlin,' he states as the retinue follow him to the transmat-receptor room.

'It appears so, Citizen Hopkins,' replies the younger man, a nephew of one of his uncles, a cousin first removed or something. 'Your trust in the woman was not misplaced.'

Of course, it wasn't nepotism that got Hopkins's cousin here, oh no, it was proven ability. There is no place for nepotism in the New Protectorate. It irks Hopkins only slightly that Carlin's moustache bears proof that the genetic hairlessness did not extend to that side of the family.

He takes his cousin's arm, 'I fancy I have a way with the weaker sex, Carlin. I pride myself I understand the warped logic of their minds. Now, they have not been arrested as yet, have they?'

'I have stationed the guard according to your orders. No one has been in there.'

Hopkins's lip curls. 'Good. Good. I want the first face he sees to be mine. So he will know exactly what will happen to him. It is said I have a particular aptitude for this kind of work, Carlin, is that not so?'

'Indeed, Citizen Hopkins, without question.'

They reach the hatch with its stencilled black lettering, the two guards swiftly acknowledging Hopkins's presence. He checks his uniform; he wants to be immaculate for this moment. 'Do I look all right, Carlin?' he asks, although he knows it sounds like a demand.

'If I may, Citizen,' replies Carlin cautiously, and straightens the neckerchief.

'Right,' says Hopkins. He takes a deep breath. Sweat is trickling down his hairless back, pooling inside his waistband. 'Open the door.'

Robert Hopkins positively runs inside the room. Where he stops.

It is not Paul Neville. That man in the transmat-receptor room is not Paul Neville. It is, instead, a clown.

The clown is flapping at the singed end of an improbably long scarf wrapped round his neck. His floppy brown hat seems to be smoking slightly. Pelham is there beside him, absolutely pale.

'So you see,' the clown is saying, with all the pomp of the circus, 'a dual transmat-activator in that bangle on your wrist would be just the thing I would use to get two people out of a hopeless predicament.'

He turns to Hopkins and offers a hand. Hopkins stares at the soot-blackened object. 'Hello,' says the clown, his eyes wide and mad. 'I'd like to thank you for saving our lives. It was you that provided Ms Pelham here with that bangle, wasn't it?'

Hopkins nods to Carlin, who promptly floors the clown with his Protectorate law-bringing blackjack.

'Who is this?' Hopkins seethes at Pelham, a fraction of the anger he will bring to bear upon her later.

'I'm the Doctor,' comes a pained, muffled voice from the floor. 'Do you mind if I get up? I feel awkward talking to a pair of boots. And boots that, if I may say so, seem a little tight. You need to watch your circulation.'

Hopkins kicks the clown, who clutches his head once more and shouts in agony. 'I was only saying,' he manages, 'you seem a little too big for your boots, no need to get the hump.'

Enraged beyond all endurance, and worried that in his ire he will kill this buffoon too quickly, Hopkins snaps his fingers. 'Bring them,' he sneers.

They had caught her with embarrassing ease. Despite Neville's warnings, despite her own experiences, Miranda Pelham had walked straight into it.

She had been back in the solar system, chasing up a lead. Word had come in that a merchant had visited a planet in the Pan-Arlington system and come away with a set of coordinates, inscribed into ancient monoliths. These coordinates, he claimed, were in pictogram form and described the final resting place of a 'black skein', a creature with twenty heads that had menaced the long-extinct race that had put them there. For a large sum of money, the merchant would divulge the co-ordinates on Charon, Pluto's twin. Two dark twins a long way from the sun.

It sounded pretty feeble, even to the desperate Paul Neville, but he was unwilling to pass up any opportunity. He and Pelham were getting closer to Ashkellia, but this would have been the confirmation of a location they already suspected.

Pelham had volunteered to chase it up. She was sick of the Elite supremacist exiles they were sheltering with; their dull, cruel, petty nostalgia for that which they had lost to the New

Protectorate. She was also becoming, quite rightly as it turned out, very frightened of Paul Neville. It was clear that he was not in his right mind. In fact, very probably, he was becoming a paranoid obsessive with some distinctly nasty tendencies. He had taken to executing a serf every morning, just to rid himself of his nightly anxieties, and their hosts were running out of servants. It was about this time she met Erik, she recalled.

The Elite supremacist movement had supplied her with false papers and given her the dun, coarse clothing of a New Protectorate citizen. The creed of the revolution was called Uber-Material, supreme rationalism, and the people of the protectorate followed this creed with the enthusiasm of zealots. Pelham dyed her hair back to its natural colour and removed her make-up. She hadn't realised how old she had become in so short a time.

Charon was as much of a toilet as she'd been informed. Nothing more than a shantytown anchored to that moon. The only view on offer was the gigantic satellite gulag, a political prison and the shantytown's *raison d'être*, a huge grey ball sharing the sky with Pluto itself. Looking up at the grey prison made her shiver.

Her only company was Protectorate prison officials, and the occasional merchant who used the ghastly place as a stopover before journeying to a more enticing part of the Terran solar system.

Pelham spent a week in fear of her life. The Protectorate guards were just the thugs she had expected; her only salvation being their brutish, genetically-reared stupidity (the rumour was that generations ago there had been some distasteful breeding experiments involving Ogrons; she didn't like to think about it). Their lack of curiosity, their lack of anything – except perhaps pleasure at the prospect of what they were going to do to certain inmates when they were

161

allowed back up to the gulag – almost made her smile. Almost.

It had been a relief when the 'merchant' arrived. A rendezvous was arranged and she walked straight into the trap. One minute she was seated in a bar right on the edge of the town, the next she was being pinned to the floor by six iron clads.

They hauled her up and she got her first view of the hunter himself: First Citizen Robert Hopkins. His skin was as pale and bald as the rumours suggested. She had fainted when he looked at her. His eyes were a pale pink and held not a trace of mercy.

Shaking with fear, Miranda Pelham had pleaded for her life. No, let's get this correct, she begged, screamed with fear for her life. He just looked at the floor, waiting for her to say the right thing. She did, in the end. She told him where to find Paul Neville.

He didn't kill her. Oh, he shuttled her up to the gulag, gave her the VIP tour of the inquisition chambers where she witnessed a number of surgical procedures that would stay with her until her dying day, but he didn't kill her. He wanted Paul Neville too badly for that.

Of course she told him where he was, the location of the Elite supremacist movement, although she knew that once he had Neville, she would be of no further use to Hopkins. And if you were of no use to Hopkins…

Only when Hopkins's men were picking through the smoking ashes of the Elite base and could not find Neville amongst the bodies, did she begin to hope that she might survive.

Hopkins sat her down at a field table in the remains of the base. All around, iron clads were sifting through rubble, scrutinising the remains for any clues. She was shivering, her hair shorn, her clothing nothing but a dirty grey blanket, her face blue with bruises.

'I want you to find Neville,' he had said, very calmly. 'You will find him for me.'

'Yes,' she nodded furiously. 'Yes.'

Hopkins had regarded her with his unblinking eyes. 'He trusts you. You have been his closest ally for three years now. There is nothing to connect you to me. We will concoct a story about where you have been.'

'Yes.' She was shivering.

'When you find him, you will contact me. From this moment on, your life is not your own. You belong to me. Nothing else exists. Once we have parted, if he is not with you the next time I see you, I will have you tortured to death. Do you understand me?'

'Yes.'

Pelham had returned to Charon, where she waited for Neville to contact her. She often toyed with the bangle Hopkins had welded round her arm, the transmat-bangle with its short-range homing beacon.

When a genuine merchants' shuttle arrived with a message from Neville telling her where to travel next, Pelham had felt like a woman in a dream. Hopkins's invisible leash was with her wherever she went; she knew he would never let her go.

In this daze, she travelled along the complex pipeline of destinations where Neville sent her until, at last, she was reunited with him on the starship bound for Ashkellia. New evidence had come to light, proof of the whereabouts of the tomb of Valdemar. Erik was terribly excited.

Pelham had stuck to the story she had concocted with Hopkins. She wondered whether Neville suspected anything, but although he certainly knew about the destruction of the base, he didn't seem to make any other connections. Despite his paranoia, he hadn't suspected a thing.

Knowing that Hopkins would almost certainly be right behind her, knowing that she was caught between two madmen, Miranda Pelham had set off on the final part of her twenty-year journey to Ashkellia – the palace of the Old Ones, and her appointment with Valdemar.

'I can understand why you were so reluctant to use that little toy of yours,' says the Doctor, rather ruefully, as he attempts to reach the bruises on his back where the iron clads have been busy.

'The New Protectorate,' he muses. 'A strange, rather anachronistic period in Terra's history. The rigours of puritanism applied to a purely materialistic philosophy. Odd really, like a toffee without an apple.'

Pelham finds that her imagination is running along other tracks, such as what Hopkins is eventually going to do to her.

'Don't worry,' the Doctor reassures her, 'it's not a permanent situation. Little more than a blip really. It'll all blow over in… oh, a couple of centuries.'

They have been led into an imposing, efficient-looking torture chamber. If the New Protectorate lacked imagination, it found its creative outlet in the multitude of ways it was possible to inflict pain on a human body. Pelham was not relishing the possibility that where Kampp left off, Hopkins would more than readily pick up.

'You do realise,' she says as they stand… well, not so much stand as hang, chained to the wall by their wrists as they are, 'you do realise that we are going to tell them everything, immediately. I don't want you getting all stubborn and brave, you got that straight?'

The Doctor ponders this. 'Well, I…'

'Because if they disbelieve even one word, suspect even a single lie, then they'll start again.'

164

'If you insist. Mind you...'

'No.'

'I was only going to say...'

'No.'

The Doctor shrugs as Pelham twists herself round to glare at him. 'Let me give you the speech, Doctor,' she says. 'Before you start going all noble on me. I'm a coward, I'm proud of my cowardice, I look after it, nourish it, feed it. The merest concept of the smallest possibility of the slightest amount of pain to be inflicted upon my person and I will go to any inconvenience to avoid it. I will put myself out; I will be proactive in avoidance of that pain. And if that includes denouncing you as a traitor or a spy or whatever Hopkins wants me to denounce you as, there's not even an issue, there's not even a list of priorities. It's done.'

'At least you're honest.'

'I'm not proud of my cowardice. In fact, I understand that it may appear morally repugnant. However, like a limp, it's a part of my life.' She raises her eyebrows. 'Sorry, just thought it would be better for you to know.'

'Thank you,' the Doctor replies. 'You have been most reassuring. I think you're braver than you think.'

'Oh!' she says with alarm. 'Don't think that! Loads of people have said that and I've denounced them all.'

The Doctor smiles, something she hadn't expected. 'Aren't you getting tired of hanging around?' he says. Is he aware of the irony or not? She doesn't know. In fact, she doesn't know anything about this lunatic. Except, perhaps, that he's the sanest man in this solar system.

He clears his throat. 'Uh huh! Excuse me! Excuse me! Could we hurry this up please? Ms Pelham and I do have other things we could usefully be getting on with whilst contemplating what you're going to do to us.'

'Doctor,' she warns.

'Failing that, how about a crossword, or a magazine? To pass the time!'

The door to the torture chamber opens. 'Ah,' says the Doctor and winks at her.

Pelham starts to tremble. She has a feeling, not dissimilar to the feeling she felt down in the entrance to the tomb when Erik and Neville's man disappeared and she was all alone with the god she had created. 'Oh God,' she moans, 'Oh God. There's no way out. I'm going to die. Please, Doctor, don't let them. I don't want to die.'

'Ssh now,' he says softly. 'I've got work to do.'

Hopkins enters. Well, whoever it is – he is wearing an inquisitor's hood – is at least a foot shorter than any iron clad Pelham has ever met, so she deduces it must be him.

'Hello,' says the Doctor enthusiastically. 'Come right in.'

Hopkins is followed by two of his officers. They are as stern-faced and grim as he must be beneath his hood. None speak as they make their way over to their prisoners.

Hopkins is holding a small, stubby club.

'Look,' Pelham starts to gabble. 'Please, Hopkins, don't kill me. I'll do anything you want. I'll tell you everything, you know that. This one here, they call him the Doctor, he can tell you everything you need to know about Neville and what he's going to do. Listen to him, you have to listen to him. The situation down there, it's just awful…'

She feels the crack of the club across her face, and her expensively capped teeth rattle. She screams, loudly, and starts to cry.

'I didn't give you permission to speak,' says the muffled voice beneath the hood. His gloved hands grab her face and lift it up to meet his hidden eyes. She knows of old that he is inspecting her tears, seeing how close she is to breaking.

'That's the trouble, you see,' says the Doctor, 'if you tell them everything all at once, any self-respecting torturer feels he's missed out on something.'

'How right you are, Doctor,' says Hopkins.

The Doctor looks up at the two officers standing behind their master. 'I'm impressed,' he says. 'Keeping a straight face with him in all this get-up.'

There is an involuntary twitch in one of the officer's cheeks.

'Silence!' bellows Hopkins and strikes the Doctor.

When the Doctor has recovered, he looks at the little hooded man. 'Can you see me all right?' he asks, concerned. 'How many fingers am I holding up?' High above his head, the digits waggle in their restraints. The offending officer turns his head away to cough. Even Pelham finds her fear retreating. It's still there but she feels more in control.

Hopkins raises the club once more. 'You are a decadent, Doctor. I know. You have that arrogant superiority common to all aristocrats. My role is to teach you the error of your ways.' He states this calmly, without emotion. 'Fetch the needles. Some say that pain is all in the mind. I don't believe that, do you?'

The Doctor is staring out, apparently distracted.

'Well?' Hopkins snuffles.

The Doctor's head jerks, as if he is just waking up. 'Oh, sorry,' he says, 'I didn't realise you were talking to me. It's that hood, I can't see your eyes and your head was more inclined to the left so naturally I assumed…'

'I asked you a question!'

'Yes, you did.' He looks up. 'No, it's gone. You couldn't repeat it, could you? My memory's terrible when I'm hung up.'

Pelham can see he has gone too far.

'I don't like your face, sir. I don't like your smug manner and I don't like your dress.'

The Doctor pauses for a moment. Then, all innocence, he replies, 'I'm not wearing a dress.'

Pelham groans, actually makes the noise. Hopkins nods beneath his hood. 'I see. I see. Lieutenant Carlin, kill this man.'

The smirking officer pulls a pistol from his belt.

'I wouldn't do that,' the Doctor says calmly. 'Not if you want Paul Neville. Pelham here won't be able to help you on her own.'

Hopkins raises an arm to postpone the execution. 'And why is that?'

'Because you're running out of time. He's not the man he used to be, you know.'

'What?'

'Oh dear,' sighs the Doctor. 'This is going to be a long story…'

'And I'm tired of listening to you,' Hopkins sneers. 'I don't know who you are and I don't care. Goodbye.'

He means it. He does. Pelham can see it even if the Doctor can't. He has made the mistake of thinking he was winding up a normal psychotic. Hopkins wasn't like that; he worked to his own rules. He could never kill enough.

'Listen to him,' Pelham shrieks. 'Listen!'

'Oh, the mouse squeaks,' Hopkins snarls, and whacks the club across the bridge of the Doctor's nose. Coldly, as if it is a new experience, the inquisitor examines the Doctor's reaction to the pain. He strikes again and this time the Doctor cries out.

'You are mistaken if you believe my treatment of you is something I enjoy, acted out to appease some delusional mental fantasy,' Hopkins tells him. 'Your death is not a pleasurable experience for me. I simply perform my duties according to my position in the state. I once slew thirty LaRoi children from youngest to eldest, one after the other, in front of their parents. It was important, historically, for them to understand their family line was to be no more. The task was unpleasant but necessary. I did not flinch.'

'The Doctor's right,' Pelham says, not hoping, not anything, just wanting to live. 'You'd better let him go. I saw some weird stuff in the palace and he's the only one who knew anything about it.'

'I don't care about palaces, I just want Neville.'

'Then for God's sake, listen!' she cries. What is she saying? Where is all this verbiage coming from? Shut up, you stupid woman, shut up!

She finds she is not stopping. 'If you kill him, then you can torture me all you like because there is no way you will get to Neville without him.'

At last, Hopkins turns. 'Torture you…'

'That's right. Go on, do it. You've done just about everything else to me. If what the Doctor says is going to happen happens, then things are going to change around here. If you kill him then torture me all you want. You'll be doing me a favour.'

She thinks, she knows, she has gone too far. There is no walking away from this. It's not bravery, nor stupidity, that has made her say these things. It is that she is tired, tired of lying, of all those months trying to balance between Hopkins and Neville. She's had enough.

'It may be wise to listen to what they have to say, Citizen,' says the officer who had been forced to conceal his amusement earlier on. What was his name again? Carlin. 'After all, we have no idea what is actually down there.'

'I disagree,' says the third man, another tall and rather dashing officer. 'We don't need to know what is down there. May I suggest, Citizen Hopkins, that the artillery officer release two Hammer class warheads on to the relevant coordinates?'

Pelham has often wondered why such a deranged, inverted snob as Hopkins should surround himself with men of such noble, aristocratic looks. Every time he looks at them, the thought of his own squat, bald physique must drive him berserk. Of course, he probably does it for that very reason.

At the moment, however, Hopkins looks pretty berserk with both men for interrupting his fun. Actually, to Pelham, this missile idea sounds pretty reasonable.

'I'm afraid your missiles won't work,' says the Doctor. 'Apart from the fact that there's bound to be some kind of psychic response from the palace, the missiles would undoubtedly be unable to manage Ashkellia's atmospheric idiosyncrasies. In other words, they'll melt before they reach their target.'

'Silence!' snarls the missile-suggesting officer.

'Only trying to help,' the Doctor mutters. A well-aimed blow from the club quietens him down.

Hopkins considers. He stares first at Pelham, then up at the Doctor. He paces the torture chamber, puffing out his chest as he does so. The two officers try not to look at each other. Pelham finds that she is annoyed that her ultimatum, her willingness to sacrifice herself for the Doctor, has met with only this reaction. This was her big moment, surely?

'You say you want to help me, Doctor. Why is that? What's in it for you?'

The Doctor shakes his head, 'You know, if Neville succeeds in opening the breach into the higher dimensions, all this, everything you know, will be destroyed. Nothing will be left unaltered. Time itself will no longer exist. I'd like to try and stop Neville doing this. How about you?'

The Doctor is detained in the brig as the ship enters the atmosphere of Ashkellia. Pelham has been whisked off somewhere and he feels alone for the first time in days.

Left to himself, he feels the burden of guilt threaten to overwhelm him. Why hadn't he realised? It was ridiculous to think he could have been so blind. Of course Neville would have known what to do once the power was restored.

The Doctor knows he is guilty of selfishness; worse, of blindness. His desperation to hurry this up, get back to what seemed of utmost importance to him, affected his perception as much as the higher dimensions affected the palace. It was almost as if someone else was putting thoughts in his head. Almost.

He cannot evade the responsibility. He is to blame, no one else. Not for the first time, he resents the White Guardian and the demands made upon him.

Still, now he is in this position, he must redress the situation. If he can. He sits himself in this dark room, pulls his hat down to cover his face and tries to clear his mind.

Romana. What has he abandoned her to? Poor young thing, so full of herself, so eager to see the universe. Well, he'd certainly given her that, all in one go.

The disgusting vaccine gurgles inside him. 'Fat lot of good you are swirling around inside me,' he berates it, out loud.

The Doctor touches his head beneath the hat. Somewhere inside it, even in the warped complexes of the Time Lord mind, there lies the organ he stunted with the… the magic potion of the Old Ones. A prehistoric link, he supposes, with the universe when all was whole; right at the start, when all things were one. He can't imagine what that would have been like - a socket waiting for a plug and a wire. Suddenly switching into the immensity of the universe in its entirety. No, it is not imagination he lacks; it is the capacity to perceive.

If only he had had more time. If only he had managed to replicate the vaccine's numbing effects and administered it to Romana. If only he hadn't started something he couldn't finish.

He thinks of the Old Ones, how they must have felt when they realised what they had released. The first alterations;

subtle, almost imperceptible. Their control room changing around them, seemingly coming to life, and then they themselves changing, feeling the world shift and widen. Were they ever aware of what was happening to them? Of course, in the end they must have been. They found a way to hold it back. Logical really.

Now all he had to do was find the same solution.

The docking process clangs around the ship. He looks up. This is no time for rumination. He must be active; he must concentrate fully on the task in hand. Forget the Key to Time. If the higher dimensions are released, time will cease to exist.

The door opens. The Doctor leaps to his feet.

A wan-looking officer stands there – Carlin was his name wasn't it? Seemed a sensible enough fellow. Saner, at least, than Hopkins.

'Now, what can I do for you?' the Doctor asks, innocently.

Carlin seems embarrassed, bemused in some way. 'We're moving into the atmosphere. You seem to know a bit about what's going on. I want you and Pelham on the bridge. Just in case.'

'What about Mr Hopkins? Can you keep him off me? He doesn't strike me as the type who appreciates advice.'

'I'll do what I can. Just don't push your luck.'

Robert Hopkins returns to his lists of efficiency percentages. However, he finds the pragmatic statistics less soothing than usual. How clever this Doctor thinks he is, how charming, how absolutely awfully terribly amusing and witty and sardonic. At some point in the future, hopefully the very near future, Hopkins would like to remind this babbling idiot of some universal truths. The breaking point of the body, the weakness of the spirit, that kind of thing. He would enjoy teaching these lessons. Iron and flesh, Doctor, talk all you like.

It had been galling to accept that he would have to do what the Doctor suggested after all. Hopkins may have been looking forward to the damage he might do to his prisoners, but he isn't an idiot. Not where Paul Neville is concerned. Any kind of trap might be waiting for them in this golden palace thing.

How he hates Paul Neville, hates everything he represents. Not only the centuries of misrule and subjugation of his own class, almost of his own race. Hopkins has long ago sated his blood lust in that particular quest for vengeance.

No, it is this spiritual, religious mysticism that he hates. This decadent belief in spirits and souls and the greater life to come – all nonsense, all lies to placate the fear of mortality.

He understands. Robert Hopkins understands, about life and death. There is no more, no less, than existence. No soul, no 'inner being', no higher purpose; just a cold, indifferent universe and the lives that pass through it. Nothing exists except that which one makes exist. Will to Power. Like it or not, that is everything.

This Ashkellia, this 'tomb of Valdemar'. Robert Hopkins looks at the statistics in the logbook and sees it for what it is. A planet, the second planet in its system, orbiting at a distance of eighty-nine-million miles; a minor star in a sparsely clustered back-end of the galaxy.

He has read the reports on the cult, their sad beliefs. The last dying breath of an obsolete social order, the final clinging to mysticism. It would make him laugh, if he were capable of laughing. How he had hated the resigned, passive faces of those at the theomantic universities, as he and his men ploughed through them with sword and shot. He had shown up their religious convictions for the falsehoods they were. Even believers could scream if you took your time and were brutal enough.

The cult is smashed now, he knows that. He wonders whether Neville does. How Hopkins would love to explain it to him – the details, the ruination, all by his hand.

Yet a nagging doubt remains, even in his selective mind. The cult isn't smashed, not entirely. And the strongest of those he had slain had still died with the word 'Valdemar' on their lips.

The downfall of Paul Neville, this Magus of a little obscure cult – a cult that stubbornly refuses to die, the symbol of all that opposes the New Protectorate – is all that he feels he has left to achieve.

Well, Hopkins himself will parade that grey-bearded head on a pole through Earth Parliament if he has to. Because Hopkins is better. Because Hopkins knows that nothing matters, that out here in the stars there is no one to judge.

Paul Neville murders in the name of evil, in the name of Valdemar, always failing to understand the true perspective. Let him do that, let him do those things. Hopkins knows better. He murders in the name of the only true universal law. He murders in the name of nothingness.

The intercom beeps. Hopkins realises he is soaked in sweat. The logbook is crushed in his hairless hands. He will have to wear the hairshirt to keep himself calm.

'Report!' he barks into the brass cylinder.

'Citizen Hopkins,' comes the voice of Carlin. 'We have broken orbit and are commencing descent. We should reach the coordinates obtained from the tracer in one hour.'

'You sound worried, Carlin.'

'Sir, sensors indicate that acidity levels contained in the atmosphere will cause severe damage to hull integrity. We will not be able to remain there for long…'

Hopkins flicks the 'send' command. 'We will remain as long as is necessary. I will not flinch from my duty.'

'Of course, Citizen.'

'Where is the Doctor?'

Carlin pauses. Hopkins listens to his breathing.

'On the bridge. We felt it would be wise-'

'What? How dare you! I'm coming up immediately.'

'Sir.' His cousin fails to keep the disappointment out of his voice.

Despite himself, despite all his knowledge, Robert Hopkins raises his head to the ceiling of his metal cage and looks up. Without even realising he is doing it, he prays. Give Paul Neville to me, he hisses at the cold void outside. *Give him to me!*

Chapter Eleven

It's funny, thinks Miranda Pelham, but before Hopkins arrived, the bridge had almost seemed a relaxed, normal place to be.

The crew had been silent and efficient, just as a crew ought to be, only speaking when they had important information to relate. This Lieutenant Carlin seemed a humane and sensible officer, overseeing the ship's descent calmly and carefully. The Doctor watched, to Carlin's right – a Gonzalo to his duke – as they entered the maelstrom. For a while Pelham had the impression that the cavalry were on their way to kick the stuffing out of the bad guys.

Hopkins's arrival changed all that.

For a start, as the hatch to the bridge opened and he strutted in, the ship lurched suddenly. As he opened his mouth to shout something unpleasant, Hopkins was totally caught out, flying over and smacking his head on the navigational consoles. Terrified officers helped him to his feet, pulling his captain's helmet up from over his eyes.

Now, the whole atmosphere has changed. The crew is nervous, over-enthusiastically studying their instrument read-outs.

'Captain on deck!' bellows Carlin, and all stand to rapt attention. Hopkins smooths out the ruffles in his silk and leather uniform, then falls over again as the ship lists.

'Hull breaches on decks three and six, Lieuten– Citizen Hopkins.'

'Get men down there and get them sealed,' barks the inquisitor, looking around, daring his men to laugh. Carlin vacates his seat and Hopkins settles himself in, neatly avoiding humiliation in the subsequent lurch.

When the ship has righted itself, he starts to look around.

Pelham knows exactly who he is looking for and attempts to shrink back into some non-existent shadows.

It does no good.

'You'd better have a damned good explanation for their still breathing, Carlin,' Hopkins hisses.

'Oh, he has,' says the Doctor, much too flippantly for Pelham's liking. 'He has. Tell him, Carlin. He's all ears.'

Carlin coughs. Before Hopkins turns too red he speaks up. 'Well, they are the only people with any idea what's inside this palace, Citizen. I thought it best…'

'Leave the thinking to me.' Hopkins glares at them. Any excuse, Pelham realises, any at all.

'We're one hundred and twenty kilometres into the atmosphere, Citizen, descending at ten kps.' Thank you, bridge technician person, she breathes, thank you.

'Activate sensor equipment,' orders Hopkins, snapping into the job. The buffoon has gone, replaced by the sinister figure she knows only too well. Hopkins is back on the hunt.

'Problems with the sensor array, Citizen,' says Carlin. 'The acid is attacking our probes.' He bends over, squinting at the sensor terminals. 'But I think we've found it. Large metallic object, some unknown elements, could be your palace.'

Hopkins looks up at the Doctor, who confirms: 'It is the palace. I would be very careful if I were you.'

'Hull breaches occurring on nine decks now, Citizen.'

There is a tearing sound overhead. A sudden bump of turbulence sends them all scrabbling for handholds.

'Visual, give me a look at the damn thing!' Hopkins orders. The crew swarm over their controls, trying to find a spectronic reading that can penetrate these clouds. Infrared reveals the column of vast heat from the planet's core, supporting the structure.

'My God…' whispers Carlin.

'Don't be stupid,' Hopkins warns him. 'It's a building, that's all. There's nothing supernatural about it. Forget the docking bay, Neville will have thought of that. Take us over the top of the thing. We'll burn our way in.'

Yeah, right, thinks Pelham, nothing supernatural at all. She is feeling the same unease, the same background ice she felt the first time that she approached this ancient structure. There is something unreal about it, a sense of ancient... what could it be... ancient evil?

'There! There it is!' Hopkins loses his cool. He leaps out of his seat and jabs like a maniac at the viewscreen.

Indeed, through the acid clouds, the clouds that even now gnaw at the New Protectorate cruiser, the bulbous shape of the palace emerges, dark no longer.

The doubts return, unbidden. It is as if the palace has become sick.

The air on the bridge has become hot, thick. Compensators whine deep under her feet as they attempt to cope with the atmospheric conditions. Pelham is drawn to remaining silent as she stares, and she realises she is not the only one. All gaze silently at this thing towards which they are driving.

The column of superheated air that sustains the palace's position high above the surface, is almost visible, glowing with an obscene light. The palace itself seems to throb with its own unearthly breath. It glistens. Nothing she can specify, it is just wrong. Something that shouldn't exist here.

She thinks of herself caught in this sticky structure, the life drained from her. She sees her own face, her own dead face staring sightlessly back at her. The palace makes her think of night and a dark, earthen crypt.

'It... it's alive...' she mutters, after an eternity.

'No,' says the Doctor. 'Not life, not in the sense that we know it. Not even an "it" as we know it. Just something that can

179

shape matter, objects, minds. Remember, we are seeing this with the benefit of the vaccine. These others, and Romana, will be affected and they won't even know it. They won't be seeing what we can see. What this palace has become is what everything will become, if the gateway is opened.'

'Whatever you say…' she replies. 'I can't go there again. You have to stop Hopkins going there. We'll die, I know it.' She looks at him, knowing the mask that fear is making of her face.

'I'm sorry, Miranda, I can't do that.'

'Don't, don't say that. You have to.'

'I've made a terrible mistake and the consequences will be catastrophic unless I can stop it. There will be nowhere to go to unless we prevent Neville opening the tomb.'

She feels like stamping her feet. 'Do you always get so high and mighty in the face of certain death?'

'It's a living.'

'Prepare an artisan team,' says Hopkins. His voice is hoarse but – and Pelham groans once more – dreadfully expectant. 'And fetch Redfearn,' he continues.

Carlin nods and, unable to tear his eyes away from the growing palace, flicks the intercom switch. 'Calling Mr Redfearn. Mr Redfearn to the airlock please.'

The ship clangs on to the roof of the palace. Hopkins selects a retinue and they all shuffle down to the airlock. The artisan team – well, some stripped-to-the-waist thugs and some welding apparatus, anyway – are already there, filling the small chamber with smoke and sparks. The work turns the cramped space into a furnace. Pelham has been kitted out in a kind of makeshift, iron clad outfit, without the iron, which doesn't help. The shirt is too rough, the breeches too tight and the boots too hard. The Doctor, meanwhile, gets to keep his mad professor's outfit, down to that stupid scarf.

Pelham can feel the buffeting of this mad atmosphere. The metal plates of the hull buckle and twist with the violence of the storm.

Mr Redfearn, it turns out, is a small, pale, rather rakish-looking man in his early forties. His main distinguishing feature, if Pelham is forced to allocate one, would be his brightly coloured, expensively tailored waistcoat, which he wears beneath a smart grey jacket. That, and the black wide-brimmed hat which he raises to the boarding party.

'Mr Hopkins. Gen'lemen,' he states formally, in an accent that has to originate from the Presley colonies. 'Ah trust y'all have a reason for disturbing mah three-card stud? Ah was in possession of a peach-like hand capable of stunning mah opponent into foregoing the game.'

'Your opponent?' asks Pelham, stunned by such an inappropriate figure.

Mr Redfearn places a hand on his waistcoated chest. 'Mahself. Worthy adversaries are so rarely to be found in this day and age.'

Mr Redfearn sees her with his his hawkish eyes and smiles. He bows. 'Ms Pelham. Delighted t'make yoh acquaintance. Mr Niles Redfearn at your service.'

Hopkins, like the rest of his boarding party, is buckling armour and weapons all over himself. He holsters his pistol. 'Mr Redfearn, your task will be to oversee this man...' he indicates a bemused-looking Doctor, 'and Pelham.'

'Why, that is not a task, that is a signal pleasure. Ma'am.'

'Never leave their sides. Not even for a moment.' Hopkins loads his shotgun and snaps its breech closed. 'Nothing must get between Neville and myself, and I don't want those two running around causing trouble.'

The Doctor snorts. 'And what do you do, Mr Redfearn, that makes you so special?'

181

White teeth gleaming in an ever-so-friendly smile, Mr Redfearn stretches. His jacket opens to reveal the two bandoliers draped around his shoulders, and the two holstered pearl-grip pistols strapped to them. 'Ah win,' he replies.

Hopkins looks the Doctor up and down. 'Mr Redfearn is a phenomenally accurate pistol marksman. His reactions have been genetically augmented. An "amusement" for the now defunct Elite. He has never missed a shot. Much to their eventual regret.'

The waistcoat closed, Mr Redfearn looks small and insignificant again. 'That's not quite true, suh. There was that time when ah was two yeahs old...'

The Doctor nods impatiently. 'Yes, yes. Can we get on with this?'

Mr Redfearn raises an eyebrow. Pelham presumes that if you're an expert marksman, you don't like being interrupted. 'Ah look forward to furthering our acquaintance, Doctor,' he says politely, and stares.

'Enough,' Hopkins barks. He looks around at the assembled company. Apart from himself, Mr Redfearn, the Doctor and herself, there are eight men including the tall figure of Lieutenant Carlin. To Pelham, this does not seem nearly enough.

Hopkins tightens the straps on his helmet. 'Keep your eyes open, men. Anyone we meet is to be considered an enemy and executed on the spot. The only exception is Neville himself. He is mine. Any man taking any action against him will be shot. Do I make myself clear?'

The company nods. Hopkins slams a gauntleted fist on to the shoulder of one of the welders. The poor man winces. 'Nearly done,' he manages through the pain.

The artisan team step away. Outside, Pelham hears the storm redouble its attack on the ship. Sledgehammers are produced and the already sweating drones start to bash and pound at the smooth metal roof of the palace. It's tougher than this, Pelham prays, no way could these people hammer and weld through its skin. Just as the first hole appears. Well done, Miranda, good to see the old luck holding out.

The airlock is a hell of echoes and metallic clamouring. The artisans kick and smash their way through to widen the hole. At last a huge plate is worked loose and it drops down, into total blackness beneath. Seconds later, too many seconds, Pelham hears it hit the floor inside.

'Ladders,' Hopkins orders. Seconds later, the ropes drop. 'After me.' Hopkins slings his shotgun over his shoulder and commences his descent.

'Let battle commence,' says Mr Redfearn as Pelham realises it's her turn.

Hopkins can feel adrenaline pumping him up. As he hits the floor, the lights come on. Immediately, he unsheaths his shotgun and swings round. This must be done efficiently. For a second, he is on his own. He can hear the others clambering down above him but there is something, something that seems to slow the moment down.

The room, or chamber or whatever, is circular. A quiet circle that seems to be waiting for something. Perhaps it was once an observatory; there is a large, inexplicable machine staring up at the ceiling from the centre. A hatch points the way down into the depths. He senses that this is where it lurks.

It? What does that mean?

The source of the decadence that is the cult; that's what it means. Not surprising really, because if all that rubbish has a source, it stands to reason it's here. He can feel Neville's influence. All these arcane colours and symbols daubed over the walls, all this burnt-orange metal.

183

It's breathing down there, waiting for him. Well, don't worry my friend, you don't scare me. I'm coming for you. I'm coming.

Time speeds up again and Carlin hits the floor behind him, helmeted and formidable. His cousin is a fine man. The others follow, readying weapons.

'Standard formation,' Carlin orders. 'Interesting.'

'What is?'

'These markings. Cult runes.'

'Are they really? Well, don't bother with them. We need to keep moving. Surprise is everything.'

The Doctor has swung down, performing his usual theatrical antics as he tries to disentangle his foot from the rope ladder. How Hopkins would love to work on him. First Neville, then him. Remember that.

'He's gone,' the Doctor says, sniffing the air.

'How can you tell?' asks Carlin.

'He can't!' Hopkins snarls. 'He's as much a charlatan as Neville.'

The Doctor grimaces. 'If you say so. I say there's no one here.'

'All right, clever man,' says Hopkins, 'which way?'

With a smile, as if to a child, the Doctor nods at the hatch in the floor. 'Well, I'm no expert but at a guess...'

'Don't push me,' Hopkins barks.

Mr Redfearn is helping Pelham from the ladder. 'Careful, my dear,' he says politely. 'Lest you entangle yourself further.'

Pelham falls into his arms and immediately pushes herself away. 'It's too late for that,' she says sardonically.

'Keep together, move quickly and quietly. I want two men at point looking for booby traps.' Hopkins moves theatrically, on the alert for danger. 'Remember,' he whispers chillingly, 'this is the Magus's lair.'

The pause makes him start. They are all looking at him. 'What?' he asks, 'What is it?'

Carlin looks at the Doctor. He doesn't like the way those two are getting thick together. 'Did... Did you say "the Magus's lair", Citizen Hopkins?'

Did he? Why would he...? 'Of course not. It's just Neville's bolthole, that's what I said.'

'Ah.' Carlin does not seem convinced.

'I should be very careful,' warns the Doctor. 'All of you. This structure will affect your minds. You won't even know it's happening.'

'But I presume only you and Pelham are immune to these "effects", Doctor,' Hopkins sneers.

'As it happens, yes. You see, we found this vaccine...'

'Shut up. As you know it all, you can be one of our point men. Open that hatch.'

As Hopkins indicates, the Doctor looks mournfully at that which he has been asked to unlock. 'Well,' he shrugs, 'if that's what you want. I think it would be better if we all went back to your ship and–'

'Open it! Or I'll kill you where you stand.'

Even now, even with that threat, the madman keeps playing the fool. He looks at each of his hands, as if weighing up the possibilities.

'Do it,' Hopkins warns.

'I'll open the hatch,' says the Doctor, nodding.

The palace opens up for them, a cross-section for searching, and it appears that the Doctor is correct. The iron clads bob and weave, and poke their guns into many a deceptive corner, but find no creature, living or dead.

Once the Doctor has shown them how, they descend the levels via the anti-grav shafts. He is intrigued by the sense of awe and wonderment that Hopkins and the others display at the alien construction. They seem overwhelmed by its colonnades, its vast halls of decorated stone, its baroque, over-embellished décor.

The Doctor feels a stab of pity, as he wonders how much further down the road of new perception Romana will have travelled by now. Why did he have to have been saddled with a companion so incapable…? No, it is his fault, there's no getting away from it.

With the vaccine de-clouding his mind, he can see the palace for that which it is – an overblown, fairground haunted house, complete with cartoon ghosts and ghoulies. As the soldiers marvel at the way the geography seems to shift and shimmer according to their desires, he sees the clunky floor moving, the rusty clanging of gears, the flora in crumbling pots hiding the cracks. It is a carnival ride at night, the machinery working to sustain a superficial illusion.

Only one of Hopkins's men is seemingly immune to the effects of the higher dimensions, and that's because he has his eyes firmly on the Doctor's back. 'Five paces ahead if you don't mind, suh,' says Mr Redfearn evenly. 'No more, no less.'

The Doctor is impatient. He is in the wrong place. He must find a way to get to the tomb before critical mass is achieved. These men will start to become affected very soon, undoubtedly enabling him to slip out of their grasp. The question is, can he wait that long?

Wait, he thinks to himself. He has to confirm that which he thinks he already knows. He indicates that they should descend to the piazza level. Hopkins nods; even the madman is susceptible to logic at times.

Neville and Hopkins make a fitting pair, the Doctor thinks. Both zealots, both utterly consumed by their own self-righteousness. Both so utterly, completely convinced that they are right. He remembers a long-ago philosophy course, Romana would know more, and an aphorism that seems apposite – 'Strive not to know thyself too well.'

There must always be more to learn, for the mind solidifies, the cerebral arteries harden if they are not busy, always striving.

The search widens and his worry increases. He leads the small unit down on to levels he remembers. He tries to walk at a relaxed pace, as if strolling through Hyde Park. However, slowly, imperceptibly, he increases that pace. He has to find his companion.

'Not too fast now, Doctor,' says Mr Redfearn, right behind him.

At last, he finds the double doors leading to the main piazza. Not quite so empty here. Something has happened. There is the same echoing space, the same trickling fountains and steamy air, the same steps and nooks and crannies. But there is also more.

'Check them,' says Hopkins grimly. 'Check if one of them is Neville.'

Pelham gasps. She has been silent on this trek but now her voice is released, revealing some kind of pent-up trauma that she has been long brooding upon. Her face turns a ghastly sheen of white, and the Doctor skips neatly to her side to catch her if she faints.

'My God,' she whispers. 'What did they do to each other?'

Awkwardly, the Doctor finds himself holding her up. Well, no choice really, better than her smashing her head on the marble steps. The soldiers prod and poke the bodies.

The children – twisted, deformed and full of bullets. And others in amongst them. Neville's guards, their wounds and the effects of the higher dimensions reshaping their faces and bodies into new, unrecognisable forms. But no Neville or Romana.

Pelham clutches the Doctor, unreasonably tightly. 'I keep

dreaming. I'm awake but I can't shake it off. I keep seeing something, a scene,' she starts to babble out of nowhere. The Doctor feels her fear shaking him. 'A hilltop. It's night. A single tree that stands over a block of stone. Somehow, I know that this block is my tomb. I'm dead. Cold and dead inside but I'm looking in on it and I can see myself looking up…I'm dead but I know I can still see. I can still see…'

The Doctor keeps a grip on her. Is this some incipient madness or are the vaccine's effects limited? He realises that the higher dimensions affect individuals in different ways and are impossible to predict.

'Put the image out of your mind,' he soothes her. 'It is nothing but a dream, your own mind rationalising new potentials. Think only of these numbers; repeat this formula I am giving you…' He then proceeds to reel off a string of equations and numbers, Time Lord exercises for clearing the mind. He forces her to obey. Her shaking subsides.

The iron clads are silent as they proceed with their checks. The Doctor watches them, his own face set in stone.

'What happened to them?' demands Hopkins. He lifts the helmet's visor. Already, his hairless face trickles with feverish sweat. He blinks, lacking the eyebrows with which to divert that sweat.

'I tried to tell them,' the Doctor replies, 'and I've been trying to tell you. The higher dimensions have been released and the palace was evolving their physical forms to embrace the new perceptions. Unless we get done with this, you will all be similarly affected.'

'Is Neville among the dead?' asks Hopkins, ignoring the Doctor.

'No, Citizen,' Carlin replies, double-checking the last of the corpses.

'Spread out. Keep looking.'

'You know what I think?' asks the Doctor, quietly.

Hopkins lowers his visor once more. 'I'm not interested in your opinion.'

'Oh, I think you are. I really think you are.'

'All right then. What?'

The Doctor, under the unerring gaze of Mr Redfearn, seats Pelham on the steps. 'I think Neville did leave a little trap for you. The guards were placed to ambush you. We're right next to the docking bay. Only the others got to them first.'

Hopkins sneers. 'These are the cloaks of the cult high guard. How could these… children have done this? The guards could have cut them to pieces.'

'I don't think they were children any more.'

Hopkins stares at him and, for a moment, the Doctor feels pity for the deranged little man. He has encountered countless closed minds in his time, met people and creatures for whom black just had to be white, and the result is always the same. They seal themselves into traps of their own devising, and wither away. Not accepting the palace, refusing to understand the truth, will be the death of Hopkins.

'Check the docking bay,' orders the Doctor. 'See if the bathyscape is still there.'

Carlin moves instinctively to obey. Hopkins raises an arm and stops him dead. 'How dare you…?'

'Check it!' bellows the Doctor, feeling his patience finally exhaust itself.

'I am sick and tired of you,' says Hopkins slowly. 'Just who do you think you are? You've just been wasting my time.' He turns away, past the worried-looking Carlin to the calm and anticipatory Mr Redfearn, who is leaning idly against a column, picking his teeth. 'Mr Redfearn, the time has come to terminate this little alliance.'

Mr Redfearn shrugs and straightens himself up. His eyes

never leave the Doctor as he adjusts his clothing. 'My pleasure, Mr Hopkins.' The gloved hands flick back the jacket, revealing the pistols within. His fingers twiddle. 'Any last words, Doctor?' he asks.

The Doctor considers. 'One word,' he replies after some careful thought.

'Hmm?' Mr Redfearn is smiling, almost interested. His eyes glitter, like those of a cobra.

'Dark,' says the Doctor, and the palace obeys, sending the piazza into utter and complete blackness.

'Light! Light!' Hopkins screeches at the top of his voice. There is a flash, and milliseconds later, the sound of the report – Redfearn firing, reacting more quickly than he would have believed possible.

There is the sound of running and scuffling and Hopkins is pushed off balance by some mighty force. He topples and finds that the ground has disappeared. Instead, there is nothing but water; one of the pools is all there is to break his fall. He hits it with a mighty clap and then the liquid is all over him.

He sits up, spitting out the foul, scented water. A light flashes on, right in his eyes, and he sees the pistol, the thumb cocking it and Mr Redfearn laughing right behind it.

'It's me! It's me!' Hopkins screams and the light flicks off. He buries his head in the water once more, panic-stricken.

Getting his heart under control, he hauls himself up. His men are shouting and dashing around in the dark. He hears iron and spur clashing in the inky blackness. 'Get some torches on!' he bellows, coughing out the last of the pool. His armour leaks like a waterfall. Someone, Carlin, finally barks orders that bring the men under control. Torchlights snake through the blackness.

This is it, Hopkins thinks. This is it! It was all going so smoothly and professionally until Pelham and her madman turned up. Since then, the whole operation has been one long catalogue of errors. He is certain Neville can see this and is laughing at him. Laughing!

Well, no more. The Doctor is going to die for this. Die.

'Are you all right, Citizen Hopkins?' asks a concerned Carlin, right by his side, making him jump, making him slip back into the pool once more.

He spits water, as eager hands help him up. 'Get away from me!' he snarls, slapping Carlin. Finally, the torrent of water stops flowing out of his armour. His boots, however, remain full. He jabs a finger where he thinks Carlin's face should be. 'I want the Doctor and I want him dead, you understand me?'

'Citizen.'

'Now get the men organised. No more mistakes. Give me that torch.'

Carlin does so. The men are bunched round him, ready for action. Hopkins shines the light, one at a time into their faces. Is he checking to see if any of them are laughing? He will not admit that to himself. One man, two, three, four… wait a minute.

'Something the matter, Citizen?' asks Carlin, as the torch stops moving.

'What's going on?' Hopkins mutters. There are more than eight men here, many more. Who's that behind Carlin? 'You,' he snaps. 'Show me your face.'

The soldier walks into the small spotlight. Where's his damn helmet? It looks more… more like a hood.

Even before the creature reveals its face to Robert Hopkins, as the lights flicker back on, he knows who this must be, and who all the others are that have risen from the floor to encircle his tiny unit.

* * *

That man Redfearn was as quick as he had feared. Almost. The Doctor's hair still burned from the furrow driven through it by the bullet. He would have to get his hat repaired... well, get Romana to do it, if he ever found her again.

'Where are we going?' asks Pelham, out of breath and clearly confused about the events of the last few minutes. 'And how did you do that?'

He tries to shut out her voice. His diversion hasn't gained them that much time. They're back where they were before, and there was the access conduit up to the control room.

Pelham sees it and stops. 'No, Doctor. Not again,' she leans against the corridor wall, her breathing hoarse with sobs.

'Yes, yes, yes,' he insists, hauling her off her feet and up on to the creaky metal ladder bolted into the conduit's side. He pushes her, egging her on.

There isn't much time, so he explains on the climb. As much to reassure himself as anything else. 'I should have realised it much earlier.'

'What's that then, Doctor?' Pelham's weary voice comes booming down the ladder.

'The Old Ones wouldn't have bothered with such a tiresome way of transporting themselves into the particle accelerator as your bathyscape. Of course they wouldn't. They were far too lazy for that.'

'And?'

'And they would have set up some kind of transmat-beam. And the control room does seem the rather obvious place to operate it, don't you think?'

'Now you mention it, not that obvious...'

'Keep climbing. Time's running out.'

She is out, back where they drank that foul potion. The Doctor practically leaps out of the hole in the floor and bounds to where he knows the beam is, where it has to be. That console, there!

'The palace operates through mind reciprocity. It attempts to cater for its host's neural wishes. Now, if you don't know it will do this, it will respond to your unconscious, emotional wishes. I worked it out and decided to affect it consciously. Just in time as it turned out. Now, quiet please, as I try to unlock the transmat's telepathic operational cyphers.'

Pelham puts her hands on her hips. 'And do you know all this, or are you just guessing?'

He shrugs. 'Well, an educated guess perhaps. Now, quiet please.'

He is just about to start when something flutters in front of him. He snatches it out of the air. It is a small rectangular piece of card. One side decorated; the other, the ace of hearts.

There is a click from behind. A sound he finds uncomfortably familiar. The cocking of two pistols. 'Very clever, suh. Ah congratulate y'all.'

The Doctor forces a huge smile on to his face as he turns to face the gunslinger. 'Mr Redfearn, how nice to see you again. I'm so sorry you missed me.'

Mr Redfearn raises a discreet eyebrow. 'An unfortunate occurrence ah intend to rectify right now, Doctor.'

'No last words?'

'Not this time.'

Pelham almost makes a move; the Doctor senses it and waves her back. Mr Redfearn is cool, completely unruffled. His aim is disturbingly unwavering.

'How about a fighting chance, to make it more interesting for you?'

'No tricks, Doctor. I couldn't miss a second time. How would I live it down?'

'Ah, but you see, I think I'm faster than you.' The Doctor stares back and nods.

'Doctor…' hisses Pelham.

At last, Mr Redfearn laughs out loud. Good-natured, a nice man. The Doctor laughs too. 'No,' says the gunman, with a finality.

'I don't mean a gun. I… I'll just use this.' Slowly, very slowly the Doctor unwinds the scarf from around his neck.

'That scrap of wool? I am not an idiot, suh, do not treat me as such.'

'Oh, I mean it. I'll wager I'm faster with this scarf than you are with that gun.'

Mr Redfearn snorts, once. He uses one pistol to raise the hat over his face.

'Well, of course, if you're afraid I'll beat you…' says the Doctor.

'I will not be goaded, suh.' However, with the merest flicker of emotion, Mr Redfearn slowly replaces his pistols into their holsters. 'Very well, you have your wager. To even the odds a little, ah will even fire using mah left hand. However, ah must warn you suh, the truth is, ah am just as fast with the left paw as ah am with the right. Draw when ready.'

The Doctor takes the scarf and loops it slowly round itself. He is not thinking about the stupidity of his action, or that Pelham is putting her hands over her eyes, or even of Mr Redfearn's sly grin. He suspects something, the Doctor realises. He thinks it's a trick.

They stare, each waiting for the other to move. The sly grin never lapses.

'Oh for God's sake, this is ridiculous,' says Pelham and the Doctor sees Mr Redfearn, with a predator's reactions, whip the pistol from its holster. He makes his move.

Chapter Twelve

If Romana had been in one of her contemplative moods, it is more than likely she would have diagnosed her psychological condition as that of transference. Transference being the displacement of negative emotional energies generated by a highly stressful external stimulus, or stimuli (let's say, for the sake of argument – two zombies pounding at the bedroom door of a highly disturbed adolescent with unprecedented psychic abilities, possessed of an unnatural fixation upon her) from that source to another (let's say, again for the sake of argument: the Doctor, who had dropped her into this mess).

Unfortunately for Romana, she is not in one of her contemplative moods. Undeniably however, the transference is definitely there as she mentally curses the being who got her into this mess. She thinks about the various punishments she has devised for his benefit. Yes, once she gets out of this room...

The banging is increasing and it seems as if the door is getting warmer. She tries an experimental touch. Oh yes, definitely getting warmer. Somehow the butler and his new playmate are burning their way in.

'Huvan,' she addresses the youth lying slack-jawed on the bed, 'if you can think of a way out of here, I really would be incredibly grateful.'

It is as if he can no longer see her. He had lain back on the bed as soon as she returned, as if her presence was enough to send him into a nice relaxed sleep. Romana realises the boy has gone into some kind of trance. She hesitates to conclude that the palace is using him as some kind of battery, a spark to kick off its own power reserves.

A rather unpleasant burning smell starts to drift in from the doorway. The metal seems to be warping in its frame. Whatever they are doing to it, it's proving very effective.

'Huvan!' she shouts. He does nothing but lie there, eyelids fluttering. She thinks briefly about the damage Neville has done to Huvan's mind, and how emotionally ill-prepared he is for this new role he has been forced to play.

The door cracks and Romana forgets her pity. A clasping black glove, Kampp's, is pushing its way through the red-hot gap. The leather chars and crisps, but if the butler feels any pain, he certainly keeps it very quiet.

'Come along, Romana,' says Kampp, reasonably in a voice that, well, to be honest, she can only describe as a cold gloat. There is something unfamiliar about its tonal qualities, as if something without any understanding of how a voice works is attempting to sound human. 'There, there... promising thee much lovely new worlds... all sunshine and music inside...'

The insincerity is so apparent it is almost funny. Almost.

Kampp pushes a burning head through the gap he has created. The black coral has utterly consumed the flesh. Nothing remains but an obscene insect mask bearing only a token resemblance to what he once was. The mouth chitters and chatters as if too full of energy to remain contained.

Before Romana can act, before she can think of any way out of this, the door collapses and the two... things that were once men stagger in. They peer around, as if trying to focus on her.

'Huvan, according to all the known rules of dramatic structure, the time has come to act. Now!'

Nothing happens.

Perhaps responding to her voice, the tottering pair reach out for her. Huvan does nothing, just lies there. Already Romana feels the tugging at her mind. A tugging she understands now, instigated by Valdemar. Her eyes begin to itch as she backs against the wall.

As the men approach she feels strangely disconnected, as if this were all happening to someone else. 'Please, no,' she tries to say, but cannot. She can feel their singed gloves as they reach her, the distorted hands clutching her face, sees the black mirrors of their eyes. But she is somewhere else, somewhere dark and cold that screams for release.

All that is certain is that we move, together.

We travel down a great, dark, rushing tunnel, understanding that it is not only space and time, but also other forms of universal movement and distance. A vista of the indescribable, of the greater.

At first, there is only a great unity, a single one Movement, brighter than anything before or since. The whole, all.

Slowly, sheets of movement become clear; spinning, immense idiosyncratic waves separating, becoming arrhythmic. More subdivision, and again, as the single harmony becomes an infinity of eccentric movements that make up the whole.

We realise (for neither 'perceive' nor 'see' can do justice) that which, although *us*, is also beyond *us*. Smaller forms, with their own crystal activities that we once thought of as separate life forms travel through their cycles, spanning centuries. A great race, conical and many-limbed, flying through the universe on membranous wings; urged on by the solar winds, scouring planets, learning, until finally the patterns coalesce on to a shining world, a blue planet soaked in ocean.

The construction, from the raw matter of the Movement. Beneath the surface, a circle constructed, controlled from the structure above – a great hammer with which to smash a way into the whole, to break it open. The race tearing and ripping a wound through the dance. We see them subsumed, their own movements zephyrs of swirling dust disseminated into the greater spinning clouds until nothing is left. The Old Ones.

('Romana')

A seal, a patch bolted over the tear, the forces which are the Movement, which are *us*, held at bay. The closing, the blue oceans changing hue, altering their patterns for ever.

('Romana')

Slowly, as the rhythm is regained, we correct ourselves. Our damage, over centuries, is repaired. Until, later in the eternal Movement, we will see the actions repeated.

('Romana!')

A sound, many sounds, harsh and angry, burst into her consciousness. There is a blinding light and something more. Romana feels severed from herself.

As she realises that she is still in Huvan's chamber, despite the centuries, something heavy and lifeless falls on to her. Kampp's corpse, his body stilled by bullets riveted into him. A black film blurs Romana's vision.

'They have been touched,' comes a voice she remembers from the distant past. When she was... Neville, his name is Neville. 'Bring them.'

Part of her mind that she recognises as her own self-will forces her to resist this new consciousness. She needs a pathway, a track back to herself. Think, think back. The basic tenets, the Seven Strictures of Rassillon. Repeat them. Repeat them! One at a time, over and over again. The Seven Strictures...

The immensity narrows and she can see herself, from above, the corpse of Kampp being lifted from her littleness. With a swoop, she is back into her own small, separate self. The Seven Strictures bounce around the box of her mind. She feels the warm, scented air of the palace fill her lungs.

A guard, white-faced beneath his visor, pulls her to her feet.

She pushes him away, trying to regain her composure. 'Thank you,' she says in her old voice. 'I can manage.'

Neville is bent over the supine Huvan, examining his eyes. Romana sees how old he has become, and also the black shadows in his face. This force, this unleashed power has touched him too. She wonders if he can see that.

As she watches, trying to regain her focus, Neville lifts the boy's eyelids. 'Valdemar is in him. He has been washed clean, ready for the possession. Praise to the Dark One.'

'Praise to the Dark One,' respond the handful of guards stationed in the room. They lower their eyes.

'Bear him with us,' says Neville, reverently. 'Gently.'

He turns and Romana sees that he has been touched by more than Valdemar. His eyes shine with madness. 'And you, his consort. It has been written.'

Despite the shock, despite what feels like near absorption into the stuff of the universe itself, Romana feels she is gaining in strength. 'Neville,' she says, steadier. 'You must end this. I'm very grateful to you, I think you saved more than my life and I wish to return the favour. Leave this place. There is nothing here for you.'

'Really?'

Romana thinks about her – call it 'communion', for want of a better word. 'I know the history of this palace, this planet. The Old Ones were mistaken. They thought they could improve themselves by opening the higher dimensions. Instead, the higher dimensions swamped them, overwhelmed their race. They, and you, were never meant to perceive the universe in its totality.'

Neville turns, ignoring her. With a crooked finger he indicates the guards are to bring her. They clasp her arms. This is ridiculous, she thinks. What has got into him?

'Valdemar isn't a god,' she cries. 'It's an experiment that went horribly wrong.'

No good. He just doesn't want to listen. She struggles as the guards haul her out of the room. 'Neville! If you don't want to listen to me, listen to the Doctor. He is infuriatingly right, you know.'

At last, as she is dragged out into the corridor, he turns and looks up. Perhaps he imagines a halo over his own head. 'My dear,' he sneers. 'Bride of the Chosen One. Fear not for the Doctor. The enemies of Valdemar attend a fool's errand, for He cannot be fought.'

Through the verbiage, the messianic rubbish, Romana understands. She feels weak and her throat dries. He hasn't… he can't have…

'The Doctor has gone, into the clouds of this blasted planet. Gone, so the Magus might live!'

Oh yea…

Listen to the words of the Magus! He is calm now as he waits in his place above, looking down on his vessel, no longer the human Neville but The Red Right Hand of Valdemar. The Becoming is nigh! Hail to the Magus!

The final act draws near, the Dark One stirs. The Magus is His rod and His staff.

He bears the body of the Chosen One, and bride, to the tomb.

The road is long and fraught with danger. The Magus may see this and understand this is how it must be, for his foes lay many traps and tricks to hold His glory within.

The mighty Valdemar has foreseen this and given human Neville the power to overcome.

Bear the bridal couple gently through the thoroughfares of His mighty palace! Bear them gently. The acolytes line the route to the metal craft that will lower them to the place of opening. Past the bodies of the fallen, the sacrificed, with their trickling streams and perfumed garden. Onwards! On! To the airlock where the Doctor was banished.

The sacrifice of the Doctor was the final act, the blood quota that brought the Magus into full Becoming. Pelham was a nothing, a pawn in the game, but human Neville realised in the end that the Doctor was the final test, the last temptation.

At the head of the procession, the Magus turns, arms raised. He stares back at the line of guards, his disciples, and the offerings they bear. Huvan and Romana.

However, there are more. The Magus seems to see more, following in their wake. Black-shrouded disciples, thousands of them from thousands of planets. A multitude of faith that terminates with him, all focused on his glory. Their numbers reveal a diversity of races, odd faces and limbs, spectral and pale, all paying tribute to him, the one who released the Dark One.

'Your suffering is almost over, my brethren!' the Magus shrieks, fired with the Word of Valdemar. 'All your work, your belief is imminently to find its reward, in me!'

The guards look around, the confusion on their faces no doubt due to the sudden realisation of the horde behind them. Even the palace walls have disappeared and the Magus sees he stands on a mount, a green, grassy mount in the open air, swarming with apostles of the cult. He roars.

Something is stirring deep inside Huvan. His last real memory is of Romana coming back to him, shutting herself in with him. Then there was nothing but a black tide and visions so shocking and obscene it would be wrong for me to detail them here.

I must tell the rest of this story quickly, Ponch, for I do not have much time left. I know it is galling that I am interrupted at this late stage, after you have been listening so carefully, so precisely. I was hoping to get to the end without further interruption, but even stories do not always travel along the paths you would wish them to. It may be months before you understand, before you realise the significance of this that I am telling you.

I tell it not because I think there is anything to learn, I tell it because I am old.

Take me back to the inn; I have my reasons. You must help me to my feet; I cannot walk in this snow.

Ah, age is a new life. When a woman is old, she feels that her body, her shell, is a different companion to the one she knew before. No longer a faithful pet, obedient to her every order, no matter how stupid or self-destructive. The body becomes demanding, selfish, unwilling to do as it is told. One day you wake up and you realise you are the slave, not the mistress. And later, you realise that, in fact, it was always like this.

Don't be impatient, Romana and Huvan and the others can wait. I need a drink. Is it far?

All right, all right, I won't stop.

How dare you! Don't you think I know the dangers of splitting up a narrative, the loss of tension it entails, the dislocation? Young people today; they want it all on a plate. Do you think I'm doing this just to be pretentious?

No, and I haven't lost the plot. It's just there seem to be a lot of characters and it's hard to get the timing right. Fair enough, Mr Redfearn. Perhaps he is a little incongruous, but I like him. You'll just have to accept it.

However – ouch, mind that stone – we aren't doing the others at the moment. We're doing Romana and Huvan.'

Oh, Huvan. He hardly knows what has hit him. Certainly, he has no idea of the forces that course through him. When Romana came back to him he felt a completion, a destiny that his addled mind was no longer able to comprehend or cope with. The demands of the palace, and the widening gap in the doorway to the tomb of Valdemar were simply too much for him. Imagine the force that is blasting through his mind, for he is one with the palace, the sole coordinator of its arcane intentions.

He is barely aware, caught in a loop of his own fantasies as he is, that he is being laid in the bathyscape, ready for the final opening of the tomb.

Neville is in the ascendance now, eyes wide and staring. He orders his retinue, his faithful followers to remain inside the palace; he says to provide a line of defence against any that might now try to stop Valdemar's rebirth, but in reality because he doesn't want to share the revelations with anybody.

Romana is subdued as she ducks into the tiny vessel, outwardly calm but a mass of emotions. Neville or, as he now knows himself, the Magus, is hardly aware of her presence, save as a symbolic fulfilment of his knowledge. It was all there, in the mythologies so meticulously collected by human Neville – the witch-bride of the Centauri, the duo consort of the Binarii, even the crude Nagwife fairy tales of the Ogrons – all clues to the symbolism and meaning of Romana's appearance.

The vessel must have his consort. The weak human Neville had failed to recognise the self-evident; his human blindness preventing him from realising the inevitable. He had groomed Miranda Pelham for that particular role.

She had risen up from the tomb itself, Pelham the bridesmaid and not the bride; the Doctor a test.

They had appeared out of nowhere in the tomb, just exactly at this moment, had they? It wouldn't have fooled a child. The problems of the past few days, the fears that human Neville might fail in his ambitions, now seem amusing. The Doctor and Pelham are nothing but liquid slops rising to the surface.

Neville pumps the sparking battery fluid, generating sufficient energy to ignite the power in the bathyscape. Romana sits quietly, a cold expression of general disapproval on her face as she supports Huvan.

The engine fires and the bathyscape lurches. Automatic, computer-controlled bundling lifts the small vessel off the ground. The technology is human, bolted on to the side of this alien palace. It is clumsy, designed for weak, soft creatures. Upon the resurrection, there will be no need for such puny devices.

For some reason, this casual thought now perturbs the Magus. He has forgotten something perhaps, overlooked something? He feels the old Neville threatening to re-emerge. What could it be?

'Mr Neville,' says Romana suddenly, 'I really believe that if you gave me the opportunity to explain the situation you would think again about attempting to open the gateway.'

The Magus can barely hear her, instead operating the controls for the exterior hatches, the ones through which the Doctor and Pelham so recently exited. The metal, telescopic arm stretches out, lifting the bathyscape away from the deadly updraught of the planet's core. The giant chains grind and rattle in the deafening gold-and-red of Ashkellia's clouds. Acid rain sprays with a hiss across the portholes, sending up spirals of liquid smoke.

'I believe the effects of the higher dimensions stored in the palace are altering our beings.' Romana is trying again, breaking into his triumphant moments. 'Your butler was what we may all end up resembling. The key is this boy. By taking him to the heart of the Old Ones' experiment, you will...'

'Hold your prattling tongue!' Neville yells at her as the bathyscape drops, making stomachs churn. At frightening speed, the chain over their heads unravels. Through the porthole, the Magus observes the palace shrink, and the clouds wrap themselves round it until it is gone from sight.

In truth, Romana knows her attempts at reason are at best half-hearted. She isn't going to change his mind. Perhaps the Doctor might have done, but the Doctor is dead.

There is something wrong with Paul Neville, something very wrong. His schizophrenia has overwhelmed his personality to the extent that the situation is probably irretrievable.

The lowering of the bathyscape is echoing the lowering in her own mind.

She feels an emotional pull she has not encountered before. One fact sits like a lead weight inside her. The Doctor is dead.

Now this whole situation, this whole mess, has become her sole responsibility. And she knows she is not ready.

The whole concept of a Time Lord, of the Doctor, being killed, dying for ever, is a fact she could theorise, could rationalise. The truth, as she is now discovering, is very very different. She has never known a life swept away like this. Even after the recent, unheard of, Sontaran occupation, she had been far enough away for the deaths of those few Time Lords involved to be little more than horror stories.

What is she going to do? Just what is she going to do?

Romana feels she is starting to understand a little more about the Doctor. He had been someone who regularly faced such decisions. She had read what little actual evidence there was of his history – the famous Master affair, Omega's dread return, his mission to Skaro. All heavyweight assignments and in each case he had returned, if not always triumphant, but at least with the situation resolved.

It is simply beyond her understanding that he should die now, at the start of a new, long and complicated mission, down a cul-de-sac not even related to that task. She had never thought the weight of responsibility could prove so traumatic.

Grief, she muses, it must be grief. Not a pleasant emotion but one so overwhelming, that it is paralysing her. She realises just how small she is compared to the universe she inhabits.

She must focus her energies, somehow and find her own Key. The Doctor, what would he have wanted her to do? Think about that. She must not let his memory die.

Her experience at the hands of Kampp was important. She remembered the pull, the temptation to allow herself to be swallowed up by the universal whole, to subsume her identity back into the raw stuff of creation.

A new thought strikes her – perhaps the Key to Time mission, the details of which she is still foggy about, is only a minor ambition. What happened to her in Huvan's bedroom, this was something that would, if released, affect reality itself for ever. If only she knew what to do.

She is not strong enough, not yet. She cannot feel it now, but the effects of the higher dimensions are inevitably warping her mind and perceptions without her knowing. This makes her unfit for the task. She must hand over the responsibility to those with clearer minds. A plan is forming in her head. They are travelling back to the tomb… no, no, the particle accelerator; there is no tomb. Here she will attempt to elude Neville if she can, and make her way back to the Doctor's TARDIS. She will have to attempt to idiosynchronise the machine to respond to her metabolism, with K-9's help, and contact Gallifrey. They will know what to do. They will relieve her of this intolerable burden. This is what the Doctor would have wanted, she understands that now.

Awake, Huvan! Awake from thy dream! Ariel, weaver of magic, the voice of your Prospero commands you to rise.

Huvan has spent an eternity here in this dream world, in which, it must be said, Romana played something of a large part.

The real world is rough and uncomfortable, the air hissing with flame and spattering heat. He feels like he has slept for twenty-two years and is rising now to his true age, possessed at last of the secret knowledge of the adult.

The Magus is calling him. Huvan dreamed him too; in fact the whole waking world seems naught but a dream. He opens his eyes to see that vision, that loveliness he would call his own, in the flesh. She seems to be weeping, though she may not be aware of that fact. Her demeanour is as elegant and cold as ever. She is a princess. He feels her arms round his shoulders. The Magus is still calling his name.

Huvan smiles.

The Magus flinches, momentarily, under the weight of that smile. He knows the protégé has outgrown the master. Something has happened to him in his sleep.

They are dropping down to the tomb, Huvan can see it. He can see as if he is in all places; above in the palace, down in the crypt, outside in the clouds.

'Huvan, my child, you have grown powerful.' The Magus bows, to him. Rightly so. Romana lets go and gives him room.

'I've seen a lot. In my dreams.' He looks at Romana and recalls some of those dreams. She recoils.

'Don't worry,' he says. 'I remember the palace. I shall not allow its like again.'

He feels the power, the new thing, coursing through him, ready for him to use. He is the book of spells, the grimoire. Now all he needs is the sorcerer. 'Command me, Magus,' he says, noting how Neville visibly relaxes at these words. 'I can do anything.'

The Magus looks around, licking his lips. He is still unsure. Huvan can see his beating heart thumping faster, the glands in his face increasing their sweaty output.

'We must release the Dark One,' Neville says hesitantly.

'In time. Command me now.' Huvan starts to feel impatient. 'I want to show off.'

'Huvan,' says Romana, 'these impulses you feel. Fight them, for they control you, not you them.'

'Quiet!' Neville barks, hysteria mounting. Huvan listens with detached amusement.

'Order me, Magus, I am yours,' he says. 'For you gave me this power. What is it you wish to know?'

The magus licks his lips. 'Tell me something, my boy. For my life, my whole life, I have searched for Valdemar. Am I worthy? Will I be the one to reawaken him?'

Huvan smiles. He looks at Romana's worried, mortal face, seeing the alienness in her. He looks back at the magus. Images flood his mind, at his summons. Nothing is hidden from him. 'Of course you will,' he says. 'Is that all you wanted to know?'

The Magus breathes out. Tears well from his eyes. He sobs, a lifetime's tears pouring out of him. 'Thank you. Praise to the Dark One.'

'What about the Doctor?' Romana asks softly. 'Is he truly dead?'

A surge of irritation. This Doctor, always this Doctor. You are mine, Romana, there is no room for another. Of course he is dead.

The words spring to Huvan's mouth but something is wrong, something blurs his thoughts. For the first time, there is something that is not of him.

Huvan tries to clear the image in his mind. He sees this Doctor, as he was. In the palace, a past event, with Pelham. They are snapping open a glass vial he knows of old… then oddly, they pass beyond his knowledge. Yes, he is gone… but dead?

A pain enters his new mind. A stinging. He can't think about this.

'Forget the Doctor. There is no Doctor.'

Romana slumps back into the padded seat. She too begins to fill with emotion.

'Then,' she says to herself, 'then we actually fail...'

'No, Romana. You will live for ever. With me.'

She shivers, inexplicably as far as he is concerned, and turns upon him a gaze that pierces his new self-confidence. Contained in that gaze, there is nothing but pity. She should be triumphant for what he has become. Not pity, not that. 'You poor boy,' she says sadly. 'Neville never gave you a chance.'

'A chance?'

'To grow up.'

Somewhere, deep inside himself, he remembers who he is. The boy he once was, before the experiments and the drugs. Just a flash, a quick memory of a time simple and uncomplicated. A time when he was happy. The simplicity of that memory throws him off balance. The power does not flow strongly. Its smooth circulation through him shudders and stutters.

The bathyscape jerks suddenly. Its swing is not as wild as it was. The tomb has taken control of the tiny craft once more.

Huvan sees that the Magus has hardly noticed. He has his face in his hands, tears running through his fingers. 'Do not weep, Magus,' he says to him. 'There is still much to be done.'

Romana stares at him, as if looking through him. He finds he cannot bear her gaze. How he loves her. She will be his. 'Avert your eyes, Romana,' he says. 'Lest I remove them for you.'

A shadow's line rises through the porthole. They are descending into the pyramid itself. He feels the source of his power close now, almost awake. The dreamer behind the gateway is shuffling in its sleep. Neville has taught him true;

Valdemar is great and good and needs him. Soon they will soar through the universe once more, flying on great wings through the cold blackness. The power he has now is nothing, unbelievably there is still more to be his.

'You must remember who you are, Huvan. Keep your individuality or you will be destroyed. What Neville has promised you is a lie. You know this.' Romana speaks softly, insidiously.

'No!' And Neville has leapt to his feet, eyes wet with joy. 'No, Huvan. Together, everything will be ours, all power. All!'

The bathyscape settles with a bump. And a new insight is gained. Huvan sees the palace, sees what will happen there, is happening there. Fear – an emotion he thought he had left behind. The one being still capable of harming him, the phantom he has feared since he could understand it. 'We are betrayed,' he whispers.

'What?' Neville, caught in mid-flow.

Again, the smooth rhythm inside Huvan is interrupted. He starts to tremble, clutching at the Magus's ringed hands. '*He* is here!'

'Who is here?' asks Romana.

'Nemesis! The Finder.'

Neville clasps his hands, tightly. 'Hopkins? Impossible.'

'I can see his angry face, his skin without hair, his flaming sword. He knows of the palace, knows we are here.'

'How? Nothing was left to chance.'

Huvan grasps the Magus's hands, unable to stem the flow of images in his mind. 'He wants us, wants us… help me, I don't know what to do.'

'Destroy him, Huvan,' The Magus is feverish, the black marks of Valdemar clearly visible round his eyes. 'Kill them all!'

'No, no!' Romana cries.

Huvan *wills*, in the new way that he can. 'It is done,' he says softly, not quite sure what it is he has done. He has an image of the palace, corroding and dying, falling from the sky, and nothing more. Somehow, he knows not how, he has done it. He thinks.

He cannot look at Romana, does not need to see her face. He doesn't understand, every time he tries to impress her he just seems to make everything worse. What more does he need to do? What will win her over? He will have her, but he would rather she came to him voluntarily. He feels it is important for him to win her rather than take her. Why, when the other way is so much easier? He realises he still has a lot to learn.

'Come,' he says, concentrating on a much easier path. He doesn't want to think too much any more.

The hatch levers click and the small doorway opens, a simple trick.

'At last,' says the Magus, stepping out. 'At last, the tomb of Valdemar. After all these years, all the work. The time of greatness is almost upon us.'

He can barely contain his excitement; so human of him despite what he thinks he has become.

Romana follows him, Huvan behind her. The three of them stand inside the pyramid, the war of Ashkellia's atmosphere crackling over their heads. 'Yes,' says Huvan, 'the tomb of Valdemar.' He takes a deep breath of the cold, ancient air. 'Let's open it.'

Chapter Thirteen

It seems worth noting that, despite all appearances to the contrary, Robert Hopkins has managed to retain his firm convictions concerning the cold materialistic nature of the universe. His stubborn existentialism remains intact, despite the horde of zombies that have risen from the dead and are now presently in the process of slaughtering his men.

He is running now, armour clanking, not entirely certain how he got away from the battening undead. He vaguely recalls giving orders as the robed ghouls descended upon his iron clads, with a savagery of breathtaking dimensions considering they were ripped and hacked-up corpses. These orders consisted, in the main as he remembers, of shouting 'Fight to the last man! Protect your leader! Get me out of here!' or something he will choose to re-remember in the future.

Hopkins recalls also the brave Lieutenant Carlin cleverly hacking through the creatures and taunting a few into following him into the empty airlock chamber. Whether he did this deliberately, Hopkins does not know. What he does know is that his cousin's actions gave him an opportunity to fight his way clear, his shotgun blasting already tattered cadavers into non-existence, and hammer on the controls that opened the bay doors. He remembers Carlin's horror-struck face as the floor gave way beneath him and he fell, three of the ghouls already fastening onto him, into the clouds.

Oh, brave Lieutenant Carlin! His sacrifice will be long remembered in the annals of the New Protectorate!

Turning away, and using his sword to strike down the snarling body hurling itself at him, Hopkins had realised his men were already doomed. They grappled with their attackers on the ground, fighting to the last as the creatures ripped them apart.

He ran. He thinks he did anyway, it all gets a bit foggy at that point.

Typically, now that he is out of that bloody piazza, anger has taken over from fear as his dominant emotion. Once more, Neville has outwitted him! He must destroy this decadent; nothing else matters.

At last, somewhere in the sumptuous living quarters, Hopkins collapses and must catch his breath. With trembling hands and heaving chest, he sheaths his black-stained sword. The shotgun has gone, lost in the mêlée, but he still has his pistol. He listens for pursuit but hears nothing except distant screaming. The noise does not last long.

What to do, what to do now? He could make his way back to the ship but then what has he learned? He must find Neville, if he has to fight his way through all the devils this palace can throw at him.

There is a noise, something that just caught his hearing. He cocks his heavy pistol and kneels, scanning the corridor both ways. Didn't sound like one of those creatures. Already he is rationalising. They weren't undead at all. Some kind of cyborg, some trick of Neville's to reanimate dead flesh, programmed to respond to their arrival. Highly original, and lethal, but nothing supernatural about it.

He hears the sound again. Definitely not the guttural screeching of the ghouls. Something else, something like a voice.

'Hello?'

Hopkins leaps away from the wall. It, the voice, came from behind him. He suspects more of Neville's trickery; another trap, this time an assault on the senses. Nothing to be afraid of, it's just another conjuring trick.

214

'Hello?' It comes again.

The wall isn't a wall. It's a door, a door with its ornate golden handle broken off.

'Have you come to rescue us?' comes the voice. It sounds like a woman.

Hopkins looks round. Nothing. All is quiet.

Then the tapping begins, on the other side of the door. 'Help us,' says the mournful voice, unmistakably female. 'We've been locked in here so long.'

Hopkins takes another look around. Nothing, no sounds, just the empty corridor. Should he respond? Perhaps they know something, whoever the people are behind that door. After all, they would undoubtedly have been locked in there by Neville; the handle snapped off to prevent their release. Anything to get to that black sorcerer is worth the risk. Anything!

In the end, it is the empty-follicled goose bumps he feels running down his arms that make up his mind for him. Despite the massacre and the voices, he will not be swayed by superstition and a lot of bumps and lighting effects. The body is weak, afraid, but the mind controls the body and that is everything he stands for.

'Did Neville put you in there?' he asks in a whisper. He's not so stupid as to announce his presence to those things that are presumably looking for him.

There is a silence, as if whoever is behind the door is not really expecting a reply.

'Hello?' it says, she says, again.

'Yes, hello,' Hopkins replies impatiently. 'Did Neville put you in there?'

'Neville... yes...' the voice comes slowly, cautiously. 'Will you free us?'

Ah. Now. That is the question. He may be desperate but he isn't stupid.

'Who are you?' he asks.

'Prisoners, that's right, prisoners. He betrayed us, tried to kill us, but we were too clever for him, oh yes. Open this door and we will help you.'

'Do you know where he is?'

'Oh yes, open the door, quickly, or he will escape you again.'

Not really listening, hearing only what he wants to hear, Hopkins draws his sword and begins to hack at the lock.

The whole process takes longer than he thinks. The door is tough and he doesn't want to make any more noise than is necessary. He hauls his helmet off to cool himself down. Finally, the lock breaks under repeated pounding from the hilt of his sword. With a crack, the door inches way open. The room beyond is dark.

Hopkins boots the door fully open, dropping his sword and pulling out his pistol. He cannot understand why his breathing should be so jerky, why he feels cold. The will, he steels himself, the will is absolute.

'Come out,' he shouts, louder than he had intended. 'I warn you, I am an officer of the New Protectorate under full jurisdictional provenance from the Civil Matriarch herself. Any attempt to impede me will result in your immediate execution.' Somehow, these familiar words in this mad place make him feel much better. 'Do I make myself clear?'

'Oh very. Our saviour,' the female voice emerges from the gloom. Or is that two voices? They sound so very much alike.

He doesn't have time for this. Forget the mumbo-jumbo, those cyborgs of Neville's making are surely prowling around looking for him. It's only a dark room, and the voices sound too weak to put up any resistance. Why is he even standing out here?

He strides in, gun first. 'All right, all right, show yourselves.'

The room is large, and dim but not totally dark. There is

fancy Elite furniture lying around in dark, black bundles. The stubs of candles flicker weakly. 'Well?' he asks, aware but not afraid. He spins around, looking for the source of the voices. 'Come out.'

'Here we are…' says the voice. Hopkins squints.

One of the ornate tables is still standing the right way up. A candle burns at its centre. There is an awful, cold smell he can't place. Two sacks sit in seats, black cowls draped over their heads. He can just make out thin bony fingers spread over the table-top. 'Help us,' says the voice.

'I just want Neville,' Hopkins says, not venturing too close. 'Give him to me.'

'Neville?' says one of the bundles. 'There is no Neville, not any more.'

'What? But you said…'

'Something else he is now, in his own mind,' says the other bundle, shaking with a terrible, thin chuckle.

'Down in the gateway he is, ready for the Return.'

'Don't give me riddles,' Hopkins snaps. 'Where is he?'

The sacks continue their amused shuddering. Hopkins glimpses faces as they turn – thin, dreadfully thin, a flash of exposed teeth, flickering yellow in the candlelight.

'Left us here he did, didn't he, sister?'

'Left us, yes. Something happened.'

'Something happened? What happened?' asks Hopkins, feeling his voice constricting with a terror he does not want to feel.

Eyes gleam beneath the cowls. 'Something to do with time. Left us here, for such a long time.'

'So long… so dreadfully long. It's the boy, you see. We were unkind and the boy, he remembers.'

Hopkins raises the gun. He begins to back out. These women, these stinking crones, they are of no use to him.

The sisters start to rise. 'So long…' says one. 'So long.'

'So hungry…' says the other and Hopkins screams. Long, skeletal arms reach for him. They move with frightening speed, droolish laughter spilling from their salivating mouths. Hopkins fires once and they're on him, teeth bared.

'No! No!' he yells, fighting off their cold clutches. He fires again and the bullet passes right through one of the hags, he sees it happen. She staggers and renews her gnawing attack. Hopkins feels his legs give away under their furious charge and the rotten robes smother his face. Their sour breath warms his body as they bite into his armour.

Then, the weight is gone and the crones scream. A high-pitched, piercing noise Hopkins will take to his grave. A fusillade of rapid shots thuds into their wasted forms. Hopkins punches himself clear, feeling the bullets whine over his head.

He rolls over to see Mr Redfearn firing, faster than even he has ever seen him fire before. The marksman is calm; shooting two-handed, pumping bullets into the witches, blasting them away from him.

'Ah suggest you crawl towards me, Citizen,' says Mr Redfearn, smoothly flicking the smoking barrels open to reload. Hopkins obeys, hearing the dreadful laughter dying behind him. Mr Redfearn helps him to his feet.

Hopkins turns and sees the riddled bundles jerk and cease their scrabbling movements. 'Nice to make yo' acquaintance, ladies,' says the sharpshooter.

The bundles begin to move. If Mr Redfearn is affected by this, he doesn't show it. He raises his guns again. 'Well, now there's a thing.'

'Get out of here,' says Hopkins, 'Get out!'

The bundles rise. 'Not polite,' says Diana.

'Most impolite,' says Juno. 'Feed us!'

Mr Redfearn fires enough bullets to bring them down once

more. The air is sickly with cordite and smoke.

Hopkins has had enough. He turns and bolts into the corridor.

He should have been more cautious. Of course he should. It is his own fault Neville has so successfully routed his entire task force. For the first time in his life, Hopkins has been guilty of over-confidence. Or perhaps over-eagerness; after all, he knows his determination to bring the cult leader in is becoming obsessive.

The element of surprise simply hadn't worked. These fiendish traps are the result of careful planning on the part of his rival. Pelham must have betrayed him. That is the only possible reasoning. Odd really – he had felt he understood the woman's weaknesses better than anyone, her morbid fear of her own mortality that underlined everything she did. This made her particularly malleable, or so he had thought.

As he waits for Mr Redfearn in the lip of an anti-grav shaft, he broods over his mistakes. Never blame others. The only failure is the failure of one's own conscious will. Still, the game is not over. Neville hasn't escaped him yet. There is still time.

Gunfire blazes down the corridor. 'Redfearn!' Hopkins bellows, no longer caring whether he is heard by anything his rival has left prowling for him. Time is of the essence; he must get back to his ship.

The gunslinger finally appears, very quickly indeed. The hat has gone, his long grey hair flows behind him. As he runs, he thrusts his smoking pistols back into their holsters.

'Ah do believe nothing in creation can satiate that partic'lar hunger,' he says, skidding to a halt. 'Even with nothing left of 'em but strung-together holes.'

Indeed, Hopkins hears even now their dreadful screeching. Without a word he leaps into the shaft, forgetting his previous suspicions concerning such devices. Mr Redfearn follows, hawk eyes trained on any potential pursuers.

'Where's the Doctor?' asks Hopkins.

Mr Redfearn allows an eyebrow to rise, a sure sign of intense rage. 'That gen'leman is full o' surprises. Used some underhand trickery to wrap that scarf o' his around my legs afore my pistol was even out of its holster. The devil take him for a quick draw; said somethin' about takin' lessons from Doc Holliday and disappeared with his lady friend into thin air. Ah look forward to sparring with that particular gen'leman again, trust me on that.'

Hopkins doesn't need to berate Mr Redfearn for his failure. He knows only too well how the marksman is feeling. If the Doctor wasn't worried about Hopkins's avowed intention to destroy him before, he will definitely be worried now. Mr Redfearn looks up at the shaft stretching ahead of him.

And then Hopkins takes in what he has just been told. The heights into which they are ascending are turning warmer.

'Did you say he *disappeared into thin air*?'

'Ah am not reputed to bandy falsehoods, Citizen. Especially where the Doctor is concerned. He muttered a few choice phrases, touched a panel on the wall and faded from view, like a phantom.'

'You mean he operated a transmat-beam.'

'Do not presume to tell me what ah mean.'

Their movement seems to be slowing. Hopkins is on the verge of replying when there is a loud boom from above. The lift suddenly shakes and all his old fears of the anti-grav return. He imagines himself and Mr Redfearn dropping to the far-distant base of this shaft. The palace rocks again, violently.

'Oh what now?' Hopkins moans. 'What more?'

Something liquid drops on to his cheek with a sizzling hiss. It hurts, a lot. In fact, it burns into his face. He screeches and clutches at the burning droplet, wiping it away with his gloved hand. All around, similar hisses send up smoke signals from the casing of the shaft. 'Acid!' he bellows. 'It's raining acid!'

'The time has come to depart this particular thoroughfare,' states Mr Redfearn.

'Oh, shut up,' snaps Hopkins. 'Why can't you talk properly?'

Before this rather unwise comment provokes a response from the icy Mr Redfearn, both hear the rumbling and look up. A great ball of cloudy acid is dropping towards them. Through it, they see that the roof of the palace has gone, the flaming sky of Ashkellia clearly visible over them.

Without further ado, both men flail their way back down to the nearest doorway.

'What is it? What could it be?' Hopkins asks as they dash away from the shaft. All around them the palace is falling apart, loudly. From far distances they hear roaring, as if the structure is a great prehistoric beast sinking into a tar pit. There is another explosion, somewhere below, and the whole palace tilts, sending the two men spinning and rolling over each other.

Mr Redfearn rolls and rights himself, whereas Hopkins cannons headfirst into a wall.

When the stars stop spinning in his eyes, he stares at the gunman, who is listening intently, his eyes narrowed to snake-like slits.

'What do you think has happened?' Hopkins asks.

'In mah considered opinion, ah have the feeling we have no more tub up there ready to ferry us out of here. Something, or someone, has exploded it and lifted the lid from this fine building in the process.'

'Oh...' Hopkins lies there and considers their predicament.

Neville has won. There is nothing they can do except wait

for this structure to collapse in on itself, or blow up or whatever it is going to do. Another few tilts and rocks and groans seem to confirm this hypothesis.

No. This cannot be the end of it. There has to be a way out. It is a question of will and intelligence. For every problem there is a solution.

The palace begins to list. All over, the bangs and crashes of the slow turn ring through the corridors. Already the angle is steep, soon they will be walking on the walls… assuming the palace holds together that long. There has to be something, some way to get back at Neville. He cannot be beaten by that fake, that bearded charlatan! He will not!

'No way out,' says Mr Redfearn. Strangely, he is smiling, pink tongue licking his lips, a gleam of triumph in his eyes. His hands dance over his pistols.

And then it comes. Yes! Hopkins grabs Mr Redfearn's arm. The gunslinger pulls away. 'Ah will not be pawed at, suh…'

'You remember the way to where the Doctor disappeared? This panel you talked about?'

Mr Redfearn nods, 'Ah do, Citizen. However, without the words he spoke aloud, we may find a similar feat beyond our means.'

Hopkins glares at the man. 'But you heard him say whatever it was!'

'Once. Ah cannot be expected to remembah the exact words.'

Hopkins thinks through his repertoire of techniques for helping people to remember. He has a small leather pouch full of *aides-mémoires* tucked away in a pocket in his blouson. Be prepared, the iron-clad motto.

'Oh, you will remember all right, believe me.'

And, for the first time ever, Hopkins is treated to the sight of Mr Redfearn turning as pale as his pistol grips.

* * *

Mr Redfearn may have derived some comfort – in fact it seems most likely that he did – from the knowledge that although he had been outdrawn, for the first time in his life, by the Doctor, he hadn't entirely missed a target.

He had still managed to fire when the scarf brought him tumbling over. However, instead of hitting the Doctor, he had planted his bullet in Miranda Pelham's upper left arm.

She lies now, on the hard ground of this strange new cavern, inside the tomb where they suddenly found themselves, the Doctor staunching the unyielding flow of blood. He has been at this for half a day now. The pyramid chamber is trembling, as if in the grip of a permanent earthquake. The Old Ones' planet-circling particle accelerator is racing round, building up for its headlong crash through reality.

Pelham is semi-conscious and, worryingly, the Doctor is not convinced the wound is entirely the cause of this.

'Help me,' she moans. 'Where are we?' She looks up at the hollowed-out rock, its banks of instrumentation matching the control room in the palace.

'The reciprocating station. A minor control centre, at a guess.'

'You were right then, about the Old Ones having a transmat.'

'Indeed, although I had my doubts. I half had a horrible thought that they could simply fly down here. I'm glad I was wrong.'

Pelham winces and looks down at her arm. 'Oh God, I'm going to die…'

The Doctor is forced to admit to himself that this is a distinct possibility. He gingerly wraps the arm in a strip of her torn clothing. 'Oh, don't be silly,' he says cheerfully. 'There are far more unpleasant potential deaths waiting for us.'

She is drifting away from him, her mind seemingly fixated on the image she unexpectedly described earlier. 'I'm cold,' she says. 'Cold in this tomb. I can see myself. Already dead.'

He thinks about saying something, then thinks better of it. He doesn't really know what is wrong with her, but can't escape the notion that somehow the vaccine isn't all it's cracked up to be. Her human mind seems to have reacted with its arcane formula after all. Like an overloaded computer, Miranda Pelham has crashed, her brain frozen on one single image. It's probably worse because she's storyteller, her imagination over-sensitive and abnormally fertile. At least, that's how he presumes writers are.

How long before he is affected in the same way?

'What am I seeing?' she asks, almost delirious. 'Please, don't let me die. I don't want to be nothing.'

'It's the pull of the higher dimensions,' the Doctor replies, seeing no sense in lying. He has never been very good at these personal moments.

'What… are these higher dimensions? Valdemar? Is that it?'

How to explain, when even Time Lords can't be sure? He looks up at the cavern around him, trying to understand the Old Ones and what they had unleashed. Did they know? Even at the end when it swallowed them, had they understood?

'Doctor?' Pelham moans, 'Where are you?'

'I'm here.' Perhaps talking about it would help him. He tries to find some definition. 'The higher dimensions,' he says after a long think, 'are everything we do not understand. The raw universe, its symbolic code broken. The total and absolute perception of primal reality.'

'I thought you were explaining this to me.' She attempts a laugh.

'I can't explain. No life we know of can. There is a myth among my own people, among many peoples, that says the universe sprang from one single entity. Not a thing, not anything we could understand, just a singularity. The Time Lords call this "the Kinetic Dance". Unusually imaginative for that lot. Others personify this force and give it names: Eru,

Azathoth, take your pick. Gradually, the singularity grew and grew until it was unable to sustain itself as a single entity. It divided, split, like...' he searches for an appropriate image, but can only rely on the facile, 'like chunks of ice falling from a glacier.'

'Ice... glacier...' She is listening. She is forcing herself to listen, he understands that. This is helping her.

'Only these chunks didn't separate from the singularity, they just became different. And these chunks kept splitting and splitting until they forgot where it was they came from. They began to form their own rules; rules we now designate the proportional dimensions – time and space and so on up to the full ten.'

'Ten?'

'Never mind. Anyway, life got itself going, not remembering that it had ever belonged inside the singularity. Well, not entirely. Many species, many individuals, feel a sense of loss, of being apart from something greater than themselves. Of being away from home. Many individuals spend their lives trying to find it again. We call this separation 'mortality'. And inside us, even inside the lowliest amoeba, dormant organs lie unused, atrophying. Organs which once bound us to the singularity. Until now, of course.'

'So... so you go back to the singularity when you die... is that it? Is that's what's going to happen to me?'

With her good arm, Pelham clutches the Doctor's coat. 'Is that what happens?' she yells, and there is fever in her voice.

He takes her hand. 'I don't know, Miranda. Perhaps. Perhaps.'

She falls back. 'I don't want it to happen to me; don't let it happen. I don't want to lose myself, in a singularity or anything.'

The Doctor cannot answer. He is unable to reassure her. Because, deep down, he feels exactly the same way?

Don't think about it. Action. There must be action to take his mind off this painful subject.

'The thing is, the Old Ones didn't want to wait until they died to find out. Perhaps they had even conquered mortality but still needed more, nearly destroying the universe in the process. We have to act to stop it happening again. Get up, you're not dying. We've got work to do.'

She is going again, head slumped back, mouth moving in cold, cosmic horror. He must break this seizure once and for all. 'Pelham!' he barks. 'Get up! I won't have you turning all weak and feeble on me! You started this whole Valdemar affair and it's up to you to stop it.' He looks around in theatrical self-righteousness, as if the idea has just come to him. 'This whole thing is your fault!'

She reacts; she has heard him. Her eyes begin to focus once more. Best keep going, he supposes. He stands up and declaims to this ancient, long-abandoned stone monument. 'The universe will end! All life will be altered beyond recognition! And all Miranda Pelham can do is sit here and whinge in her own self-pity…'

He doesn't need to go on. He grins as he hears her scrabble up to her feet. He spins round.

'Who the hell do you think you are? I'm dying here!' She is shouting, but stops as she spots the smile.

Actually, he realises, she looks dreadful. Face grey and ashen, eyes shrunken with agony. Her clothes are in shreds and he is doubtful she will ever use that left arm again. Still, she is up. Amazing what a bit of willpower can do – in moderation of course.

'I can't believe you did that,' she says, grumpily. 'That's low.'

'Shall we go?'

She staggers and he rushes to help her. Pelham pulls away from him. 'I can manage, thank you very much.'

'Funny, I have the uncomfortable feeling you're not the first who's said that to me.'

'I'm not surprised. Where are we going, anyway? I'm not quite sure where I am any more.'

The Doctor points a finger towards the only way out, a dark tunnel leading down into blackness.

'Oh, right,' says Pelham. 'Look... look, before we go rushing around getting into more trouble, can't we use this stuff in here to blow everything up? There must be something in all this fancy machinery with dials and countdowns and things. I mean, that'd stop this higher dimensions whatever, wouldn't it?'

She already appears to know the answer. Her expression is hopeful rather than realistic.

'It might,' he replies. 'It might. But it's the boy we need. I doubt if Neville understands his importance. He is the key to everything. The power of the palace is all that has been released so far and it's all flowing through him. Immense power. In fact, I'm surprised the gateway isn't already open. Huvan could easily have done it. I'm hoping that's Romana's influence, calming him down. We're going to have to be extremely careful dealing with him. He's undoubtedly been driven mad and probably possesses the ability to destroy the entire solar system. It's a comforting thought, isn't it?'

There is a tremendous thump from somewhere. The cavern shakes even harder than it has shaken before. That tickle, that fear in the back of his mind hardens into certainty. He's too late. The boy knows, knows everything. The roof feels like it is about to cave in. Dust and blocks of stone rain down on them. Pelham has fallen over again and he rushes to help.

The Doctor can guess what has happened. Somehow Neville has found out about Hopkins's incursion into the palace, probably from Huvan. With his fear of the New Protectorate

227

official, Neville would immediately have ordered the palace to be destroyed. What they're getting here is the resulting energy wave. This whole situation needs getting under control, and never mind the blessed Key to Time for now. He knows it's going to have to be his job to sort the whole mess out. Once again, he'll be the one who has to get his hands dirty.

'Doctor,' groans Pelham, sinking to her knees. 'Leave me. I'm dying. I mean it this time.'

'Nonsense,' he replies and lifts her up. He is certain she has more to contribute in this game. He'll carry her if he has to.

He does have to. With the aeons-old cavern falling to pieces behind him, he makes his way to confront Paul Neville and the boy who has become a god.

Miranda Pelham is starting to forget who she is. Some of the time she is aware that she is being carried but, much more of the time, and increasingly so, she is certain she is staring up at a cold, grey, marble stone, sealing her in her coffin.

You can't be dead yet, she muses, your arm still hurts. And anyway, there's no room in death for the Doctor. If anyone had been chosen to represent life in its most energetic form, it would be this manic bohemian with his buoyant hair and lunatic manners.

He represents the only colour in her increasingly small and grey universe. What the hell good is she going to be anyway?

Fear wants her. It really wants her, burning its way through her skull and down into her stomach. A cold, sharp fire that never lets go. She is going to die – the tree and the black bird perched on this hilltop, the eternal nothingness. Feeling the Doctor's arms gripping her, she wants him to help, wants him to make everything better. If anyone can cheat death it's him, she's sure he's done it for himself. Why can't he do it for her? Because when it comes to death, you're on your own. She thinks of the black nothing waiting for her *(that is going to happen and there's nothing you or anyone else can do about it,* whispers a dry, dusty voice) and the ice freezes her solid.

And then something, some impulse, awakens inside her. It's been buried deep one hell of a long time, so deep she'd forgotten she'd ever had it. Now it has woken up, perhaps stirring in Hopkins's torture chamber; she can feel its warmth. What *it* is, is a refusal to go quietly.

For what seems like her entire adult life, she has been threatened, criticised, ordered, attacked and scared. Well, no more. She has had enough. Sod you Paul Neville, sod you Robert Hopkins, sod the lot of you.

She realises the Doctor is carrying her. The caverns are booming with explosions of some kind. She opens her eyes and feels free for the first time in thirty years.

'You can let me down, Doctor,' she says. He gapes in surprise. Her legs feel strong as they touch the ground once more. She ignores the pain in her arm, and the blood. 'I've got something to finish that I should never have started.'

'That's my line,' he replies in astonishment.

She strides along the tunnel, following its upward slope, leaving the Doctor behind.

Only when he doesn't follow at all does she turn, her breast full of grit and determination. 'Well?' she demands.

The Doctor puts his hands in his pockets. 'Well, I'm so glad you're feeling better,' he says, almost regretfully. 'But that's the way we came.'

Chapter Fourteen

The old woman is dead.

She, Miranda Pelham, died in the snow, on her way back to the inn, her story uncompleted. Ponch, the last listener, had submitted to her final wish and carried her to the Janua Foris, forgetting to make the sign of vigilance as he set her down on a table. Why she had wished to be brought back to this place, he cannot imagine. He had tried to tell her that once the others of his settlement knew of her death, they would descend on her corpse like jackal-birds. She had just smiled in that mysterious way of hers.

'This body is a mere shell,' she had replied. 'A way station. Don't worry about what will happen to me. You know what you have got to do.'

With that, she had closed her eyes and fallen into a snowdrift. Ponch had watched as life left her. Her skin so pale, papery and white as the thin chest ceased its fragile movement. He couldn't resist touching her face and had been surprised at how warm it still felt.

Much to his amazement, Ponch does know what he's got to do.

He walks around the growing town for a while, watching as his companions argue and fight and rob each other. He is so tired of this life. Even his own hard-gained, once-treasured furs are now revealed as nothing but shabby, rotten hides.

Why does he have to collect them for these unknowable guild sleds? What does whoever is inside do with them?

He cannot help returning to the inn. Only an hour has passed since he left it but already the scavengers have done their work. She is gone – clothing, flesh, bones; nothing remains. Nothing is wasted here.

As time passes, Ponch cannot concentrate on his work. The feeble orange autumn drags on. Oh, he helps Ofrin, Tavron and the others because they will kill him if he does not. He digs the pits, scrapes the stinking hides, soaks them down, spreads them with dung and stripped bark. He melts snow and carries bucket after bucket after bucket of water for the endless boiling. He covers this year's skins with earth, and hauls the previous year's hides, now tanned leather, from their mounds. Ready for transportation to the sleds. Ready for that food and the little bags of coins left in shabby sacks for those strong enough to take them. All the time he is wondering why.

The story has worked on him.

He believes now that it is about seeing things, seeing the world around you, the smallness you create for yourself. The Doctor and Romana and Neville and Hopkins and Huvan and the others, they all have to force themselves to look beyond their own needs. The ones that make it to the end are the ones with the courage to search for a wider… a wider… what did the old woman call it?… perspective.

One day, a cold morning in this endless cycle, Ponch makes up his mind to go into the mountains. There is something there he needs to see.

He is aware that Ofrin will attempt to prevent this desertion. He anticipates this, so the night before he leaves, he creeps up on the giant and splits his skull with an axe.

Ponch returns to the place where he buried his pony all those weeks ago. He carves enough meat from its sad old bones to last him a fortnight. If he hasn't found what he is looking for by then, he will be dead.

As he walks up into the foothills, he thinks about the old woman's story, about how it must have ended.

The three groups – that mad Neville with his idiot boy and Romana, the vengeful Hopkins and Mr Redfearn, and finally the Doctor, desperately wanting to reverse the wrong he has done, with the wounded and bleeding Pelham, the instigator of the entire business.

Ponch cannot fully comprehend what it is all about, but is aware that there is some kind of symmetry here, three points merging to create a whole, all converging on this mysterious gateway of the Old Ones. The tomb of Valdemar.

How does it end? The final riddle, a riddle he must solve, for it feels like the key to his own life, to his whole existence. Why couldn't she just have told him?

Where he wants to get to is not far, but it will take him a week. He knows the others will come looking for him and he must stay out of sight. He has broken a code, the only code they live by – that no one deserts; everyone must stay in the township after summer's call. You may get yourself killed in a brawl over a crust of bread when you're there, that's perfectly all right, but you can never, ever leave. Clearly, this rare and astonishing pact of communal agreement exists to guarantee mutual survival. If the hides are not delivered, the guild sleds might wipe out everyone instead of the annual few whom the guild, in its obscure wisdom, decides has come in under quota. Another stupid thing he has never thought about before.

How does it end?

The question pursues him through the scrubby tundra. Somehow, the old woman has convinced him; he feels the outcome is within his grasp. It is there, at the edge of his consciousness – accurate, inevitable. He needs time, time for the end to come. And after a while, after a day or two of exhausting walking, it does come.

The Doctor, he is the key; has to be where you start. Walking with the collapsing Pelham down that long black corridor to the gateway. Throughout, the Doctor has been the focus, the point of contact. He seems to know so much, to be so aware, despite his funny ways.

What would he do in this situation? Ponch feels he knows so much about how the Doctor would deal with this situation. He has a... what is it?... a goodness about him. You always know what he's going to do. Yes, that's it, he'll try and do the *good* thing.

Start there and you can't go far wrong.

All right then, the Doctor will walk to the gateway, ready to meet Neville and Huvan and Romana.

Oh wait, hang on a minute. *They* have to get there first, don't they? Otherwise it won't make sense. Perhaps it would be better to start with them.

Yes, that is what he will do.

The gateway itself, straining and buckling and warping under the influence of the mighty forces inside it, must be impressive. Oh yes, it has to be huge!

Romana, tagging along behind the impatient Magus and the besotted boy, finally gets to see this doorway they have so long been involved with, but not actually seen.

The gateway is metal, a huge slab of metal, that screeches and strains with its contained forces. It's probably wise to stop thinking of it as a door, however, as it is actually embedded in the floor of the tomb. More like a huge trap door, stretching away into the distance. Irregular bubbles grow out of its metal skin, as if pummelled from below by giant fists. Arcane symbols have been embossed into its surface, free from the ancient dust that covers the rest of the slab. Small intertwined markings, linked by some strange meaning. And in the centre, one evil-looking five-pointed star, the sign of the Old Ones.

'The tomb of Valdemar,' breathes Neville, dropping to his knees.

234

Romana knows he is wrong. But not by much. Perhaps there is something in what he says. Mighty forces do reside behind this metal plate. Not Valdemar, no. Something much more impressive.

Romana stares at the star. The symbol actually seems quite comforting, reminding her of that balmy immersion in the Kinetic Dance that she experienced in Huvan's bedroom. Perhaps the Doctor is wrong; perhaps opening the tomb doesn't mean universal Armageddon after all. He doesn't know everything and is prone to some rather impetuous value judgements.

The thought, now here, is logical. The Kinetic Dance, that ancient belief, implies a separation from the primal universe. This separation is the cause of all conflict, all war, all chaos. Why shouldn't we all return to that universe? There wouldn't be any need for the Key to Time then; life would be back to its natural pure state. All would be One, one divine state of grace.

Yes. Despite his misconceptions, Neville's plan might actually result in something good, something great.

She thinks about her plan to rush back to the Tardis and enlist the aid of the Time Lords. What a silly, immature, futile plan. To work against the opening. How could she even have thought such a thing? One has to separate oneself from emotion, perceive things as they really are. Her own people are so conservative, so reactionary, they would undoubtedly oppose such an inevitable, sweeping action. They just wouldn't understand, would fail to see the logic.

'Romana?' asks Huvan. 'Are you ready to open the gateway?'

She ponders the question. How can anybody be ready for that majesty?

It's funny, but she wonders how she ever found him repulsive.

'Open it,' Neville orders. 'Release Valdemar!'

Romana looks at him kneeling on the filthy ground. How small he now seems to her, how pathetic. The idea that this vain, ageing idiot could be any kind of spiritual leader is amusing. How little he knows of the truth of this greatness.

Huvan holds out a hand to her. 'I'm doing this for you,' he says sincerely. 'Everything I've done is for you.'

Romana smiles.

'At last,' Neville mutters to himself. 'The Dark One, reborn at my bidding, my will!' He laughs, a booming laugh revealing precisely the extent of his insanity. 'Valdemar reveals himself to me! I see planets crumble! Stars themselves beg for mercy as we sweep by on our black wings! Release Valdemar!' His voice rises in a tiresomely theatrical crescendo. 'I command you! Release him now!'

'Erm, excuse me,' comes a familiar voice. A voice from someone Romana knows to be dead.

'Doctor?' she asks, not sure whether she is pleased at his arrival or not. He emerges from the shadows, nonchalantly inspecting the symbols on the tomb.

'Hello Romana. You look a little tired. Now be careful if you walk near it. I don't think this tomb is safe. You think there'd be a rail or something.'

Pelham is there too, walking into the light. Although 'staggering' might be a more appropriate verb for the way she is moving. 'Give it up, Neville,' she says, bolder than Romana has ever known her. 'There's nothing here for you.'

Neville is staring at them, open-mouthed. 'You,' he hisses. 'You're dead! I killed you.'

The Doctor smiles. 'Well, I won't tell anyone if you won't.'

Neville takes a deep breath. He is trying to take in this impossibility. 'You certainly won't, Doctor,' he replies. 'In fact, you won't do anything ever again. Huvan...'

'Oh, is that the best you can do?' The Doctor seems upset, let down. 'Surely you want me to witness your great triumph, the culmination of your life's work? I mean, what's so special about unleashing a great god of destruction if you don't leave anyone alive to gloat about it to. That's half the fun in my opinion.'

'Huvan, kill him.'

'Of course, that's just one opinion.' The Doctor raises his hands.

'Cease your prattling.'

'You see, I don't believe you can do it. I don't think you control Huvan as much as you think you do.'

'He's right, Huvan,' says Romana suddenly. She is glad to see that the Doctor is seeing reason.

At last Huvan himself, who has been watching this squabble with the detached amusement of a boy burning ants, acknowledges the Doctor's entrance. 'You are perceptive, Doctor,' he concurs.

Neville's face is the epitome of crestfallen astonishment. 'What? What did you say?'

The Doctor continues. 'You have become a man, Huvan. The higher dimensions have allowed you to see yourself as an adult. Isn't that right, Romana?'

She is forced to agree.

The white-faced Pelham makes her contribution. She clutches at the stained bandage on her arm. 'You know that Valdemar is a child's dream. I just made it up. He never existed except in your mind.'

Huvan smiles. 'You are correct, Miranda.'

'Yeah, careful with the familiarity and everything, Huvan.'

Neville interrupts. He obviously cannot believe what he is hearing. 'But…' he stutters, 'but I gave you this power. I raised you for this destiny. To become Valdemar. Without me, you were nothing, a slave. You owe me everything!'

237

'No,' says Huvan. 'You gave me everything except the one thing I ever wanted – to be myself. You have used me cruelly, Paul Neville, and I owe you nothing. Look at yourself. There is no Valdemar and there is no Magus. There is only you and your blinkered dreams.'

Neville will not be crushed. 'You are mine, Huvan, body and soul. Obey my commands.' He is so angry, he literally shakes his fist at his protégé. 'I will not be defied!'

'Oh, shut up,' snaps the Doctor rudely. 'It's all over. Romana, say your goodbyes, we've got work to be getting on with. And I really think we need to get you away from this place.'

Old habits die hard, goes the cliché, and Romana takes a step forward before she realises she cannot go with him. She does not want to go with him.

Huvan turns his placid gaze upon the Doctor. 'Oh no,' he says. 'It's not like that at all. The tomb will be opened, Doctor. Have no fear of that.'

For once, for the first time ever, she sees the Doctor at a loss for words. 'What?' he mutters, regaining his composure. 'What do you mean, "it will be opened"? Of course it won't.'

He is wrong. They all know it. He is wrong to be upset by this. 'Doctor,' Romana says, 'don't be afraid. Huvan here is about to perform a wondrous act. He will restore the universe back to its natural state.'

The Doctor shakes his head, as she knew he would. 'My poor Romana,' he replies softly. 'What has he been telling you? Didn't I warn you about boys? They'll say anything to impress. I'm sure it was on my list of "a thousand and one universal constants to warn Romana about".'

'I am no longer a child,' says Huvan, coldly. 'Do not treat me as such. The tomb will be opened. Now.'

Romana hears the psychically-operated locking mechanisms click apart with a great echoing screech. The embossed symbols, sleepy with age, sink into the buckled plates. All across its surface, the metal begins to soften, to alter form. Deep inside the planet, the particle accelerator screams with even more violent energy. She feels the ground shake, feels the ultimate release of energy approaching. Soon, she realises. Soon. Happiness fills her with light.

At this point, it would probably be wise to initiate the reappearance of Robert Hopkins and Mr Redfearn. Let us assume they escaped from the collapsing palace via the transmat and have found their way here, just at this crucial moment. They bring an almost comic element to the proceedings, as we imagine their soot-blackened faces and wide blinking eyes. Let's face it, they've been through a lot.

They are watching from the wings, Hopkins astonished to realise he has finally caught up with his arch rival. Mr Redfearn instinctively lines up a shot, but his master knocks his arm away.

He wants to savour the moment.

At last, however, he dares wait no longer. The rending screeches of shifting metal that reverberate throughout the cavern imply that this drama is moving into its final stage. All attention is on the gateway as it grinds open. Hopkins doesn't like the look of what seems to be happening here, this blurring mist that rises from the big metal slab.

He and Mr Redfearn step out of the shadows and duck and weave their way towards the group. They are all there – Neville, Pelham, the Doctor, some young woman and that boy, who seems to be running the show. Hopkins instinctively understands how dangerous he is going to be.

'Take the boy,' he snaps.

At about twenty metres, and quick as ever, Mr Redfearn fires. Huvan turns and is the first to see them, but the bullet drives into his heart before even he can react.

239

As Huvan falls, a ball of energy blasts out from him, an energy that snakes along the ground in a line of orange balled fire.

'Mercy me,' Mr Redfearn says, smiling, as the zigzagging flame converges and bursts him out of his boots.

This achieved, Huvan, a romantic to the last, falls into Romana's arms.

Hopkins is beyond triumph as Mr Redfearn's remains sizzle beside him. He cocks his shotgun, just to ensure full co-operation and steps into the limelight.

They face each other, the players united at last. So many, and such history between them! We have assembled our archetypes, laid out the cards (albeit with one or two little tweaks and adjustments) – the sorcerer, the knight, the enchantress (Pelham, whether she likes it or not, for did she not enchant Neville with her stories?), the tragic, star-crossed lovers.

And the Doctor? What is the Doctor's archetype, his suit, his number? Not the hero, no, although he is, of course, heroic. He is too complicated for such a role. The Doctor is outside the archetype. Beyond such categories as suit and number. Only one card befits him and that is the zero, he who stands outside and sees all. Where wisdom and idiocy are combined and become the same thing. Finally, that is the card that suits the Doctor best. He is the fool.

Is it destiny that these should be here all at this time? Perhaps the tomb of Valdemar needs all of them to reveal its secrets. Perhaps they provide some kind of arcane, critical mass, cogs and gears in a greater machine? Who knows? Well, perhaps somewhere in the cold cosmic forces of the higher dimensions there is something, some spark of mischievous intelligence, that understands this game, and laughs.

* * *

Neville, no longer the proud Magus he once was, can only stare at Huvan's body, at the death of his dream.

To be foiled at this last possible moment, and by Hopkins. It isn't fair. It isn't fair!

Ignoring the shotgun, and Hopkins's gloating, he launches himself at his rival. If his enemy gets a shot out, Neville doesn't hear it. He smashes the gun from Hopkins's grasp and grapples him to the ground.

He could have been great; the universe should have been his! As he tears at Hopkins's flesh he is gripped by a fury worthy of Valdemar himself. All the planning, all the endless waiting, all the dreams, gone in an instant. Dark One! Protect your servant, he begins to pray. The Magus is there, distant but not yet departed. He cannot stop now. Neville is thy rod and thy staff, thy instrument of holy vengeance. Rise, Valdemar. Rise!

Hopkins head-butts him, and the stars in his dreams burst open.

The Doctor uses the opportunity to wrest Romana away from the gateway. He hauls at her arm and Huvan drops with a thump to the ground. Romana is dazed, the black coral round her eyes flaring with anger. 'No, no!' she yells as he pulls her away. Miranda Pelham comes and provides what little aid she can.

'Don't touch me!' Romana shouts. 'Let me go!'

At last, they restrain her furious struggling form. The Doctor piles on top of her, pinning her down. 'Romana, Romana,' he insists. He tries to keep his voice even, hypnotic, desperate to ignite whatever spark of herself remains inside her. 'Don't let it work on you, remember who you are. It's all over, it's all over.'

He looks at Pelham and the fear on her face mirrors his own misgivings about whether this is actually the end of the matter.

* * *

Neville tumbles backwards. Hopkins finds he is laughing, laughing with relief. He has triumphed!

He ignores the pain in his face, where the other man attacked him. They stand, the rivals, facing each other. Neville's beard is streaked with blood that pours from his nose, but his eyes glitter with hate. Hopkins punches him but he does not fall. Instead, the blow is returned and both men stagger.

All Hopkins's thoughts of a long, lingering death for Neville have been displaced now. Forget the long session on the rack, the lingering pain; forget even the broken man paraded round the New Parliament. This is a fight to the death, and one he does not intend to lose.

Neville backs away, racing towards the gateway which is steaming but now silent. Hopkins passes the others, ignoring them. No one else matters, just Neville. Just Neville.

The magician's feet sink into the undulating gateway, and he falls.

'Valdemar! Hear me!' Neville screams, arms raised. 'Live! Live and strike down the heretic!'

Hopkins, hot and boiling in his ruined armour, sprints to the metal slab. In his madness, he is braying with laughter. 'Your god is dead, Neville!' he screeches. 'There is only me!'

He reaches his quarry on the flimsy cover that is the burning gateway. The metal feels soft, like soup beneath his feet. He stumbles, like he is running through glue. Yours is a just cause, he says to himself; you are a true paladin. Nothing can stop you.

Neville swings round to him, and the insanity on his face stops Hopkins for just a second. The magician doesn't even look human. Then battle is rejoined.

The pair thump, kick, flail at each other with a frenzy beyond any rational control. Hopkins smashes a metal fist into the other's face, utterly shattering his nose. Neville returns the blow with a swinging kick that hits Hopkins's thigh like a hammer. Both drop, sinking knee-deep into the swampy, hissing surface of the slab. Neville grasps Hopkins's arm and twists. Bone cracks but Hopkins feels no pain. He responds with another blow to Neville's face.

The ground shifts and a blast of hot steam scalds both of them pink. They sink further, lost to their descent in their struggle. Only the glue that suddenly grips their limbs interrupts their rage.

Through a red mist, Hopkins realises he is now waist-deep in this mire. He redoubles his efforts and hooks his good arm round Neville's slippery neck. His opponent's robes are starting to smoulder. His own armour spits as it fries blood and sweat. Slowly, Neville raises his hands and they end up facing each other, choking the life out of their mutual selves. Their eyes bulge as the mist threatens to overwhelm them.

Together in this final stranglehold, unable to harm each other further, they sink down until only their heads are left, glaring at each other in absolute hatred.

Hopkins feels the warm stuff rise up over his chin and the pull from below. His last view is of Neville's eyes, glaring. 'VALDEMAR!' shrieks the sorcerer. Then neither man can see anything.

Romana's struggles subside with the final descent of Neville and Hopkins. Perhaps, and the Doctor is not going to be drawn on this, perhaps it really is finished.

Now, how is he going to return his companion to normal?

Pelham topples over. Blood loss, it was only going to be a matter of time. Another one who needs his help.

All of a sudden, he realises he is the last one. He raises his hands from Romana. She has retreated into herself, whether because of his words or not he does not know. The Doctor stands

Interesting how quiet this cavern can be when it wants to. He takes a deep breath of the hot salty air, and wonders what

243

happened to Neville and Hopkins. The last he saw of them they were banging heads on the molten slab of that disassembling gateway.

Whatever process it was going through seems to have stopped.

Of course, with the unfortunate death of Huvan, the power to open the gateway would have ceased as well.

He looks down at the boy's corpse. If there could have been another way, if he had had the opportunity, he is certain he could have resolved all this in a less violent manner. Despite Huvan's age, Neville had ensured he remained a child. He really hadn't been given the opportunity to grow up.

Huvan smiles. The Doctor goes cold.

As he watches, the boy raises his arms over the small wound in his chest. Huvan breathes and the bullet pops out into his waiting fingers. 'Still think you can convince me, Doctor?' he says brightly.

As the boy floats up and rights himself, the Doctor feels intensely weary. This isn't over. It's never over.

'What do you want, Huvan?' he asks, readying himself.

The boy considers for a moment. It is intensely disconcerting to see that his feet are approximately fifteen centimetres from the ground. What has he become?

'I want Romana. That's all I ever wanted.'

The Doctor glances at his supine companion. 'I'm sorry,' he says. 'But I can't allow it.'

'Can't allow it?'

'You will not control the higher dimensions, Huvan. It's not a place; it's the primal stuff of the universe. You will not be able to control it through force of will. Everything that is you will be lost. And Romana too.'

'She wanted to come with me, she wanted me to release the higher dimensions. You know that.'

244

'Ah, but you could say she wasn't herself. She must give herself willingly. I will not allow you to force her.' Something explodes inside his head. He clutches his temple and sinks to his knees.

'A fraction of the pain I can inflict, Doctor. I don't need your permission.'

The agony leaves him. Its intensity was phenomenal and total. The Doctor knows he won't survive another attack. He's going to have to be good. Very good.

'You still have a chance, Huvan,' he says. 'You possess the power to do it.'

'Do what?' The ghost of a smile still plays over the boy's pale lips. He looks altered; it's not the black shadows of the higher dimensions, but a self-induced improvement in his appearance. It is as if Huvan has given himself a charisma injection. The Doctor muses that it was true he needed one. Still, it might be enough to work on his vanity.

'To live the life of a normal human being.'

'Why should I want to do that? I, who possess the power of an entire universe.'

'Because you would still be alone. Because there would be no one your equal, and believe me, you will never be happy until you find that. Otherwise, you're just another Paul Neville.'

'Don't mention that name. I made me what I am. Not him, I!' Around the cavern, something like thunder rumbles. 'Anyway, what would be so wrong? I wish only to enter the gateway.'

The Doctor shakes his head. 'No, Huvan. I can't allow you to do this.'

A flare of anger. The boy could kill him any minute. Instead, however, the Doctor is surprised to see him smile.

'How about this?' Huvan says, a cold, humourless joke. 'I won't release the higher dimensions, I shall just give myself up to them. Your reality will be safe. All I want is Romana to join with me, so we may become one.'

'And if I refuse?'

'No, Doctor. There is no refusal. Do this or I open the gateway and take her with me anyway. Only then, you lose everything. How about that? What do you say?'

The smile is mocking now, insidious.

When the Doctor replies, he is unhesitant. 'I will not make that decision, Huvan,' he says. 'You know it is beyond my power.'

'But the universe depends on your answer, Doctor.'

'I will not answer. I cannot be held responsible for the fate of another.'

'Then you have condemned your whole universe. Everything you know, space, even time itself will alter.'

The creaking, the giant, booming, echoing process of release starts up again. Only this time, great sheets of something like thick black rain blast upwards from the gateway. Strands like the black fibres around Romana's eyes. The higher dimensions revealing themselves. There is nothing emerging, the Doctor knows that. It is the reality around him that is changing; the particle accelerator initiating a process for which there is no reversal.

'Huvan!' he bellows. He must make the boy change his mind. There is no choice. Before the process begins to affect him.

'Huvan, listen.'

The boy is humming to himself, a sound that is eerily similar to the deafening waves of energy spilling out from the gateway. Soon, he will be beyond listening.

'Why can't you allow Romana to make the decision for herself, of her own free will?'

Nothing, no change. 'You're afraid, aren't you? You're afraid that without your influence or the higher dimensions, she'll say no. And then, for all this so-called power of yours, you will still just be… a spoilt teenager who couldn't get his own way. Who failed to mature. Is that what you want? Is that *all* you want? You would destroy all life for that?'

The boy's smile disappears. The Doctor has got through. Although, judging by the gaze Huvan now turns on him, whether that particular achievement could be called a success is debatable.

'You dare?' Huvan snarls.

'Yes, I dare,' the Doctor replies angrily. Might as well, nothing left to lose. 'Of course I dare! You're nothing but a frustrated little brat who didn't get his own way. Too scared to even try. A coward. Ask Romana. Go on. Ask!'

Huvan's mouth opens and closes and for a moment the Doctor thinks he has won. Certainly, and let's not get over-confident, he has knocked Huvan back on his heels, given himself some time to think.

'No, Doctor. Nice try.'

'Wait…'

'Too late, Doctor. You had your chance.'

Still unconscious, Romana rises from the ground. 'We will be one,' Huvan cries. ' If I need maturity, she can give it to me. My bride. As it was meant to be.'

'No!'

The Doctor makes a move but a force harder than a brick wall pushes him over, sending him sliding along the shifting ground.

Huvan and the insensible Romana float towards the solid rain. The noise is tremendous. The Doctor looks up. He cannot believe he has failed. It can't be true. 'Romana!' he yells, 'You can fight him! Romana!'

'Goodbye, Doctor,' laughs Huvan as the two of them disappear into the wall of solid energy.

Chapter Fifteen

And so it came to pass that, after all, Valdemar was released to destroy the universe. OK, he doesn't have horns and a tail, and the universe will be altered rather than destroyed, but who's going to split hairs?

And the really nice thing, the real dandy thing, is that you, Miranda Pelham, are the cause of it. How's about, if you can concentrate with all that blood spilling out and your arm being on fire, how's about going back in time, back to Proxima 2, and instead of following that black procession you just toddle off to some bar and get pleasantly drunk. Yeah, that's a good idea. Let's do that instead.

Which would mean that this... this slow, painful death on the edge of the gateway is nothing but a bad dream, too much cheese before bedtime.

The noise and the expanding cloud of whatever it is issuing up from the ground, remind her that if this is a dream, it's time to wake up.

She is going to die. Nothing can stop that now. As the universe around her changes, as the huge walls, the air itself, become somehow thinner, transparent, she understands that she too will change. Something is emerging from reality, or rather through reality. Miranda Pelham is left to face the raw stuff of life. I don't want to die; I never want to die. Please Doctor, stop it.

She forces her eyes to open, to get one last look at the man she wants to save her. He is kneeling by her side, staring at the hole in the floor, perhaps grinding one final possible solution, some last brilliant idea, through his mind. He has to come up with it; he's going to live forever.

But the Doctor looks old now, very old. The lines on his face have deepened, that funny scar on his lip puckered with weariness. 'Romana,' he says. Hope dies inside Miranda Pelham.

'Doctor,' she croaks. 'It's all over, isn't it?'

He snaps his head round to her. 'Never,' he says softly.

She lies back and realises her mind is feeding her images of the past, of her life. The old cliché about the flashing-before-your-eyes thing? Or the unravelling effects of the higher dimensions?

She sees the dullness of childhood, the discovery of the myths, writing the book, her time with Neville. The legacy of the Old Ones, the discovery of the palace that had been lying around for some idiot, her, to find it again. Perhaps there is a clue in this, something to help them. Right, unfortunately this blacking out and pain and dizziness don't exactly help matters.

A million years ago, the Old Ones broke a hole in the higher dimensions and flooded the universe. They stopped it, they staunched the flow, why can't she?

'How did they do it?' she asks.

'Do what?' he replies, distracted.

'How did the Old Ones stop Valdemar?'

'How am I supposed to know?' he barks, then immediately cuts himself off. In all this turmoil, this change, he still finds time to smile his smile. 'Yes, you're right. They did find a way, and so must I.'

How? How? Now Huvan and Romana have gone through the gateway, what could she and the Doctor possibly do?

A thought, perhaps *the* thought, enters her mind. 'Doctor?' she asks.

'Yes?'

'Why did Huvan have to go through the gateway? I mean, I'm probably being stupid…' She feels something liquid well up in her throat. Christ, not yet, not yet. The Doctor places soothing hands on her head, lifting it up. She coughs out the blood.

'Keep going, Miranda,' he says gently. 'What are you saying?'

If only the noise and the lights and everything would just let her concentrate. It's not dark in here now, it's light, blinding light.

'Miranda!' comes a voice from miles away. She keeps this thread, this final thought going.

'Why didn't he just wait?' she manages. 'If the whole thing is going to change anyway, why didn't he just stay here and wait for it to wash over him? These higher dimensions?'

The gentle grip suddenly tightens. 'Yes,' says the Doctor. 'Why didn't he wait?'

She hacks out a coughing laugh. 'I was asking you.'

'There must be something he needs. Something in there. I don't see... how could there be anything in there? Unless... a point of stability, something artificial.'

The voice is soothing, containing an energy that keeps her going. His words haul her back to the land of the living. Don't let me go, Doctor, she prays. Save me.

'Of course!' He is laughing, and it sounds like silver bells to her damaged mind. 'The Old Ones. Oh, that's cunning, that's ever so cunning.'

'What's cunning?'

'They wouldn't leave a palace lying around like that, ready to trigger that which they spent so long trying to prevent. Not without a safeguard. I mean, you wouldn't would you?'

'I don't understand.' She lifts her head and opens her eyes again for the first time in what seems like ages. The world around her is not the world she remembers. Like a badly tuned picture on a viewing screen, the solid world is being consumed in a blur of static. Only the Doctor remains whole, corporeal, a brightly coloured fly crawling across the screen.

Of course – the vaccine, the vaccine.

'Is it possible that the higher dimensions is a place in its own right after all? No, not a place – a realm. Impossible, of course, but we haven't had breakfast…'

'You're rambling.'

He lifts her up, his strength seeming incredible after all his exertions and knock-downs. She feels his vibrancy, his energy, flooding through her. He puts her on her feet and she realises she can stand.

'They left something else, one more barrier. Come on Miranda, we're going exploring. We're going to complete your book.'

She feels her hand grasped in this torrent of grey lines and he yanks her along. 'Hold your nose!' he yells cheerfully, and then the ground goes and she is falling, falling.

The infection spreads, call it Valdemar, call it what you will. Reality fades, like paint melting away, the colours draining to leave only the bare canvas behind.

High above Ashkellia, the palace is in its last throes. Since Huvan's command, just after he exploded Hopkins's starship, whatever intelligence lives within its brass confines is politely turning out the lights. Metaphorically speaking.

In fact, if an intelligence does lurk there, it is undoubtedly surprised and, presumably, very upset. After all, for over a million years it has kept the place in order, maintaining and repairing itself without complaint, without dissent. Now, as the roofless metal hull is deliberately dissolved away by the acid clouds, the palace makes itself heard with groans and screeches of pain that ring out across the planet. All that time, and this is its reward? At last, it can no longer manage and simply falls apart, tiny hissing pieces of this legacy of the Old Ones raining down to the surface. There is no one left to hear its death cry.

Except… except down in the gateway there is, unbelievably, movement. In the colourless stain of the higher dimensions, something happens.

A hand, misshapen and strangely deformed, emerges from the lip of the giant aperture. It slams down on to what is only just solid ground. From below, there is the bellow of some agonised animal.

Following the hand comes another, and arms, more than two. The animal, whatever it is, hauls itself screaming from the pit. Tattered remains of a thick purple robe, now melted into what appears to be, of all things, armour, shroud its strangely doubled body. Two heads, two bodies, fused into one by some odd process known only to the mocking higher dimensions.

It climbs back into our universe and howls with the pain of birth. Once Paul Neville, once Robert Hopkins, it is a new life, cursed with the blinding rage of both minds. Does the creature think? Can it know what it is? Who can tell, for only one impulse drives it to survive. Hate. Hate for itself, for its two warring halves.

It should have been swallowed up into that which is consuming everything. There is no reason why this new creature should not be subsumed. Perhaps it is ego, will, perhaps supreme arrogance, a refusal to be beaten by its other half, that keeps it from going down with the universe.

Through this changing state, like a thick grey rain, it charges along disappearing tunnels, fighting its own internal, insane war. A war that never ceases, a war from which there is no respite or release.

It feels like one of those sensory deprivation tanks they sometimes use on starships, thinks Miranda Pelham. If she believed she was dreaming before, she was wrong. This is the dream. Her pain has gone, just a numbness remaining; no sensation but her own heart. Perhaps, she thinks, she is dead. Is this all? Is that it?

She hangs on to the Doctor's scarf as they swim, or walk or something, through this nothingness. If she is dead, then the Doctor is dead too.

Time passes. How much she cannot say. He seems to know where he is going, so she just grips the scarf. Part of her, a giggling daft part that's already given up and retreated into madness, is wondering whether they are the last two separate entities left in the universe. Just how strong and long-lasting is this damn vaccine?

They are in another palace. How they got there, she doesn't want to know. All she does know is that this palace is the spitting image of the other. Or is it the same one?

If the Doctor is as dazed as she is, he isn't showing it. 'I was right,' he mutters. 'I mean, I'm invariably right but this time I was really right.'

For him, this is probably relief.

She is feeling OK again, somehow. Her arm feels normal and the only blood is the blood that's dried over what remains of her clothing. 'What's happened?' she asks. 'How come I feel...?'

'Some kind of purging process, engineered by this palace, at a guess. Presumably to ensure that those who travelled over would be fit enough to survive whatever was waiting for them.'

'And whatever's waiting for us?'

'We'll worry about that when it finds us, shall we? We have plenty of other things to worry about.'

He bites his lip and looks around. 'This is the equivalent to the airlock at the other palace,' he says. 'Not hard to guess where Huvan and Romana would have gone.'

Pelham thinks. She hasn't felt this clear-headed in months. 'Control room.'

The Doctor nods and bounds away. 'We haven't a moment to lose!'

Oh God, it is getting all melodramatic again. Shame that this purging thing couldn't purge the mind as well. Her old friend, 'being scared stiff', is still hanging around.

'Wait for me,' she says weakly, and jogs after him.

Same piazza, same anti-grav shaft, same slow ascent.

Everything is the same until they hit the control room. Then there is something different. Something really different.

'What the hell is that?' Pelham breathes.

In quieter moments, the Doctor would sometimes cheerfully wonder whether he really had seen it all, whether there was anything left in the universe to surprise him.

There was.

The architecture is the same, down to the benches and consoles that the Old Ones had clearly never needed or used. The palace had designed it all for the humans who came blundering in much, much later. The Old Ones hadn't been humanoid, not even close.

The creature is massive. Huge, the size of a building. It sits or lies or whatever it's doing, right in the centre of the control room. Its bulk stretches out everywhere.

It is green, as such a creature should be. All right, there are veiny purple stalks growing out of one end, and a bluish head shaped like a globe, but in the main its fibrous body is green. Vast tentacles lie supine in and around its complicated, pulsating form, some plugged into the softly blinking instrumentation in the control room. The Doctor realises that the creature is alive, patched in to the palace. Sensory apparatus... biomechanics and all that. It must know exactly what is going on. Or perhaps its perceptions are so totally alien, that it simply has no conception of the life forms that have just invaded its space.

One couldn't really tell whether it was animal, vegetable or a mixture of both. As for the smell, well, he didn't really want to go into that. Strangely, it isn't frightening; in fact there is a soothing, placid quality about this behemoth.

'What's it doing?' asks Pelham, just after her initial studied inquiry.

'Dreaming,' the Doctor replies, lost in wonder at this million-year-old creature. How much could it have learned? How much did it know? Only now does he feel he is beginning to understand the final days of the Old Ones; just exactly what it was they did.

'You think I'd be terrified,' Pelham states, similarly stunned by the sight. 'According to all the rules of Pelham behaviour, I should be, but it's not like that at all, is it? To think – an Old One.'

She walks forward, mesmerised by its alienness, its serenity.

'No,' the Doctor replies. 'Not just any old Old One. This is someone much more familiar. Someone I was convinced did not exist. It appears that, actually, I'm not always right.' He makes a show of it, lifts his arms up in front of the creature. 'This, Miranda, is Valdemar.'

Before she is allowed any kind of reaction to this statement, there comes the sound of hands clapping, somewhere in the recesses of the control room.

'Very good, Doctor,' says Huvan. '*Very* good.'

'Hello Huvan,' he replies, trying to spot exactly where the boy might be, whether there is still time to bring things back. 'We were just passing so I thought, why not drop in?'

Huvan emerges at last, from round the bulk of the creature. He is looking up at it in wonder. 'Of course, strictly speaking, you're not absolutely correct.'

'Oh, really?'

'You see, this lovely old thing,' he pats the giant's side, 'was Valdemar. Until I arrived, that is.'

'Ah!' The Doctor nods. 'I understand.' He makes his speech deliberately slow and patronising. 'So you think *you're* Valdemar now. Oh dear, I don't think that's very wise. Names get mixed up, people forget which dark god it is that is controlling their destiny. How about altering the spelling?'

'Silence! How dare you talk to me like that? You know what I have done.'

'You sound more like Mr Neville every day. He would have been proud of you. By the way, how is Romana? The earlier question remains unresolved, you know.'

'And what question is that?'

The Doctor scratches his chin, trying to appear indifferent to the proceedings. 'Oh, what Romana's decision would be if she were given a free choice. Would she want to stay with you?'

Something is bothering Romana. The blissful togetherness she has helped set in motion does not seem as blissful as she had believed.

Someone is nagging at her, someone she knows. A man, old and distant as the hills. A discord amongst the concord. She tries to ignore that voice but it won't go away.

It is telling her to fight the submersion into the Kinetic Dance. Telling her it isn't right, that she isn't meant for this.

How can that be? Huvan is the true saviour; the light pours from him, putting the universe to rights. Bringing everything back to its primal, unified state. How could that be wrong? Even now, the warm pull of the dance is washing through her. Cleansing her.

Yet, the voice remains. It tells her she is Romanadvoratelundar and that she was proud when she earned that triple first, excited when chosen by the president of the High Council himself to accompany the Doctor... but isn't this the Doctor's voice?

She can see him now, trying to converse with Huvan, at the side of the old Valdemar, the one who renounced greatness. He is telling her to choose, to remember who she is. There is a decision to be made, a really quite important decision. If only she could remember what it is…

'Romana,' comes the voice of Valdemar. Valdemar. Not Huvan. 'Romana.'

All at once, the spell is broken. She gasps, literally gasps, as self-realisation floods back to her. The gasp is enough to make Huvan and the Doctor turn.

There are no lights any more, no dance, nothing. Just her standing in a metal room with a monster at her side. She feels full of energy, totally rejuvenated. Just what has she been thinking lately?

There is something she has to say, something she cannot hold back any more. Romana puts her hands on her hips and strides up to Huvan.

'Let me tell you my decision, my friend,' she spits.

For all his power, all this greatness he possesses, Huvan shrinks away from her, quailing beneath her anger. 'My… my love,' he murmurs.

'If you think for one minute I could have any kind of emotional attachment to any creature that would dare do what you did to me, then believe me you are very much mistaken.'

The Doctor smiles. 'Romana…'

'Doctor. Quiet. I haven't finished. Let me say, Huvan, that ever since I was forced to endure that abomination you call poetry, I have attempted to get as far away from your presence as I possibly could.'

'I think that is sufficient…'

'And furthermore! Whatever sympathy you may have engendered in me concerning your sad upbringing, you have done your best to remove it. Leave me alone in future; in fact don't even talk to me. Believe me, you'll be safer that way!'

Finished. She crosses her arms and glares at the cringing boy. 'That's my decision. Doctor?' She looks up at him.

The Doctor just stares, open-mouthed. Somewhere above, the familiar sound of thunder commences.

He is of course overjoyed that Romana is herself once more. However, it would have been nice if she had been a little more diplomatic when making her decision.

The Doctor finds that he feels sorry for Huvan. He is surprised that the boy had the courage to release Romana from her transformation; he must have known the outcome of his action. Let us just hope his temper holds.

Unfortunately, this isn't looking a likely possibility. Huvan is red-faced and angry, clenching and unclenching these new elegant fists he has designed for himself.

'You all hate me! You always hated me!' he hisses at them.

'Don't be pathetic,' says Romana. 'No one hates you.'

'Well,' Pelham begins, then realises what she is saying and closes her mouth again.

Despite everything, despite his new improved physique and facial features and his smart haircut, Huvan reveals himself with every breath for the adolescent he really is. The fate of everything ever in the hands of a lonely teenage boy. Hmm, not a particularly pleasant prospect.

'It's not fair. You should be on your knees in front of me! I should destroy the whole stinking universe!'

'But you won't, Huvan,' the Doctor says. Come on. Come on, this is the last hurdle, nearly there now.

'Why not?'

'Because nothing would change for you. You would still be alone. Look at this poor creature here.' He indicates the somnambulant Old One towering over them. 'Like you, he was the psychic channel for the higher dimensions. He had the same power. You know, the answer to the riddle of how they contained Valdemar is really quite simple. He contained i himself.'

'What do you mean? If he had the power, why would he…?'

'He changed his mind. He decided he didn't want to destroy everything. I mean, who would?' Don't mention Sutekh. Don' even think about Sutekh. 'So he reversed the process and locked himself up here for all this time. Dreaming, learning. should imagine there's an amazing amount of knowledge stored here in this palace.'

'What do you mean, Doctor?' asks Pelham.

'Well, look around. Fred here is connected to all the sensory equipment the Old Ones could muster. With his abilities, he' probably been soaking up information for millennia.'

'Never mind about him! What about me? We're talking about me! Why should I put myself to sleep for a million years? No.

The Doctor looks at Romana, who looks back. She is calm now, determined to help. 'All you ever wanted was to be normal to fit in,' she says. 'If you don't stop the higher dimension spreading, that's an opportunity you will never experience.'

'I don't want to give up all this, I can do anything.'

'Anything except that which you really want,' Romana replies.

Huvan sits down, blinking away tears. 'I don't know what to do. What should I do?'

'Oh, for God's sake, put an end to it, Huvan!' Miranda Pelham suddenly shouts at him.

He looks up. The anger has gone from him; now there i nothing but sorrow. He sinks to the floor.

The Doctor sympathises, sympathises but doesn' empathise. 'I understand that this is a phenomenally difficul decision, Huvan. Not one I would like to make. However, it's time to grow up. You're not an evil man, you won't make the wrong choice.'

There, that's everything, all he's got to offer. Everything now is in the hands of the boy.

'All right. All right,' Huvan mutters. 'But what happens to me? How can I be normal?'

Again, the Doctor swaps a glance with Romana. They both know what has to be said. 'That's the phenomenally difficult part. There is a way. You won't like it, but it's definitely a way.'

Cleverly, Romana seats herself next to Huvan. 'It's your decision. We don't have the power to stop you. You must do what you feel is right.'

'What happens to me?' He is shouting again, frightened. 'Who sorts me out?'

'You do. You do it to yourself. Your powers are almost limitless. It is possible to start again, a new man who doesn't remember any of this.'

Unsurprisingly, Huvan is not best pleased to hear this. 'What? A new man? That... that's as good as killing myself. Don't be so stupid.'

'No,' says Romana. 'One day you will remember. I promise.'

'You will be different but you will still be you,' says the Doctor. 'The man you should have been. Otherwise, look at Valdemar here. A million years of solitude before the next curious lot turn up. I said it wasn't easy and I didn't lie. Make the decision, Huvan, before you destroy everything.'

'I can't... I can't...'

'Decide!'

So Huvan decides. Miranda Pelham weeps for him, surprising herself. The spectre of death still hangs over her, having so nearly taken her. What he had to do to himself... would she

have had the courage? Yet another life ruined, all because o
her own idiocy and short-sighted ambition.

She cannot help looking at the giant creature that dream
here. Valdemar, the real thing, her fiction become reality.

There is a nagging thought, a thought that won't leave he
All those years ago, stumbling over the cult, writing the book
Had she really been the one doing the writing? If this big guy
here has been asleep and dreaming and gathering all thi
knowledge for a million years, who's to say he didn't…? No, i
can't be true. They couldn't all be characters, could they
Who's writing whose story here?

'Of course,' the Doctor is saying, 'of course I knew all th
time that my hypnotic suggestion would enable you to shake
off his influence. You mustn't take the credit for that.'

Romana folds her arms once again. 'Oh yes? So it had nothing
to do with me at all, I suppose?'

'Well, you're young, inexperienced. You must expect to trip
over occasionally.'

'If you must know,' Romana states calmly, 'I think I had help
from another source.' She pats a tentacle that is wider than
her. 'Our friend here. I don't think he's quite as dormant as he
makes out.'

'What absolute poppycock!' the Doctor bellows. 'I'll have to
teach you humility, Romana. If you've any chance of becoming
as clever and resourceful as I am–'

'I don't believe you,' says Pelham. 'The universe nearly
ended, all this around us and you two just stand there
bickering.'

They stand in front of her, unrepentant. 'Miranda,' says the
Doctor. 'You must learn to see things from the correc
perspective. Now, what are we going to do with you?'

MIRANDA PELHAM

She reels. The voice is deafening, booming round her head

She feels herself falling.

MIRANDA PELHAM

'What is it? Are you all right?' Romana helps her to her feet.

'I don't know. Didn't you hear it?'

The Doctor shakes his head. 'Hear what?'

MIRANDA PELHAM STAY

She puts her hand to her mouth and backs away from the
body of the Old One. 'It... it's him.'

'Him?' snorts the Doctor.

'Doctor,' hisses Romana.

'I was only saying...'

MIRANDA PELHAM STAY LEARN

The words are more than words. She finds the language
unfamiliar but there are pictures too, stories told by Valdemar
beamed directly into her mind. He has been so far, understands
so much, even knows about that which she fears so much. He
can help her, teach her. God, there is so much they could do.
She could learn to lose that fear. He knows how.

'Miranda?' asks the Doctor.

She is laughing now, tears blurring her vision. 'He needs me,
Doctor. He wants me to stay... so much I can learn from him.'

'Well, I'm not sure.'

She clasps his hands. How to make him understand, how?
'Don't you see? There's nothing for me back there. Just that
lousy Protectorate trying to kill me. Either that or old age.
Valdemar wants me to stay, be his companion. And that's what
I'm going to do.'

'Are you sure?' asks Romana. 'After a while, it may become
impossible for you to return. Realistically...'

'Realistically? You call that real? Well if that's reality, give me
the dreams any day. I'm staying.'

'You have to be sure...' the Doctor begins. She cuts him off.
She is manic, unable to stop laughing.

'Oh just go, for heaven's sake, before I wake up and change my mind.'

'As long as you're all right.'

The laughter is crippling her, sending an agony of convulsions through her chest. 'All right? I'm bloody terrified! Go, go now!'

And, at last, they do go. All three of them. Miranda Pelham wipes the tears away and sits down next to her creation. There's a lot of catching up to do.

'Isn't it amazing,' says the Doctor, 'how quickly things recover? Not just things either.' He nods at Romana, at how fresh and young she is again. Too young, inexperienced. No, she is absolutely wrong as a companion, won't do, won't do at all.

The world of Ashkellia is just as it is supposed to be. Unpleasant, hot and filthy.

However, the gateway has disappeared, nothing there now but a patch of bare rock.

'I hope she'll be all right,' says Romana, looking at the patch. 'She seemed very nice.'

'I suppose so,' says the Doctor. 'I do hope you're not going to get all maudlin on me, I really can't be doing with it, you know.'

'Doctor,' she replies with a warm, genuine smile. 'Just once, try and be nice.'

He mutters to himself, as if the suggestion that he is ever grumpy is the utmost presumption.

'Well?' says Romana.

'Oh, all right. Just once. Come on, let's get Huvan here into the TARDIS.'

The boy, eyes betraying his childlike state, follows meekly behind. The Doctor gently – one could say respectfully – takes his arm. He and Romana both feel remorse, and guilt. They prompted Huvan to commit this devastating action upon himself. His trance-like emptiness is a sad reminder of his bravery. No matter what they do, he will never be the same again.

They usher Huvan along to the blue box they left all that time ago. The Doctor pauses, perhaps hearing something in the tunnels. He shakes his head and unlocks the door. Together, he and Romana help Huvan inside.

The door closes, just a blue box again.

'Mas-ter?' comes a welcome metal voice.

'Hello K-9, you look much better.'

'Doctor?' asks Romana.

'Oh, what now? Do you have to keep asking me so many questions? We do have a Key to Time to find, you know.'

'What are we going to do with Huvan?'

'Don't rush me, don't rush me. I'll think of something. I always do. Now, where's that first segment? What? Well, find it. Quickly!'

And then, with the sound, the TARDIS disappears. Nothing is left, not even an imprint in the ground, to tell anyone they were ever there.

Ashkellia is silent, unthinking. Outside the tomb the atmosphere still boils, the clouds still rain their perpetual orange showers. Nothing is left here; no palace, no space ships, no Valdemar. Even the hole in the planet's crust, that provided the updraught to keep the palace afloat, has somehow healed over.

Far away, a New Protectorate establishes itself over humanity, unaware of the fate of its best agent. And the Magus? Oh, the cult will live on, as cults do, but diluted and broken, eventually splitting and dividing into a thousand fragments. Undoubtedly, Paul Neville will gain a martyr's reputation that may, in time, become as infamous as the myth of Valdemar itself.

We digress. Back to Ashkellia, where to detect any kind of movement we must return to the tunnels. Follow the howling and bellowing from that inhuman hybrid throat, the sound the Doctor so nearly heard. Through the tomb of Valdemar, it chases itself; the two become one, perpetually enraged, constantly fighting itself, tearing and mauling and rending. Its wounds are horrendous, yes, but somehow, never fatal. Ever.

Chapter Sixteen

And that was Ponch's ending; simple as that.

Strange, it hadn't gone the way he'd expected it to at all. I mean, where was the big climactic fight? Yes, that would have been good: hordes of armoured soldiers suddenly appearing to help Hopkins, and then an invasion from the higher dimensions by the Old Ones, who had engineered the whole thing as a way of conquering the universe. That was more like it, a whole sight better than what he had actually come up with. For a start, this ending didn't make sense; there were loads of holes in the plot if you looked for them. So the Doctor just realised there would be an alternate palace through the gateway, did he? And miraculously just happened to be right. Who would fall for that one? How come Hopkins and Neville got fused together and avoided the effects of the higher dimensions entirely? What is this higher dimension thing anyway?

The real reason it doesn't work is, of course, obvious. If Miranda Pelham had stayed behind in the higher dimensions with that big green thing, how could she have turned up here to tell him about it? Eh? Answer that one!

Lots of reasons why this ending is no good. There are hundreds of better ones he could think of. Anything rather than that.

Except, for some reason, Ponch knows he cannot change the ending. This is how it happened, he couldn't change it even if he wanted to. There is a correctness, a smoothness, an… *what was that word*… an inevitability about this ending. Even that thing about Pelham seems right. Don't ask him how he knows, he just does.

He has been out in the tundra a week now. After three days he was caught by a couple of hunting ur-dogs, sent out after him.

He had been sleeping inside one of the ancient barrow mounds, determined not to be afraid of the dusty bones and metal that were stacked inside, sculpted into strange ornate shapes from another, ancient age.

The ur-dogs, rare and valuable tracking hounds, with long snouts and two tireless stringy legs, had sniffed him down to the grassy mound. Ponch remembers the fear that woke him, the snuffling outside. He had known exactly what had come for him.

The old men of the township would have instructed the ur-dogs to keep his head unmarked. They would see to that first, ready for the fun they would have with the rest of him. He imagined their salivating muzzles, their sour breath over him as one held him and the other ripped, feeling his muscles stretched tighter and tighter until...

Only their eagerness to make the kill had saved him. The ur-dogs whooped and gibbered, lit by the gleaming moon outside, savouring their rush into the barrow mound.

Ponch remembers finding the rusty pike, running it through the first of the beasts: a stubby, yellow, furred thing with an almost human face beneath the hair. He had screamed like a beast himself.

The second animal had dropped to its tiny, wizened forepaws and breathed short jolts of night steam towards him, its long tongue lapping up the stench of its partner's howling death.

It jumped, hard and quick, at him but Ponch was ready. He had clubbed its snout with the dagger he had grasped in his left hand. The force of its jump meant the blade sank deep. It was scrabbling all over him, screeching and biting with pain and anger. Ponch kept stabbing, given an advantage by the beast's reluctance to sink its teeth into his face.

At last, with the thing lying on top of him, breathing its sickening innards all over him, it stopped, and died, and that was that.

He left two heads on top of the barrow mound, so they would know who had done this.

Apart from that, Ponch has to admit to himself that the journey has been pretty quiet.

For some reason, the story makes him think of his past. Perhaps it had been the old woman, perhaps she reminded him of his mother.

Except that he remembers nothing about a mother. No family whatsoever. He tries to think about his childhood and can't. Not that it has worried him before. Memories are a luxury here and, anyway, nothing ever changes. Just the same old foraging for furs in summer, the township in autumn, and the holing up for the inevitably terrible, culling winter. Waiting for the sun so they could start the whole thing off again. Only one day mattered, right at the end of the autumn, the one day around which all other days revolved; the day the guild sleds came out of the mountains to collect their treasures and distribute those precious gifts.

Now, Ponch can clearly remember last guild day, and definitely one before that. Vaguely, there is the recollection of a third but he cannot be certain. Before that, they all blur into one. He guesses he would say he had fifteen or so summers behind him, but is sad that this life has ground memory from him like chaff from a millstone, scattering the details. How can Pelham's story feel more real to him than his own past?

He knows now why he has come here. The old woman, Miranda Pelham, wanted him to discover the real secret. He had come to the mountains, to the home of the guild sleds, to find out who he is. Why he lives the life he does.

There is no mistaking that he is in the right place. The mountains here are oddly formed, regular, occasionally fortified with gigantic blocks of black stone.

He sees the cylindrical watchtowers, the battlements and ramparts Ofrin once boasted of seeing when he claimed to have visited this place once long ago.

No one has ever known people on these battlements. There is no movement of any kind. Of course, Janua lives here, the great god of the guild.

But there are other stories.

They say that it is the dead who inhabit the citadel of Janua, all the people that ever died, that this is where everyone goes when they eventually get killed; that they're deep underground, and that the living provide furs for their warmth, to stave off that particular eternal cold. He remembers imagining their skeletons wrapped in fur, the teeth grinning and chattering.

So this is where he must travel. There is a sharp drop to a faraway cave, right at the end of a long, overcast, snowy valley. Ponch can see it now. This is where he must travel.

He thinks of the old woman, how kind and vibrant she was, despite her great age. How she laughed all the time, even when she was angry, if that's possible, even when Ofrin threatened to kill her. She would not be afraid now, not of ghosts and phantoms.

Even better, think of the Doctor, always jumping feet first into trouble, always ready to take on the worst with a smile, a quip and that familiar mocking 'Well…?'.

Yes, be like the Doctor. You don't know the dead live in there, you don't know what lives in there, so until you do, what is the point in being afraid? You always have to find out for yourself.

Bolstering himself up with this and many other new styles of thought, Ponch pulls the axe from his filthy fur coat and starts off into the valley.

* * *

The wind blows hard against him as he plods along. The permanent daylight of the summer sun is partially obscured by the sharp crags. There are more shadows, more dark spaces to worry about. Ignore them, ignore it all and keep going.

Ponch begins to hear sounds, noises he has never heard before. A grinding of metal, a kind of muffled roar of flame, deep below. He thinks of a fire, of the warmth and the lovely light on the cold long nights of trapping. The loneliness of so many months on your own, the constant vigilance and mistrust. Fire provides more than a physical warmth and he could really do with it right now.

Nothing here in this wilderness but rock and snow, except that which you make yourself. You had to grow up very quickly here. He hasn't seen many children. They are kept well hidden, along with the priceless child-bearers. How many make it, get to have any kind of life? How did he make it?

He wonders about the story. How old had Pelham said she had been? Forty-three? Was it possible people could live so long? So many questions. Despite his wariness, and the knowledge that he may never return from this place, Ponch thinks about a childhood he can no longer remember. It's about time he sorted out the answers.

He takes half a day to reach the black smudge at the far end of the valley. The ground here is weathered but artificial, smoothed and covered in some unfamiliar black substance. The guild sleds have worn tracks into its skin and Ponch follows them.

All around him, the mountain has given way to the ancient citadel built into it. There is no natural rock left, everything has been shaped and carved, designed as a defence against some massive besieging force. Some time ago though, Ponch realises. The ironwork has rusted completely, the bricks and fortifications and steps have crumbled and worn smooth with age.

271

Who does live here, he wonders? Who drives these sleds? Why do they need the furs so greedily?

Ponch stops. No more questions, forget the questions, they'll only get you killed. All you must do now is keep going.

He moves into a dark cave, seeing it is actually an ancient archway, an entrance into the citadel. His breathing is hoarse and he can feel himself settling into a familiar watchful state of awareness, almost a trance, nothing but senses and instincts. The conscious mind, far too slow, must be subdued.

The tunnel is lit, somehow. Ponch sees great rusted metal runners in the floors, tracks of some long-lost technology. Odd skeletal structures, with hooks and chains and levers, clink in the cold breeze. Still he has seen no life, not one living creature.

He smells the familiar oily smell of the guild sleds. They are here somewhere.

And something else, an odour that is familiar to him, maddeningly familiar, just different somehow.

He follows this scent along the huge open floor of the metal wreckage. Just coming here has sentenced him to death amongst his own people. There is no going back for him.

And then, there they are.

The guild sleds, like giant tracked slugs, quiet and still. They are parked in rows over an area bigger than the Janua Foris.

Instinctively, Ponch rolls behind cover, his movements echoing round the empty hangar. He knows only too well what those stubby nozzles at the front of the sleds can do. He was an idiot to come here, what the hell was he doing listening to that stupid woman? His life was fine until she arrived. After all her words, he is going to end up shot to pieces by the sled operators.

He realises he is grasping the little idol of Janua, still round

272

his neck on a string. The two-faced god, he who sees before and after. 'Protect me,' Ponch whispers, even as he accepts that as he has trespassed into the god's own house he can hardly expect the protection he's asking for.

Ponch lies there, behind this broken machine thing, for a long, long time. It's nice. It's safe.

He has heard nothing from the sleds, nothing at all. A trick? Perhaps, but he can't sit here for ever, can he? He has to find the answers and this is as good a place as any to begin.

That odour drifts into his nostrils again. What is it? Like an itch, it just sits there, working away at him in a place he can't reach.

So familiar, yet also so... so strange.

He risks a peep over the machine. The guild sleds are still there, just as he left them. Their skin is smooth, completely sealed, like big kidney beans. The thought makes him chuckle, until he realises the seriousness of the situation and calms himself.

The nozzles on the fronts of the sleds still protrude, but they're not twisting and waving like they do outside, hunting for prey.

The sleds are empty, he decides. They have to be. Perhaps this is his chance to get past them.

He remembers the way they roll over the fur bundles left for them by his people. The way the bundles disappear. He can't see any visible doors, so how do the operators get inside?

There must be some kind of hatchway underneath, between the runners and the tracks. As Ponch squints he calculates there is probably just enough room for him to fit under a sled. Might as well try it, better than waiting here for them to start up.

He does so. Moving, sneaking as quietly as he can, Ponch darts to the leading guild sled. He slides himself under its bulk, trying to control the rather sensible instinct to run away as fast as he can.

He shuffles underneath on his back, arms over his head, probing. There is a large metal hole leading into the sled. He grips with his fingers and pulls himself to it.

Awkwardly, and banging his head on more than one occasion, he manages to sit up, into the hole, then stand. A couple of steps up and he is inside.

Artificial lights flicker into life. Ponch flinches, expecting an assault of some kind, but it doesn't come. Instead, the interior of a guild sled is revealed to him. He is in a bare metal box, with a small opening leading to what appears to be a cramped compartment. There are no seats, just large boxes that Ponch guesses are a control system.

No one drives the sleds. They drive themselves.

How can this be? It cannot be true. Ponch is stunned by the revelation. What does that mean? Where are the operators?

There is nothing in here but dormant machinery and the lingering smell of furs. There is never anything but machinery and furs in here.

Furs. The smell of furs, that is the odour he couldn't place. It was just so concentrated, so rich, as if, as if… and already Ponch suspects what he is going to find.

He drops back out of the sled and slides his way to the rear of the machine. Then he is up and running, almost feverishly, towards the odour of leathered skins that envelops him as he races in the dark.

The ground gives way and his heart stops in its tracks as he plummets. Some kind of smooth metal chute steers him faster and faster towards the smell which becomes too strong, making him retch.

Ponch tries to grip the sides of chute but they are worn smooth with age. He yells in fright, scrabbling to escape the descent.

At last, the chute ends and he flies through the air, spinning and spiralling, his axe dropping from his hand. He hits something soft and the breath is knocked out of him.

Ponch lies there for a while in the dark, bathed in the overpowering, all-encompassing stench. Is this it? He wonders. Is this everything my life is worth?

He sits up. As he knew he would, he can see nothing but hides and skins and furs, thousands upon thousands of them, stretching out as far as he can see, the precious collections of generations of his people moulding and rotting through the years.

Ponch looks down on them. What to make of it? What to make of all this wasted work?

There isn't any guild, any operators, any Janua. There is nothing but empty ritual and wasted lives.

He looks up at the twinkling chutes over his head and bellows with laughter. 'I understand! I understand everything!'

He knows why he understands, why he feels that the final events in the palace of the Old Ones are so true to him. Why there is no other possible ending. Of course. He is such an idiot, such a child; anyone else with half a brain would have guessed it ages ago.

The story, Miranda Pelham's story, is real because it happened. He knows because he was there.

Ponch stays throughout the long, cruel winter. He uses the time to explore the remains of the citadel. What its function may once have been, he never discovers.

The only event, the only change in all the time he is here, occurs early, at the end of the autumn. Night is coming in as he stands on the battlements. The sun is a giant orange eye, sinking over the valley, sending down a shadow that is longer and longer every day. On this particular evening, he hears a multitude of clattering coughs from inside the hangar, the noisy coming to life of the guild sleds. It must be the time of the Gathering. One by one they snake out of the hangar and into the darkening valley. A line of metal beetles, on their way to their annual, mindless collection.

A week later they are back. Ponch has prepared a hiding place for himself inside their nest and watches as they drop the useless furs down the chutes, where they will rot.

A year's back-breaking labour, all he has ever known. In this life.

He wonders how many they killed for coming in below quota this time.

There is food to be found within this silent, dead space: strange metal canisters that he hacks open. Also insects and beetles and, once, a large black bird that somehow made its unlucky way to him.

Ponch doesn't mind the loneliness, the cold, the hunger. This life is a dream and it is time to wake. He is waiting for spring.

Look both ways, that's the creed of Janua, and he knows that this is what he must do.

When the snow has melted sufficiently and the orange eye peeps its way over the mountains again, he prepares a small pack of provisions and leaves the citadel behind.

The inn is still standing, though he knows it will be deserted. He walks through last year's township; its smoking ruins are charcoal bones. No bodies, no remains of any kind that will be of use to him.

Only the Janua Foris stands intact. Not so much an inn as a shrine to the trappers' life. A life Ponch is heartily sick of.

He tries to remember the poetry he must once have written, but recalls not one single word. Just a story, that's all.

Inside the Janua Foris, a light is spilling through the gloom from one unfamiliar door in the wall. He had asked himself a thousand times how Pelham had got herself here, but all the time he was thinking of boots and sleds and snow. He should have realised she would have no need for these things.

He walks through the shining door.

The warmth is uncomfortable; he is already sweating, so he hauls off his outer layers. He won't need them any more.

The room is impossibly large. He had walked around the whole inn in the past and seen no evidence of its existence, so he must already have travelled somewhere beyond the Janua Foris.

The white walls are decorated with hangings and a vast shelf of books, nearly obscuring the roundels behind them. A gently humming block of metal, plastic and glass sits snugly in the room's centre.

Ponch inspects the room with wonder, seeing doors that reveal corridors branching away eternally. Candles flicker and a… a… what is it called?… a clock ticks.

'You made it then,' comes a woman's voice.

Ponch turns, almost panicked. It has been so long since he has heard another's voice that it seems like a shout in his ears.

She is sitting in a rocking chair, a book in her lap. 'I've been waiting for you. Gave me a chance to catch up with some reading. Stories.'

Open-mouthed, Ponch points at the woman. She is young, beautiful, with dark eyes and clear ebony skin. 'Are you Miranda Pelham?' he asks, haltingly.

She smiles and shakes her head. 'Sorry about that. All that confusion. No. Not Miranda Pelham.'

'But you showed me the picture, you had a book.'

'I've done it before, I'll do it again, no doubt. She was such a lovely-looking woman.'

So many miracles, so many of these dreams, he doesn't know where to begin. 'You're the old woman who told me the story,

277

you've got the same – I don't know – the same something How…?' he stumbles, 'how did you get so young again? I saw you die.'

The woman stands. She picks up a jug of water from the table in front of her, pours a glass and offers it to Ponch. 'My dear,' she replies, amused with herself. 'You of all people should know about the disposal of dead skins.'

Ponch takes the glass, unfamiliar with the niceties of such behaviour. He drains it greedily. 'You came back for me,' he realises. 'That's what this was all for.'

'I said I would and I did. I always keep my word.'

'And the Doctor?'

She laughs and looks up at the high ceiling. 'The Doctor? You do surprise me. I don't know; that's the answer to that. Haven't seen him for years, centuries even. I suppose he's out there somewhere, getting himself into trouble. He never really liked having companions foisted upon him, you know. I prefer my method, much more thorough. Don't you think?'

Ponch shrugs. 'I don't know.'

The woman walks elegantly to the complicated machine in the middle of the room and commences pushing buttons and pulling levers. The glass column within begins to rise and fall, with an odd, faraway juddering sound.

'It's time to go,' she says.

Behind Ponch, the door to the Janua Foris shuts. The cold wind of his home is cut off abruptly. 'Look both ways,' says the woman.

The ground rocks and Ponch has to keep his balance. 'I don't know what… I don't know what's real any more,' he says. 'Is this a story too?'

The woman winks. 'Let's find out.'

PRESENTING

DOCTOR WHO

ALL-NEW AUDIO DRAMAS

Big Finish Productions are proud to present all-new *Doctor Who* adventures on audio!

Featuring original music and sound-effects, these full-cast plays are available on double cassette in high street stores, and on limited-edition double CD from all good specialist stores, or via mail order.

Available from October 1999

PHANTASMAGORIA

A four-part story by Mark Gatiss.
Starring **Peter Davison** as the Doctor and **Mark Strickson** as Turlough.

The TARDIS lands in London, 1702, where travellers are being terrorised by the charming highwayman, Major Billy Lovemore. And patrons of the notorious Diabola Club have been disappearing – shortly after playing cards with the sinister Sir Nikolas Valentine.

Is a supernatural horror stalking the streets of the city? The Doctor is soon enmeshed in a deadly game – and someone else is holding all the aces...

If you wish to order the CD version, please photocopy this form or provide all the details on paper if you do not wish to damage this book. Delivery within 28 days of release. Send to: PO Box 1127, Maidenhead, Berkshire. SL6 3LN.
Big Finish Hotline 01628 828283.

Still available: THE SIRENS OF TIME starring Peter Davison, Colin Baker & Sylvester McCoy.

Please send me [ ] copies of *Phantasmagoria* @ £13.99 (£15.50 non-UK orders)
[ ] copies of *The Sirens of Time* @ £13.99 (£15.50 non-UK orders) – prices inclusive of postage and packing. Payment can be accepted by credit card or by personal cheques, payable to Big Finish Productions Ltd.

Name...

Address..

Postcode..

VISA/Mastercard number..

Expiry date..Signature...

For more details visit our website at **http://www.doctorwho.co.uk**